Colonialism and the Emergence of Science Fiction

THE WESLEYAN EARLY CLASSICS OF
SCIENCE FICTION SERIES

General editor
Arthur B. Evans

The Centenarian
Honoré de Balzac

Cosmos Latinos: An Anthology of Science Fiction from Latin America and Spain
Andrea L. Bell and Yolanda Molina-Gavilán, eds.

Caesar's Column: A Story of the Twentieth Century
Ignatius Donnelly

Subterranean Worlds: A Critical Anthology
Peter Fitting, ed.

Lumen
Camille Flammarion

The Last Man
Jean-Baptiste Cousin de Grainville

The Battle of the Sexes in Science Fiction
Justine Larbalestier

The Yellow Wave: A Romance of the Asiatic Invasion of Australia
Kenneth Mackay

The Moon Pool
A. Merritt

Colonialism and the Emergence of Science Fiction
John Rieder

The Twentieth Century
Albert Robida

The World as It Shall Be
Emile Souvestre

Star Maker
Olaf Stapledon

The Begum's Millions
Jules Verne

Invasion of the Sea
Jules Verne

The Kip Brothers
Jules Verne

The Mighty Orinoco
Jules Verne

The Mysterious Island
Jules Verne

H. G. Wells: Traversing Time
W. Warren Wagar

Star Begotten
H. G. Wells

Deluge
Sydney Fowler Wright

Colonialism
and the EMERGENCE of
Science Fiction

John Rieder

wesleyan university press
middletown, connecticut

Published by Wesleyan University Press, Middletown, CT 06459

www.wesleyan.edu/wespress

© 2008 by John Rieder

All rights reserved

Printed in the United States of America

5 4 3

Library of Congress Cataloging-in-Publication Data
Rieder, John.
Colonialism and the emergence of science fiction / John Rieder.
 p. cm. — (The Wesleyan early classics of science fiction series)
Includes bibliographical references and index.
ISBN-13: 978–0–8195–6873–1 (cloth : alk. paper)
ISBN-10: 0–8195–6873–2 (cloth : alk. paper)
ISBN-13: 978–0–8195–6874–8 (pbk. : alk. paper)
ISBN-10: 0–8195–6874–0 (pbk. : alk. paper)
 1. Science fiction, American—History and criticism. 2. American fiction—19th century—History and criticism. 3. American fiction—20th century—History and criticism. 4. Science fiction, American—History and criticism. 5. English fiction—19th century—History and criticism. 6. English fiction—20th century—History and criticism. 7. Literature and science—English-speaking countries. 8. Imperialism in literature.9. Colonies in literature. I. Title.
PS374.S35R45 2008
823'.0876209—dc22   2007041722

To David F. Rieder, who gave me science fiction;
and, with love, to Cristina Bacchilega

The country that is more developed industrially only shows, to the less developed, the image of its own future.

—Karl Marx, Preface to the German Edition of *Capital*

Contents

	List of Illustrations	ix
	Acknowledgments	xi
Chapter 1	Introduction: The Colonial Gaze and the Frame of Science Fiction	1
Chapter 2	Fantasies of Appropriation: Lost Races and Discovered Wealth	34
Chapter 3	Dramas of Interpretation	61
Chapter 4	Artificial Humans and the Construction of Race	97
Chapter 5	Visions of Catastrophe	123
	Notes	157
	Works Cited	165
	Index	177

Illustrations

Fig. 1. Alonzo Gartley, *Native Hawaiian Fisherman with Throw Net*, 1903 — 8

Fig. 2. Frank R. Paul, front cover illustration, *Amazing Stories*, August 1927 — 11

Fig. 3. Harold V. Brown, front cover illustration, *Thrilling Wonder Stories*, June 1939 — 12

Fig. 4. Frank R. Paul, front cover illustration, *Amazing Stories*, August 1926 — 120

Fig. 5. Frank R. Paul, front cover illustration, *Science Wonder Stories*, October 1929 — 121

Acknowledgments

Several people have read entire drafts of this book and made comments and suggestions that helped me make it better. To my best writing ally and old friend Craig Howes, thanks yet again. A special acknowledgment is due to John Huntington, whose incisive reading of the manuscript as originally submitted to Wesleyan University Press resulted in an extensive revision that, I hope, greatly improved it. Arthur B. Evans read the entire revised manuscript carefully and made many helpful suggestions. The book is definitely more clearly written and carefully argued because of Art's generous help. Carl Freedman and Cristina Bacchilega also read and responded to portions of the manuscript, and to both of them I owe larger thanks that I will return to below.

Although my research on this project began as early as my sabbatical year in 2001, the book only started to take its present shape in response to an hours-long conversation about genre, plot, and the history of science fiction with Samuel R. Delany and Carl Freedman at the Rethinking Marxism Conference at Amherst in November 2003. To Chip for that memorable conversation, my warm thanks. As for Carl, this was only one in a long series of such conversations, and only one example of the many intellectual, professional, and convivial benefits I have enjoyed as collateral effects of our friendship.

I had the good fortune to present papers that grew into parts of this book at the Modern Language Association meeting in 2002, and at the International Association for the Fantastic in the Arts meetings in 2004 and 2005. I want to thank everyone who asked me questions or gave me encouragement about the project at those meetings, especially Chris Kendrick. Special thanks are also due to Eric Rabkin, who gave me excellent feedback on the project proposal. Thank you to Jack Zipes, Kenneth R. Johnston, and Jerrold Hogle for their support of the proposal as well.

I have had the good fortune to work in a fine, intellectually vibrant department since 1980, and it is a pleasure to have the opportunity here to thank my colleagues at the University of Hawai'i at Mānoa in the Department of English and in the International Cultural Studies program for their responses to colloquium presentations on this material. I also owe a debt to my students, especially those in my undergraduate and graduate courses on science fiction, but also to all of the students I have taught in my twenty-seven years in Honolulu, because this book's focus on colonialism is rooted in that teaching experience. Finally, I want to thank Bruna Rieder, who gave me encouraging news about how the opening pages would strike a bright college student who was not particularly interested in science fiction.

Some portions of "Science Fiction, Colonialism, and the Plot of Invasion," originally published in *Extrapolation* 46 (2005), are reused in chapters one and five. Thanks to Javier Martinez for his encouragement and enthusiasm about this project.

A grant from the University of Hawai'i Humanities Endowment allowed me to spend a month during the summer of 2003 reading at the Eaton Collection at the University of California, Riverside, Special Collections Library. The wonderfully helpful and well-informed staff at the Eaton helped me to make that stay very productive. Acknowledgment is also due to the Eaton for providing me with the image from the cover of *Thrilling Wonder Stories*. I thank the Bishop Museum Archives of Honolulu for providing the Alonzo Gartley image and permission to use it. Thank you to Frank Wu who very generously shared his expertise on Frank R. Paul. The Cushing Memorial Library and Archives at Texas A&M University provided the three Frank R. Paul images, and the Frank R. Paul estate granted permission to use them. For expert advice about the cover art, thanks also to Robert Weinberg and John Gunnison.

I want to acknowledge the efficiency, energy, and courtesy of the editorial and production staff who helped me see this project through at Wesleyan University Press, especially Eric Levy for shepherding the project from proposal to book and Leslie Starr for her work on the cover and other publicity materials. Thanks also to the attentive copy editor at University Press of New England and to those who oversaw the production process there.

No one has had a stronger impact on the way I have learned to think about narrative than Cristina Bacchilega. For the last twenty-four years, she has encouraged and supported my writing in every way possible—professionally, intellectually, and emotionally. But of course that is only a small part of it. If, as our friend Lynn says, this book has been a work of passion, my passions have flourished in the still-unfolding plot of our love.

Colonialism and the Emergence of Science Fiction

chapter one

Introduction
The Colonial Gaze and the Frame of Science Fiction

The question organizing this book concerns the connection between the early history of the genre of English-language science fiction and the history and discourses of colonialism. Consider first a brief example. Those searching out the origins of science fiction in English have often pointed to classical and European marvelous journeys to other worlds as an important part of its genealogy (e.g., Philmus 37–55; Aldiss 67–89; Stableford 18–23). It makes sense that if science fiction has anything to do with modern science (I am deferring the problem of defining "science fiction" until the fourth section of this chapter), the Copernican shift from a geocentric to a heliocentric understanding of the solar system provides a crucial point where the ancient plot of the marvelous journey starts becoming something like science fiction, because the Copernican shift radically changed the status of other worlds in relation to our own. An Earth no longer placed at the center of the universe became, potentially, just one more among the incalculable plurality of worlds. Of all the marvelous journeys to other worlds written in Galileo's seventeenth century, Cyrano de Bergerac's *The Comical History of the States and Empires of the Moon and the Sun* (first translated into English in 1656) is the one that science fiction scholars have expressed the greatest admiration for (see Suvin, *Metamorphoses of Science Fiction* 103–106). All the scholars I've cited would agree that the main work of Cyrano's satire is hardly a matter of celestial mechanics, however. Its crux is the way it mocks, parodies, criticizes, and denaturalizes the cultural norms of his French contemporaries. The importance of his satire has far less to do with Copernicus's taking the Earth out of the center of the solar system than with Cyrano's taking his own culture out of the center of the human race, making it no longer definitive of the range of human possibilities.

The example of Cyrano suggests that the disturbance of ethnocentrism, the achievement of a perspective from which one's own culture is only one of a number of possible cultures, is as important a part of the history of science fiction, as much a condition of possibility for the genre's coming to be, as developments in the physical sciences. The achievement of an estranged, critical perspective on one's home culture always has been one of the potential benefits of travel in foreign lands. In the fifteenth and the sixteenth centuries, Europeans greatly expanded the extent and the kinds of contacts they had with the non-European world. Between the time of Cyrano and that of H. G. Wells, those contacts enveloped the world in a Europe-centered system of commerce and political power. Europeans mapped the non-European world, settled colonies in it, mined it and farmed it, bought and sold some of its inhabitants, and ruled over many others. In the process of all of this, they also developed a scientific discourse about culture and mankind. Its understanding of human evolution and the relation between culture and technology played a strong part in the works of Wells and his contemporaries that later came to be called science fiction.

Evolutionary theory and anthropology, both profoundly intertwined with colonial ideology and history, are especially important to early science fiction from the mid-nineteenth century on. They matter first of all as conceptual material. Ideas about the nature of humankind are central to any body of literature, but scientific accounts of humanity's origins and its possible or probable futures are especially basic to science fiction. Evolutionary theory and anthropology also serve as frameworks for the Social Darwinian ideologies that pervade early science fiction. The complex mixture of ideas about competition, adaptation, race, and destiny that was in part generated by evolutionary theory, and was in part an attempt to come to grips with—or to negate—its implications, forms a major part of the thematic material of early science fiction.[1] These will be recurrent topics of discussion in *Colonialism and the Emergence of Science Fiction*.

The thesis that colonialism is a significant historical context for early science fiction is not an extravagant one. Indeed, its strong foundation in the obvious has been well recognized by scholars of science fiction. Most historians of science fiction agree that utopian and satirical representations of encounters between European travelers and non-Europeans—such as Thomas More's *Utopia* (1516), Cyrano's *Comical History*, and Jonathan Swift's *Gulliver's Travels* (1726)—form a major part of the genre's prehistory. Scholars largely (though not universally) agree that the period of the most fervid imperialist expansion in the late nineteenth century is also the crucial period for the emergence of the genre (Suvin, *Victorian Science Fiction in the UK* 325–26; Clareson, *Some Kind of Paradise* 4; James, "Science Fiction by Gaslight" 34–35; for one who disagrees, see Delany, *Silent Interviews* 25–27). Science fiction comes into visibility first in those countries most heavily involved in imperialist projects—France and England—and then gains popularity in the United States, Germany, and Russia as those countries also enter into more and more serious imperial competition (Csicsery-Ronay 231). Most important, no informed reader can doubt that allusions to colonial history and situations are ubiquitous features of early science fiction motifs and plots. It is not a matter of asking whether but of determining precisely how and to what extent the stories engage colonialism. The work of interpreting the relation of colonialism and science fiction really gets under way, then, by attempting to decipher the fiction's often distorted and topsy-turvy references to colonialism. Only then can one properly ask how early science fiction lives and breathes in the atmosphere of colonial history and its discourses, how it reflects or contributes to ideological production of ideas about the shape of history, and how it might, in varying degrees, enact a struggle over humankind's ability to reshape it.

From Satirical Reversal to Anthropological Difference

We can start from Edward Said's argument in *Culture and Imperialism* that "the novel, as a cultural artefact of bourgeois society, and imperialism are unthinkable without each other" (70–71). His thesis is that the social space of the novel, which defines the possibilities allowed to its characters and the limits suffered by them, is involved inextricably with Western Europe's project of global expansion and control over non-European territories and cultures from the eighteenth century to the present. One could no more separate the psychological and domestic spaces represented in the novel from this emerging sense of a world knit together by Western political and economic control than one could isolate a private realm of emotions and interpersonal relationships from the history of class and property relations during the same period. Said does not argue that imperialism determines the form of the novel, but simply that it provides a structure of possibilities and a distribution of knowledge and power that the novel inevitably articulates.

Emergent English-language science fiction articulates the distribution of knowledge and power at a certain moment of colonialism's history. If the Victorian vogue for adventure fiction in general seems to ride the rising tide of imperial expansion, particularly into Africa and the Pacific, the increasing popularity of journeys into outer space or under the ground in the late nineteenth and early twentieth centuries probably reflects the near exhaustion of the actual unexplored areas of the globe—the disappearance of the white spaces on the map, to invoke a famous anecdote of Conrad's. Having no place on Earth left for the radical exoticism of unexplored territory, the writers invent places elsewhere. But this compensatory reflex is only the beginning of the story. For colonialism is not merely an opening up of new possibilities, a "new world" becoming available to the "old" one, but also provides the impetus behind cognitive revolutions in the biological and human sciences that reshaped European notions of its own history and society. The exotic, once it had been scrutinized, analyzed, theorized, catalogued, and displayed, showed a tendency to turn back upon and re-evaluate those who had thus appropriated and appraised it. As the French philosopher Jacques Derrida put it, "Ethnology could have been born as a science only at the moment when a decentering had come about: at the moment when European culture ... had been *dislocated*, driven from its locus, and forced to stop considering itself as the culture of reference" (282, Derrida's emphasis). Emergent science fiction also articulates the effects of this dislocation. The double-edged effect of the exotic—as a means of gratifying familiar appetites and as a challenge to one's sense of the proper or the natural—pervades early science fiction.

Although, as we will see further on, much early science fiction seems merely to transpose and revivify colonial ideologies, the invention of other worlds very often originates in a satirical impulse to turn things upside down and inside out. A satirical reversal of hierarchies generates the comparison of extraterrestrials to colonialists in an episode from Washington Irving's *A History of New York by Diedrich Knickerbocker* in 1809, for example. Irving invents a race from the Moon who arrive on the Earth "possessed of superior knowledge in the art of extermination," on the basis of which, after "finding this planet to be nothing but a howling wilderness, inhabited by us poor savages and wild beasts," they "take formal possession of it, in the name of his most gracious and philosophical excellency, the man in the moon" (252). Human savagery consists not only in having the wrong skin color (white, not pea-green) and anatomy (two eyes instead of one) but also in humans' perverse marriage customs and religious beliefs (monogamy and Christianity instead of communal promiscuity and ecstatic Lunacy). Irving's point is entirely explicit. When the savages ungratefully resist receiving the gifts of civilization, the lunarians convert them to their own way of thinking "by main force" and "graciously permit [the savages] to exist in the torrid deserts of Arabia or the frozen regions of Lapland, there to enjoy the blessings of civilization and the charms of lunar philosophy, in much the same manner as the reformed and enlightened savages of this country are kindly suffered to inhabit the inhospitable forests of the north, or the impenetrable wildernesses of South America" (254).

In the course of the nineteenth century, Irving's strategy of satiric reversal persists in a number of important proto-science-fiction texts, such as Samuel Butler's *Erewhon* (1872), with its reversal of the values of disease and crime, and James De Mille's extraordinary lost-race novel, *A Strange Manuscript Found in a Copper Cylinder* (1888), with its systematic reversal of the values of light and darkness, wealth and poverty, and life and death. The most famous such reversal in the history of science fiction closely resembles Irving's. At the outset of H. G. Wells's *The War of the Worlds* (1898), Wells asks his English readers to compare the Martian invasion of Earth with the Europeans' genocidal invasion of the Tasmanians, thus demanding that the colonizers imagine themselves as the colonized, or the about-to-be-colonized. But in Wells this reversal of perspective entails something more, because the analogy rests on the logic prevalent in contemporary anthropology that the indigenous, primitive other's present is the colonizer's own past. Wells's Martians invading England are like Europeans in Tasmania not just because they are arrogant colonialists invading a technologically inferior civilization, but also because, with their hypertrophied brains and prosthetic machines, they are a version of the human race's own future.

The confrontation of humans and Martians is thus a kind of anachronism, an incongruous co-habitation of the same moment by people and artifacts from different times. But this anachronism is the mark of anthropological difference, that is, the way late-nineteenth-century anthropology conceptualized the play of identity and difference between the scientific observer and the anthropological subject—both human, but inhabiting different moments in the history of civilization. As George Stocking puts it in his intellectual history of Victorian anthropology, Victorian anthropologists, while expressing shock at the devastating effects of European contact on the Tasmanians, were able to adopt an apologetic tone about it because they understood the Tasmanians as "living representatives of the early Stone Age," and thus their "extinction was simply a matter of . . . placing the Tasmanians back into the dead prehistoric world where they belonged" (282–83). The trope of the savage as a remnant of the past unites such authoritative and influential works as Lewis Henry Morgan's

Ancient Society (1877), where the kinship structures of contemporaneous American Indians and Polynesian islanders are read as evidence of "our" past, with Sigmund Freud's *Totem and Taboo* (1913), where the sexual practices of "primitive" societies are interpreted as developmental stages leading to the mature sexuality of the West. Johannes Fabian has argued that the repression or denial of the real contemporaneity of so-called savage cultures with that of Western explorers, colonizers, and settlers is one of the pervasive, foundational assumptions of modern anthropology in general. The way colonialism made space into time gave the globe a geography not just of climates and cultures but of stages of human development that could confront and evaluate one another.[2]

The anachronistic structure of anthropological difference is one of the key features that links emergent science fiction to colonialism. The crucial point is the way it sets into motion a vacillation between fantastic desires and critical estrangement that corresponds to the double-edged effects of the exotic. Robert Stafford, in an excellent essay on "Scientific Exploration and Empire" in the *Oxford History of the British Empire*, writes that, by the last decades of the century, "absorption in overseas wilderness represented a form of time travel" for the British explorer and, more to the point, for the reading public who seized upon the primitive, abundant, unzoned spaces described in the narratives of exploration as a veritable "fiefdom, calling new worlds into being to redress the balance of the old" (313, 315). Thus when Verne, Wells, and others wrote of voyages underground, under the sea, and into the heavens for the readers of the age of imperialism, the otherworldliness of the colonies provided a new kind of legibility and significance to an ancient plot. Colonial commerce and imperial politics often turned the marvelous voyage into a fantasy of appropriation alluding to real objects and real effects that pervaded and transformed life in the homelands. At the same time, the strange destinations of such voyages now also referred to a centuries-old project of cognitive appropriation, a reading of the exotic other that made possible, and perhaps even necessary, a rereading of oneself. How does science fiction organize this play of the fantastic and the critical?

The Colonial Gaze

Although the reversal of perspective in Wells's *War of the Worlds* transposes the positions of colonizer and colonized, the framework of colonial relations itself remains intact in an important way. Wells switches the position of his white Western narrator from its accustomed, dominant, colonizing one to that of the dominated indigenous inhabitant of the colonized land. This strategy makes not only the political, but also the cognitive effects of the framework of colonial relations visible in a tellingly distorted way. The narrator no longer occupies the position usually accorded to the scientific observer, but instead finds himself in that role historically occupied by those who are looked at and theorized about rather than those who look, analyze, and theorize. We can call this cognitive framework establishing the different positions of the one who looks and the one who is looked at the structure of the "colonial gaze," borrowing and adapting Laura Mulvey's influential analysis of the cinematic gaze in "Visual Pleasure and Narrative Cinema."[3] The colonial gaze distributes knowledge and power to the subject who looks, while denying or minimizing access to power for its object, the one looked at. This structure—a cognitive disposition that both rests upon and helps to maintain and reproduce the political and economic arrangements that establish the subjects' respective positions—remains strikingly present and effective in spite of the reversal of perspective in *The War of the Worlds*. Let me illustrate by way of comparison with another, pictorial representation of a colonial subject.

Consider the combination of exoticism, realism, science, and ideology in Alonzo Gartley's 1903 photograph, *Native Hawaiian Fisherman with Throw Net* (fig. 1). Gartley's photo orients itself towards its subject, the Hawaiian net fisherman, according to conventions that draw upon both anthropology and ethnography. The man's clothing and the technology he is using draw attention to his cultural difference from an implicitly Western viewer who occupies the position of the photographic apparatus itself. The clothing and fishing tools identify the man as a primitive, and so, according to the dominant model of ethnographic and anthropological discourse at the time, establish his presence before the photo's audience as a kind of anachronism that allows them to view their own cultural past. The fisherman becomes an object of knowledge, an exhibit for the contemplative gaze of the photographer and audience to work upon. The archaic figure of the Hawaiian fisherman is no mere curiosity, however, but rather is meant to call out to us across the gulf of the ages. As Morgan writes in his introduction to *Ancient Society*, "The history of the human race is one in source, one in experience, and one in progress" (xxx). The fisherman's cultural difference is balanced by his universality. He represents man-the-hunter, confronting an elemental nature rendered power-

FIGURE 1. Alonzo Gartley, *Native Hawaiian Fisherman with Throw Net.* 1903. *Courtesy of Bishop Museum.*

fully present in the breaking surf and the bright sunlight. The image's archetypal quality implicates the audience in a commonality between the fisherman searching for his prey and the photographer capturing his image, and this commonality in turn exposes a second difference. For, if the scene articulates the photographer's technological superiority over his subject, it also lays bare the photographer's relative loss of immediacy in relation to the natural world. Capturing (or viewing) an image is a mediated, delayed gratification compared to netting a fish. Thus the universalizing frame both assigns the native an inferior position and gives that position critical, reflective power in relation to its superior.

The photo's combination of anachronism and universality conforms also to a dramatic proximity and yet emphatic separation from its subject that reproduces the convention of the invisible fourth wall of proscenium theater. We spectators are placed in the "realist" position of onlookers at a scene that is wholly absorbed in itself and therefore does not and cannot look back at us. This one-way quality, shared by dramatic, photographic, and later cinematic conventions, is likewise crucial to the ethnographic and anthropological conventions that treat such a figure as an anonymous, un-self-conscious representative of a type of society or a stage of human development. These assumptions might be disrupted, however, once one notices the photo's elaborately posed artificiality. For instance, one might suspect that the rough surf area and precarious rocks where the hunter crouches are chosen more for their picturesque qualities than for their appropriateness to the fisherman's task; nor would it be easy to explain what prey the fisherman can be stalking in this particular stance, since his keen eyes are directed at the shore, not the water. The self-consciousness of the pose therefore belies its apparent status as ethnographic evidence of a spontaneous practice. Although the photo may masquerade as a form of knowledge about the Hawaiian fisherman, then, it is evidently a piece of exoticism that, whatever Gartley's artistic or ethnographic intentions, was quickly put to service promoting a nascent tourist industry in the newly annexed American colony of Hawai'i.[4]

If noticing the artificiality of the model's pose begins to undermine the image's ethnographic significance, what would happen if we were to rearrange more actively the positions that establish the colonial gaze? If one were to introduce a reciprocal gaze into the scene, for instance, so that the model could be allowed to stand up straight, look back at the camera, and address himself to the audience, the generic conventions would switch from those of the ethnographic image to what Mary Louise Pratt calls autoethnography. This reversal of narrative point of view would yield a story about the Hawaiian fisherman's experience that would, quite likely, have less to do with subsistence fishing than with trying to earn money by posing for a white photographer, and it would have correspondingly less to do with the social and economic organization of precontact Hawai'i than with its disruption by the economic and political dominance of the white settlers. But such an account also would be something rather different from the reversal of narrative perspective accomplished in *The War of the Worlds*. *That* generic turn would happen, not if Gartley's model were to take over the narration, but rather if the imaginary subject, the primitive man enveloped in nature, were to reconstruct from his point of view the scene of the impossibly alien, futuristic, and invasive photographer capturing his image. The resulting pictorial representation might look similar to the cover illustration of the August 1927 issue of *Amazing Stories*, which depicts Wells's Martian fighting machines astride their tripods attacking the English countryside with their heat rays, not wholly unlike so many giant photographers (fig. 2). (A more literal resemblance to the reversed photographic scenario appears on the cover of *Thrilling Wonder Stories*, June 1939. [See fig. 3.])

The Wellsian strategy is a reversal of positions that stays entirely within the framework of the colonial gaze and the anachronism of anthropological difference, but also highlights their critical potential. In *The War of the Worlds*, we should remember, the "native" human narrator himself occupies not only the position of the dominated, dehumanized colonial subject, but also that of the scientific observer, especially when he becomes an ethnographer in the marvelous chapter on the Martians' anatomy and technology. This ethnographic chapter is at least as crucial a register of the relation between colonial discourse and science fiction as the famous comparison regarding genocide at the novel's beginning. Thus the science fiction novel, while staying within the ideological and epistemological framework of the colonial discourse, exaggerates and exploits its internal divisions. Although it does not demystify the colonial gaze by bringing it into contact with history, as autoethnography would, nonetheless it estranges the colonial gaze by reversing the direction of the gaze's anachronism—science fiction pictures a possible future instead of the past—and setting the hierarchical difference between observer and observed swinging between the poles of subject and object, with each swing potentially questioning and recoding the discursive framework of scientific truth, moral certitude, and cultural hegemony.

FIGURE 2. Frank R. Paul, front cover illustration, *Amazing Stories*, August 1927.
*Courtesy of Cushing Memorial Library and Archives, Texas A&M University.
Used with permission of The Frank R. Paul Estate.*

FIGURE 3. Harold V. Brown, front cover illustration, *Thrilling Wonder Stories*, June 1939. *Courtesy of The Special Collections Library, University of California, Riverside.*

"Looming through the Mists"

One of the later and less well-known novels of H. G. Wells, *Mr. Blettsworthy on Rampole Island* (1928), can help us to further elaborate and refine this analysis of the critical potential of science fiction. In part three of this novel, we find Wells at his most Swiftian, as he depicts the castaway Arnold Blettsworthy's stay among the savage, cannibalistic, and heretofore undiscovered Rampole Islanders. As in so many exotic adventure tales, like Arthur Conan Doyle's *Lost World* (1912) or RKO's *King Kong* (1933), Wells's isolated islanders share their island with dinosaurs. But Wells's dinosaurs are not spectacular predators. They are megatheria, sloths the size of elephants, who destroy all flowering plants, no longer even reproduce, but survive through sheer inertia. Blettsworthy explicitly compares the megatheria to legal and political institutions in his home society and uses these prehistoric survivors to illustrate that Darwinian "survival of the fittest" (a popularizing paraphrase coined by Herbert Spencer and endorsed by Darwin himself) by no means always favors the better species. Any discerning reader will see that the political and religious institutions of the Rampole Islanders also parody those of contemporary Europe, as in the "howling sessions" where the military leaders whip up hatred against their enemies. Blettsworthy himself survives among the islanders under the sponsorship of Chit, the interpreter of the Sacred Lunatic. Blettsworthy fills the post of Sacred Lunatic in an ideal fashion, since the things he says make no sense to the islanders and therefore are entirely amenable to Chit's construing them in ways that enhance his personal power. Chit's opportunistic manipulation of the cultural other is one keynote of the whole episode, and it casts its shadow on the third chapter of the section, "The Evil People," which stands back from Blettsworthy's personal narrative to perform an ethnographic survey of the Rampole Islanders' appalling cultural institutions.

In part four, it turns out, however, that this entire society is a delusion suffered by Blettsworthy, who actually is living in a mental asylum in Brooklyn. When he awakens to his actual reality and is convinced of his delusion, he responds with the key generic and theoretical principles behind the novel's construction: "'This is the real world and I admit it.' At that he [Dr. Minchett, i.e., Chit] looked relieved. 'And also,' I added, 'I perceive that it is Rampole Island, here and now! For, after all, what was Rampole Island, doctor? It was only the real world looming through the mists of my illusions'" (267–68). Thus Rampole Island's grotesqueries represent the realistic material in the other three parts of the novel—including Blettsworthy's betrayal by his first business partner and his fiancée; his grisly career in the trenches of World War I; his deliberate abandonment on a sinking ship by a brutal captain who previously has beaten a cabin boy to death; and his exploitation by Minchett, who discovered Blettsworthy on the real Rampole Island while Minchett was searching unsuccessfully for survivors of the megatheria, and has been using this serendipitous specimen to further his scientific career—all "looming through the mists" of Blettsworthy's illusions. It would be wrong to dismiss the strategy that Wells takes for placing the Rampole Island sojourn into the coherently realist satire as merely a version of the tired "it was only a dream" device. Instead, *Blettsworthy*, like Philip K. Dick's *Confessions of a Crap Artist* (1975), is a realist narrative that takes on fantasy and delusion as its subject matter in such a way as to produce a metafictive commentary on the author's better-known nonrealist work. Blettsworthy's delusional system, which functions realistically as a defense that shields him from the traumatic reality he has lived through (this is Minchett's explanation), simultaneously exposes and comments on the social delusions all his countrymen share.

In fact, isn't Blettsworthy's fantasy construction of the social order of Rampole Island closer to reality than the normal social understanding of the world itself in precisely the same way as a theory pierces through appearances to depict fundamental principles or structures of interaction? I think that the way fantasy and reality play against one another here is meant by Wells as a comment on the critical potential of the combination of realism and impossibility in fictions such as Part Three of *Blettsworthy*—which is to say in fictions like *The Island of Dr. Moreau* (1896) or *The Time Machine* (1895).[5] But there is a temptation to be avoided here, which is that of reducing the Rampole Island episode to the hidden truth of the rest of the narrative. Such a reading would content itself with the moralizing conclusion that civilization is the true savagery, an anticlimax we can avoid by resisting the equation of the "real world looming through the mists" of Blettsworthy's illusions with truth unmasking falsehood. For what we are presented with is a metafictive structure, a fiction commenting upon another fiction. "Looming through the mist" is not a way of exiting from the narrative's frame to find a truth outside of it, but instead a way for the narrative to double back and comment upon itself. Moreover, what makes it possible for the fantastic adventure fiction of Rampole Island to be written over and against the realist fiction that contains it is the displaced cultural reference provided by the island and its people. It resembles a science-fictional displacement as soon as the island is exposed as a fantasy of the West, but its critical potential depends on the island's not being simply a disavowed, elaborately disguised self-portrait. Instead, Wells's metafiction sets into play about the image of the exotic other a set of tensions alternately assigning to the other the status of discovery or projection, datum or fantasy, the epiphany of radical difference or the disguised representation of the same.

This play of antithetical possibilities is an important measure of science fiction's engagement with colonial history, ideology, and discourse. But these ideological and discursive effects are not so much a matter of topical references as they are results of the way the narratives of colonial history and ideology "loom through the mists" of science fiction. It is as if science fiction itself were a kind of palimpsest, bearing the persistent traces of a stubbornly visible colonial scenario beneath its fantastic script. Or, to change the metaphor, it is as if science fiction were polarized by the energies of the colonial field of discourse, like a piece of iron magnetized by its proximity to a powerful electrical field. Both of these metaphors are ways of saying that science fiction exposes something that colonialism imposes. However, to repeat a point, colonialism is not simply the reality that science fiction mystifies. I am not trying to argue that colonialism is science fiction's hidden truth. I want to show that it is part of the genre's texture, a persistent, important component of its displaced references to history, its engagement in ideological production, and its construction of the possible and the imaginable.

Genre, System, and Text: Defining the Object of Study

Before venturing further into analysis of the relation between colonialism and the emergence of science fiction, however, it is necessary to explain exactly what I mean by "science fiction" and its "emergence." By "the emergence of science fiction," I mean the coalescence of a set of generic expectations into a recognizable condition of production and reception that enables both writers and readers to approach individual works as examples of a literary kind that in the 1920s and after came to be named science fiction. This process involves a historical shift in the system of recognizable literary genres, the emergence of a set of conventions and expectations that presented itself as a market niche, on the one hand (as the publishing entrepreneur Hugo Gernsback, the man most responsible for promulgating the term "science fiction," recognized), and as a creative possibility, on the other (as Verne, Wells, Conan Doyle, London, Burroughs, and many others recognized in the half-century before Gernsback launched his first "scientifiction" magazine). During a seventy-year period beginning around 1870 and ending with the outbreak of the Second World War, a steadily increasing number of texts prominently featured characteristics of science fiction, and a fairly coherent, long-term change in form accompanied this rising volume. At one end of the period, for instance, Verne's *Twenty Thousand Leagues Under the Sea* (1870; translated into English in 1872) and Bulwer-Lytton's *The Coming Race* (1871) set themselves in the contemporary world and began in a realist mode. The narrator or protagonist then stumbled into a remarkably nonrealist setting—Nemo's submarine and the underwater realm to which it gives access in Verne, the underground world of the Vril-ya in Bulwer-Lytton—which the rest of the narrative explored and explained. At the other end of the period, say in a typical issue of *Astounding Stories* in 1937, a whole set of nonrealist conventions was taken for granted from the outset. Alien beings, futuristic settings and technology, and the neologisms that name such nonexistent things are standard devices often casually dropped into the prose without explicit explanation. The first words that greet the reader of Eric Frank Russell and Leslie J. Johnson's "Seeker of Tomorrow" in the July 1937 issue of *Astounding Stories* (in Ashley 2:96–136) are "The Venusian city of Kar." Don A. Stuart's (i.e., John W. Campbell's) "Forgetfulness," in the June issue (reprinted in Campbell 161–91), opens with an astronomer standing in a "lock gate" breathing in "the strange tangy odors of this planet" (Campbell 161)—an unmistakable signal that he is not on Earth. The emergence of science fiction is the long, winding path leading from certain narratives that carefully disrupt realist conventions in the mid to late nineteenth century, to ones that assume science fiction conventions in the 1930s.

I am not going to define science fiction. This is a theoretically informed decision, lucidly proposed by Paul Kincaid in his essay "On the Origins of Genre." Kincaid's thesis is that we can neither "extract a unique, common thread" that binds together all science fiction texts, nor identify a "unique, common origin" for the genre (415). Pointing to the notorious proliferation of conflicting and even contradictory definitions of science fiction, Kincaid argues that science fiction, or any other literary genre, is best understood as a group of objects that bear a "family resemblance" to one another rather than sharing some set of essential, defining characteristics. He borrows the notion of family resemblance from Wittgenstein, whose example in the *Philosophical Investigations* is the term "sport." Wittgenstein shows that we can point to any number of activities that we consider sports, but we cannot point to any essential feature that all sports share. Applying Wittgenstein's notion of family resemblance to science fiction, Kincaid concludes that "science fiction is not one thing. Rather, it is any number of things—a future setting, a marvelous device, an ideal society, an alien creature, a twist in time, an interstellar journey, a satirical perspective, a particular approach to the matter of story, whatever we are looking for when we look for science fiction, here more overt, here more subtle—which are braided together in an endless variety of combinations" (416–17).[6]

Science fiction is "a web of resemblances" that can be traced backward from Gernsback's baptism of the genre along a variety of paths, and that can be extended in an unpredictable number of new and different ways. Its fluid boundaries have been defended and contested in many ways for many reasons, but the existence of the category as a condition of literary and cultural production and reception is incontrovertible.[7] Approaching science fiction as a web of resemblances, rather than a set of defining characteristics, puts the questions of inclusion and exclusion that have preoccupied definers of the genre from Gernsback to Darko Suvin into their proper place. When Gernsback, in the first issue of *Amazing*, reprints stories by Edgar Allan Poe, Jules Verne, and H. G. Wells alongside reprints of more recent pieces by G. Peyton Wertenbaker, George Allan England, and Austin Hall, and then declares Poe "the father of scientificiton" in his opening editorial (3), the question to ask does not concern the common defining characteristics of the six stories or their relation to Poe as source and font of science fiction, but rather it concerns the motives for Gernsback's construction of this group identity and its genealogy. The question about motives applies equally to Suvin's construction of a tradition of the "literature of cognitive estrangement" in *Metamorphoses of Science Fiction* that reaches back to Lucian and includes Percy B. Shelley and William Blake. To use the terminology and analysis mapped out in Pierre Bourdieu's "The Field of Cultural Production, or: The Economic World Reversed," both constructions of science fiction's identity attempt to capture and defend economic or cultural capital by staking out and laying claim to certain positions in the field of literary production. The difference between Gernsback's construction of a generic tradition and Suvin's has to do with their historically and culturally different positions and projects—most obviously, between Gernsback's attempt to establish conditions of profitability for his magazine venture by establishing a set of predictable and attractive expectations for the potential buyers of future issues, and Suvin's attempt to give the study of science fiction academic respectability by including canonical Romantic poets and excluding "subliterary" texts like those by Wertenbaker, England, or Hall.[8]

Any literary text can be read as a similar kind of project. Citation, imitation, allusion, and so on inevitably perform some kind of position taking (Bourdieu, "Field" 312), so that the pressures of the market, the dynamics of prestige, and the construction of genealogies are intrinsic features of the web of resemblances that constitutes a genre. Genres are best understood by way of the practices that produce these resemblances and the motives that drive those practices. Pigeon-holing texts as members or nonmembers of this or that genre is intellectually frivolous, whatever consequences it might have in terms of market value or prestige. This is doubly true because, first, genre itself is an intertextual phenomenon, always formed out of resemblances or oppositions among texts, and second, no individual text is generically pure. Every text produces within itself a set of generic values in tension with and interacting upon one another.

Because genre is always determined by a distribution of resemblances and differences across a field of cultural production, to speak of a genre is always to speak of a system of genres. Generic identity is always generic difference as well. The emergence of science fiction is both the historical process of the coalescence of a set of narrative innovations and expectations into a coherent generic category, and, necessarily, a shift that takes place in the entire system of genres, so that science fiction's web of resemblances becomes meaningful—emerges—as a distinct, conventional set of expectations different from those in its proximity. The "dialectical self-production of new forms," according to Hans-Robert Jauss, proceeds from innovation in individual texts to "changes of the system of literary genres and forms," that is, to changes in the "horizon of expectations," the literary and social conditions for the reception and transmission of cultural material (17, 22–24). Thus, over and above its mere existence as an ahistorical formal possibility, the value of a genre shifts with the changes that take place in the genre system. It means a different thing to write a first-person lyric poem in the early twenty-first century, within a system of genres that includes television commercials, tabloid journalism, and mass-market romances, than it did to write one in the early nineteenth, when such poetry was not a subject of college pedagogy, but was a standard feature of *The Gentleman's Magazine*. By the same token, the generic identity of individual works changes over time. Wells's scientific romance about alien invasion of Earth meant something different in 1898 than it did when Gernsback reprinted it in 1927, because what was surprising innovation in relation to the future war genre in 1898 could be read as the establishment of science fiction conventions in 1927.

The idea that a genre consists of a web of resemblances established by repetition across a large number of texts, and therefore that the emergence of science fiction involves a series of incremental effects that shake up and gradually, cumulatively, reconfigure the system of genres operating in the literary field of production, precludes the notion of science fiction's "miraculous birth" in a master text like *Frankenstein* (1818) or *The Time Machine*.[9] A masterpiece might encapsulate an essence, if science fiction had one, and it certainly can epitomize motifs and strategies; but only intertextual repetition can accumulate into a family of resemblances. In fact, the very notion of the founding instance or origin of a genre is self-contradictory, because the work in question is in an important way not an example of the genre it establishes, but rather a peculiarly influential violation of some pre-existing set of generic expectations.

Mary Shelley's *Frankenstein* is an excellent case in point. In 1818, on its first publication, it was read either as an example of Gothic romance or as a political novel in the vein of her father William Godwin's *Caleb Williams* (1794). Walter Scott wrote an important, perceptive review about Shelley's innovative combination of a fantastic premise with a realist development of it, but through most of the nineteenth century the story was better known in its melodramatic stage adaptations than its novel form. Only when the novel was released from the restrictive copyright under which it languished from 1831 to 1881, and sold four times more copies in the decade of the 1880s than it had in the previous six, did it become an important literary influence within the emergence of science fiction — most notably on Wells's *The Invisible Man* (1897) and *The Island of Dr. Moreau*. This influence was exercised within a genre system that included the 1880s' romance revival as well as a drastically different scientific and political context, which is to say, an entirely different horizon of expectations than greeted the publications of the novel's first edition in 1818 or the revised edition of 1831. Thus those who have identified *Frankenstein* as the first important piece of science fiction in English ought to add the proviso that it only became important in this way within the changing genre system of the 1880s.[10]

Another important corollary to the proposition that genre cannot be recognized as such on the basis of a single text, but only in the repetition of generic devices or qualities across a number of texts, is that generic resemblances have a collective, and therefore anonymous, character. For instance, the figure of the "advanced" alien race or of the man from the future with an enormous brain and atrophied body, despite the fact that it can be traced back to Wells's humorous essay "Of a Book Unwritten" and the Martians of *The War of the Worlds*, appears in magazine science fiction and cover art of the 1930s with a frequency that cannot be accounted for adequately by the widespread influence of Wells's essay or story. Instead, the figure acquires an anonymous quality, comparable to that of a legend or a joke, and one needs to explain its repetition in social terms. What is so fascinating, or so attractively repellent, about it? What collective fantasy, based on what shared desire, or trauma, or both, does it embody? Such repetition in magazine science fiction must be attributed in part to the pressure of commodification. But recognizing that the pursuit of sales to a target, niche audience determines a certain number of the choices that writers and editors make only returns interpretation of such stock figures to the question about reiterated desire, and emphasizes all the more the desire's anonymous, collective quality.

A better way to read such figures symptomatically and socially at the same time is to regard them as "mythic," not in the interest of seeing some kind of persistence of the Eternal in popular culture, but in Claude Lévi-Strauss's sense of myths as imaginary solutions to real social contradictions. These symbolic acts can be considered solutions, it must be remembered, only in the sense that the mythic narratives weave together distorted representations of socially intractable material in such a way as to render its intractability invisible. It must also be remembered that this kind of solution to a social contradiction, as Lévi-Strauss's discussion of the methodology of myth interpretation in his essay on Oedipus argues, only appears in the comparative analysis of multiple versions (206–31). One of the chief virtues of Lévi-Strauss's thesis, in fact, is the way it delivers a collective intelligibility and coherence to the often cryptic events and details of individual narratives. Applying Lévi-Strauss's methodology to the emergence of science fiction, then, involves tracing the paths of various commonplace devices, identifying the most insistently reiterated patterns, and interpreting them as cosmetic solutions to real social contradictions.

The social contradictions that underlie the desire and trauma motivating generic repetition are various. The shifting social horizons within which science fiction emerges are far too complex for us to single out any "key" element, be it technological change, class tensions, or the relative authority of science and religion. Writing the history of the genre's emergence must be a matter of weaving together disparate social, economic, and literary narratives. This book will demonstrate that many of the repetitive motifs that coalesced into the genre of science fiction represent ideological ways of grasping the social consequences of colonialism, including the fantastic appropriation and rationalization of unevenly distributed colonial wealth in the homeland and in the colonies, the racist ideologies that enabled colonialist exploitation, and the cognitive impact of radical cultural differences on the home culture. These range from triumphal fantasies of appropriating land, power, sex, and treasure in tales of exploration and adventure, to nightmarish reversals of the positions of colonizer and colonized in tales of invasion and apocalypse. When we return to the figure of the large-brained, small-bodied man of the future in the fourth chapter, it will be in the context of this pervasive ambivalence, which I earlier called the polarization of science fiction by its proximity to colonial ideology.

But we are not dealing with myths or dreams or neurotic symptoms. We are dealing with conscious works of art. The anonymous reference of generic expectations to social contradictions is complicated when one approaches individual texts, because the particular embodiments of those expectations are not merely repetitions of the generic ideology but also an antithetical form of expressing it. Just as any individual who possesses average qualities remains, as an individual, antithetical to the average as such, the relation of the generic to the particular in a literary text is never simple. On the contrary, in becoming the particular embodiment of a generic motif, the text simultaneously cancels out or sublates the generic quality of the representation. A similar situation arises, as folklorists have long recognized, when individual storytellers inevitably perform their relation to genre and their repetition of anonymous material in distinctly authorial, idiosyncratic ways. Using conventional material always involves taking a position towards it, so that interpretation needs to shuttle between collective ideology and the more or less complex repetition and resistance of it enacted in the individual text. This point and its implications will bear a full illustration.

The Map in the Lost-Race Motif

I will draw my example from the late-Victorian and early-twentieth-century lost-race motif—stories where a traveler or group of travelers encounters a previously isolated race or civilization in an exotic, nearly inaccessible setting. From around 1870 to World War I, there were two major strains of the lost-race motif. One, drawing largely on utopian and satiric traditions, ran from Samuel Butler's *Erewhon* (published in 1872) to Charlotte Perkins Gilman's *Herland* in 1915. The other, more commercially successful and numerically predominant strain of lost-race fiction ran from H. Rider Haggard's attempt to out-do Robert Louis Stevenson's adventure fiction in *King Solomon's Mines* (1885), to Arthur Conan Doyle's attempt to out-Haggard Haggard in *The Lost World* in 1912.[11] Of all the sub-genres that have been recognized as important to the genealogy of science fiction, perhaps none is more predictable than the commercially oriented adventure strain of the lost-race motif. It presents us with a plethora of widely repeated elements, including the map or document that initiates the expedition, the perilous journey to a nearly inaccessible destination, and a strictly circumscribed set of locations for the lost land itself (the underground world, the polar paradise, the isolated island, plateau, or valley). In the lost land, we find a beautiful princess, a corrupt priesthood, an architecturally impressive pagan idol, and a treasure or a fabulously rich mine. The plot often will include the return of an important native in the company of the explorers, the instigation and resolution of a civil war, and of course romantic involvements between the explorers and the princesses. Critical reception of the genre these days (although there is little written about it aside from work on Haggard) is as close to unanimous as one could ever expect to find in agreeing that it is fundamentally grounded in and expressive of an anonymous, collective, colonialist, and imperialist ideology (Katz, Stiebel).

My illustration concerns the way that the commonplace figure of the map or document figures in the lost-race motif. Its collective ideological character is grounded in the relation of the lost-race motif to the history of colonial exploration. The lost-race motif appeared on the scene just as one of the great eras in the history of cartography was drawing to a close. In the early part of the nineteenth century, the British Admiralty oversaw a comprehensive project of mapping the world's coastlines. The impact of the mapping expeditions on the world was not confined to making navigation safer or opening new coastlines to British commerce; Darwin's voyage to the Galapagos Islands on the *Beagle* was part of a coastal mapping expedition. The mapping of the non-European world proceeded inland later in the century under the leadership of the Royal Geographic Society, spearheaded by Sir Robert Murchison, who had also identified the Devonian, Silurian, and Permian stratigraphic systems in British soil and sought confirmation for his geological findings elsewhere (Stafford). The lost-race motif of finding living dinosaurs (cf. *Blettsworthy*) and long-lost fragments of European civilization in new lands is a sensationalist exaggeration of the actual project of reading the flora, fauna, and the very soil of foreign lands as the texts of a gradually developing scientific story of the world's history. Haggard's fiction of dark-skinned natives living in the midst of the ruins of King Solomon's civilization, ignorant of the significance of what surrounds them, echoes the European understanding

Introduction: The Colonial Gaze ○ 23

of indigenous people in a natural world they seemed to barely understand or know how to take advantage of. Thus the map that instigates the adventurers' expedition, often pointing the way to a hidden treasure, indicates the way that European knowledge gives the adventurers both the means and the right to claim the hidden treasure as their own.

Yet a closer look at the treasure map in *King Solomon's Mines* reveals a more complex situation. Written in blood on a scrap of clothing by a dying Portuguese explorer, the map enjoins its European readers to raise an army, invade the isolated African country, and thereby reap unimaginable wealth. One might recall that the treasure map no doubt inspiring Haggard's use of this device, the one found in Stevenson's *Treasure Island*, is discovered amidst the businesslike accounts of a career pirate. Haggard, who hyperbolizes everything about the map and the treasure alike, raises piracy to the level of state policy. The picturesque name for the mountains that form a nearly impassable barrier to the explorers, Sheba's Breasts, is also the invention of the Portuguese mapmaker. This sexualization of the African land, a typical enough feature of colonialist ideology and of adolescent fantasy, also disturbingly associates the explorers' entering and attempting to carry away treasure from King Solomon's mines with vainglorious sexual conquest, at best, and at worst, rape (McClintock 1–4). Thus, along with representing the isolated African land as a kind of legacy bequeathed by the Portuguese explorer to the white travelers, the map undermines that claim and its supporting ideology in significant ways. The relation of the generic motif to the particular text is here a dialectical relationship between the imaginary solution of a social contradiction—here, the contradiction between the adventurers' claim to the treasure and the rights of the local inhabitants—and the social conflicts that stubbornly cling to that imaginary solution.

One might argue that, rather than an example of the antithetical relation between the generic and the particular, what one finds in the example of the map is the subtle undermining of predictable adventure formulas by Haggard's literary art. Deliberately undercutting adventure story formulas is indeed a typical feature of satirical versions of the lost-race motif, especially after the remarkable proliferation and commercial success of the adventure formulas in the 1890s. Perhaps the best example is Wells's brilliant short story "The Country of the Blind" (1904). In this story, however, as in Charlotte Perkins Gilman's *Herland*, one finds alongside whatever complications or ironic twists that are given to formulaic elements, a quite deliberate avoidance of central adventure material: the explorers are not heroic, the society they enter is stable rather than riven by an internal conflict that their coming helps to solve, and so on. In fact, both Wells and Gilman make their explorers into naïve readers. The satires both turn on the fact that the strangers in the strange lands expect things to work out as if they were in a typical lost-race fantasy. There is nothing of this in *King Solomon's Mines* or *She* or *Allan Quatermain* or — to move to an example more contemporaneous with Wells and Gilman — in Conan Doyle's *The Lost World*. I would suggest, however, that in Haggard's and Conan Doyle's enthusiastic exploitation of the predictable, the fault lines of the formulaic solutions show up in ways that register the emotional ambivalence and historical complexity of colonial situations just as richly as the more explicitly critical satirical-utopian works do. Theirs is a different achievement, and the difference is one worth thinking about.

There is a social dynamic at work in the attitudes of the academic world toward Haggard and Wells, as measured by the amount and kind of scholarly attention each has received, that has to do with the privilege and distinction afforded to "literature" in the sense in which that category is produced by a class practice based on taste and discernment.[12] Pierre Bourdieu's survey of musical likes and dislikes in *Distinction: A Social Critique of the Judgement of Taste* suggests that an important feature of the reception and distribution of different types of music is the way they convey the sense that understanding and appreciating them marks one as being in the know, a member of what he calls "the aristocracy of culture" (11–96). Similarly, more "literary" texts, such as "The Country of the Blind" and *Herland*, demand that their readers be in the know. These stories call upon their readers to understand that a popular convention is being alluded to, and simultaneously to see beyond it, relishing both its invocation and its sophisticated dismissal. But if the more commercially oriented narratives, intent on fulfilling generic expectations rather than subverting them, are for that reason in closer, or rather, more explicit contact with the popular ideologies that they repeat and exploit, this does not prevent them from exposing, mocking, and criticizing those ideologies at the same time. As literary critics, we should not allow the dynamics of prestige to fool us into thinking that commercially oriented narratives actually aspiring to fulfill popular generic expectations are, merely for that reason, written or necessarily read naïvely.

The difference between the satirical-utopian and the commercial strains of the lost-race motif bears much more than an accidental resemblance to the difference between Hugo Gernsback's commercially motivated construction of a science fiction tradition and Darko Suvin's critically and academically motivated genealogy. For the emerging genre of science fiction, especially in the venue of the pulp magazines, generic expectations were primarily conditions of profitability, promises to the reader of a certain sort of satisfaction. But Suvin's genealogy, with its insistence on dividing "literary" and "sub-literary" texts from one another, is possible because the genre of science fiction, like any narrative genre, is a diverse phenomenon, one whose web of resemblances is scattered all across the field of cultural production that is structured by the tensions between commercial profitability and class-oriented prestige. Therefore, there is always more than one kind of profit at stake in the operation of its generic conventions, and the strategies for capturing those profits vary accordingly. The description and analysis of the emergence of science fiction conventions and of a reading audience attuned to them cannot be restricted to the niche market identified by the entrepreneurial pulp publishers. Such an audience is always going to be shadowed by and overlap with another group that is happier reading *against* generic expectations than *with* them. By the same token, the large-scale tensions that structure the entire field of cultural production also reappear within individual texts with effects that sometimes coincide with and magnify the polarization and ambivalence of ideology.

Colonialism, Class, and the Reading Audience

I have so far used the terms "colonialism" and "imperialism" without pausing for definition or discussion of them, and without acknowledging that for some historians they denote distinctly different situations: colonization and settlement versus rule by proxy governments or bureaucratic administration from afar (the British in Australia versus the British in India). The sense in which colonialism is used in the title of this book is a very broad one that includes both of these situations and more. It refers to the entire process by which European economy and culture penetrated and transformed the non-European world over the last five centuries, including exploration, extraction of resources, expropriation and settlement of the land, imperial administration and competition, and postcolonial renegotiation of the distribution of power and wealth among the former colonizers and colonized. In this sense, colonialism describes something as pervasive and complex as capitalism itself, and in fact, I ascribe to Immanuel Wallerstein's position that "the appropriation of surplus of the whole-world economy by core areas" is not merely an extension of European capitalism into the rest of the world but rather an integral feature of capitalism throughout its development (18–19). Without reducing the complex political and cultural history of colonialism to mere secondary effects of a primary economic process, one still can say that one of the most comprehensive and inclusive ways to think about colonialism is by way of its role in the construction of a world-wide, unified capitalist economy, a process that gets seriously under way in the sixteenth century and reaches a climactic fulfillment and crisis in the period with which we are most concerned here, from the mid-nineteenth century through the world wars.[13]

Two aspects of the construction of a world-embracing capitalist economy are particularly relevant to the relation between colonialism and the emergence of science fiction. The first is the realignment of local identities that accompanied the restructuring of the world economy. As local economies ravaged by the new extractive industries (oil, rubber, tin, copper, precious metals) and regional specialization of agriculture (cotton, sugar, pineapple) became "underdeveloped" and dependent, so too the cultures that the traditional economies had supported often were thrown into shock and disarray. What the dominant ideology recognized as the relation between civilization and savagery, and between modernity and its past, can be read at least in part as a misrecognition of the corrosive effects of capitalist social relations on the traditional cultures of colonized populations and territories. Understanding the non-Western world as an earlier stage of Western social development, in this line of interpretation, serves the apologetic function of naturalizing the relation of the industrialized economic core to the colonial periphery and rendering its effects as the working out of an inexorable, inevitable historical process. But the scientific study of other cultures—what Derrida calls the decentering of Europe as the culture of reference—is intimately bound up with the same economic process. I therefore will be arguing both that ideological misrecognition of the effects of economic and political inequality has a strong presence in the ideas about progress and modernity that circulate throughout early science fiction, and also that early science fiction often works against such ethnocentrism.

The second pertinent effect of the construction of a global economy is a ramification of the international division of labor. Lenin famously quotes Cecil B. Rhodes's opinion that "if you want to avoid civil war, you must become imperialists" (79). The point, for Lenin, is that imperialism produces a division of the international surplus that ameliorates class antagonisms in the imperialist nation-states. The imperialist country's exploitation of the rest of the world creates inside the nation a privileged category of workers whose interests have been aligned with the bourgeoisie at home rather than with the proletariat abroad (106–8). For the historian of science fiction, the point has less to do with the sharing of real wealth than with the reading public's vicarious enjoyment of colonial spoils, as attested to in Victorian England by the popularity of travel accounts and adventure stories. This sharing of imaginary wealth will be a major concern in the reading of lost-race fiction presented in chapter two. At the same time, the contradiction between domestic class formation and international inequality sometimes can complicate the mechanisms of identification that such vicarious enjoyment would seem to depend upon. For instance, the usual reading of Wells's *The Time Machine* is that the Eloi and the Morlocks enact the long-term logic of the relation between the bourgeoisie and the industrial proletariat, but Eric Hobsbawm refers to the Eloi and the Morlocks as a more or less obvious representation of the "parasitism at the centre" of imperialism and fears of "the eventual triumph of the barbarians" (*Age of Empire* 83). It is not a case where one reading cancels out the other. The ambiguous class position of the imperial public makes them look like the Morlocks in the context of the domestic economy, and like the Eloi in the global one. This is a problem we shall return to at greater length in the section on *The Time Machine* in chapter three.

It is difficult, of course, to provide evidence about what segments of the imperial public purchased and read early science fiction in sufficient numbers to encourage the growth of the genre documented in Bleiler's, Clareson's, and Suvin's bibliographies. But what evidence there is, particularly the biographies of Victorian authors of science fiction compiled in Suvin's *Victorian Science Fiction in the UK*, indicates a predominantly middle-class audience with a strong disposition towards technical occupations. From this tentative evidence, we can draw three correspondingly tentative conclusions.

First, we can say that such a reading audience could have come into shape only with the second phase of the industrial revolution, at which point the economically predominant industries became steel and coal rather than textiles. The industrial economy demands a sector of the work force that has some scientific training, and the members of this middle-class, technocratic-managerial milieu, or, perhaps more likely, the younger readers whose interests and education tended to direct them toward this milieu, seem likely to have comprised an important, perhaps even dominant, element in the reading audience of early science fiction. Science fiction's fascination with technological innovation surely would make sense in this connection.

Second, it is also during the second phase of the industrial revolution that the exploitation of labor power—with the passage of the Ten Hours Act in England in 1847—tended to become intensive rather than extensive, depending on increasing productivity, primarily through automation, rather than on lengthening the working day. If the early readers of science fiction were clustered in the technically advanced sector, they also would have been the part of the population most closely associated with this orientation toward increased productivity. This is significant for two reasons. First, an orientation toward productivity and efficiency certainly conforms both with the popularity of stories about marvelous inventions and scientific discoveries, as we just mentioned, and also with ideologies of progress, which we will look at more closely in the next section of this chapter. Second, modern mass culture in general depends upon the development of a certain type of leisure tied to this regime of increased productivity. The strong interest that a capitalist economy has in occupying leisure time with consumption of the commodities that are being churned out in ever-growing number by its ever-more-productive workers is what lead Max Horkheimer and Theodor Adorno, the twentieth century's most caustic theorists of mass culture, to call the entire phenomenon "the culture industry" (120–67). The early science fiction reading audience—middle-class, educated, and provided with leisure—seems to be one well placed to put into action the consumerism at the heart of modern mass culture.

Finally, the dominance of steel and coal in the second phase of the industrial revolution is also inseparable from the building of the world-wide railroad system, and the rocketing exportation of heavy machinery from the industrial core countries, which characterized the extended economic boom of the 1850s through the early 1870s that decisively established capitalism as the single unifying world economy. This was followed, however, by an extended economic downturn from the 1870s to the end of the century, provoking the frantic imperialist competition that culminated in the First and Second World Wars. While the period's improvements in communication and transportation bound the world economy more tightly together, they also marked out ever more clearly the boundaries separating the developed world from the undeveloped one. The most spectacular form of the widening difference between the developed and undeveloped nations was their military technology. If science fiction emerged in the context of the industrialization of the core economies, its corresponding international context was the imperial competition that gave birth to the first modern arms race.

The Ideology of Progress

The arms race is one of any number of sites where ideas about "progress" link the various threads of colonial discourse to one another and to science fiction. Thomas Clareson, the least fussy of all major scholars of science fiction when it comes to generic definitions, nonetheless insists that belief in progress is an absolute prerequisite to the formation of science fiction ("Emergence" 5). Fredric Jameson offers a more complex and ambitious theory that links progress and science fiction via the historical novel. For Jameson, progress is what he calls an ideologeme, "an amphibious formation, whose essential structural characteristic may be described as its possibility to manifest itself either as a pseudoidea—a conceptual or belief system, an abstract value, an opinion or prejudice—or as a protonarrative, a kind of ultimate class fantasy about the 'collective characters' which are the classes in opposition" (*The Political Unconscious* 87). Progress, says Jameson, is the form of social memory demanded by capitalism, an awareness of qualitative social change that links the past to the present under the narrative logic of growth or development. Moreover, progress is the ideologeme that is fundamental to the historical novel, a genre that is "the symptom of a mutation in our relationship to historical time itself" ("Progress versus Utopia" 149). Jameson follows George Lukács's famous argument in *The Historical Novel* that from the middle of the nineteenth century on, the historical novel begins to lapse into naturalism, its critically powerful linkage of past and present tending to degenerate into mere antiquarianism or exoticism. Science fiction, Jameson proposes, then emerges as a counter-strategy that revitalizes the notion of progress by "transforming our own present into the determinate past of something yet to come" ("Progress Versus Utopia" 152). A straightforward example of such a strategy is Edward Bellamy's *Looking Backward* (1888), with its vision of a utopian future attained by centralized industrial production and rationally administered distribution of its products. Surely Bellamy's commitment to a certain version of technological and administrative progress must be called upon to help account for the novel's enormous popularity and influence. In the 1890s, as we will see in chapter three, the future was called upon repeatedly to establish a critical perspective upon the present. In the process, because of the ideology of progress, the relation of the present to the future inevitably took some of its tone from colonial discourse.[14]

The pseudoidea or protonarrative of progress pervades the ideologies of colonialism that code the non-European world in all its diversity, not simply as the Other, but in various ways as the veritable embodiment of the past: wild, savage, tribal, barbarous, despotic, superstitious, and so on. From the moment Darwin's *The Origin of Species* appeared in 1859, pre-existing ideologies of progress imposed themselves on the theory of natural selection to produce "Social Darwinian" justifications of racism and of ruthless territorial expansion. The protonarrative of progress operates equally in the ideology of the "white man's burden"—the belief that non-whites are childlike innocents in need of white men's protection—and the assumptions that undergird Victorian anthropology. From the most legitimate scientific endeavor to the most debased and transparent prejudices runs the common assumption that the relation of the colonizing societies to the colonized ones is that of the developed, modern present to its own undeveloped, primitive past.

The way that the "collective characters" of the ideology of progress act within science fiction is one of the most important features of the intersection of colonialism and science fiction. The persistence of the structure of the colonial gaze in the frame of science fiction often boils down to this, and in much of what follows I will be arguing that science fiction addresses itself to the ideological basis of colonial practice itself, by engaging various aspects of the ideology of progress. By the ideological basis of colonial practices, I mean a set of beliefs of the sort that Slavoj Žižek calls ideological fantasies—beliefs that we consciously disavow, recognizing them as untrue, but nonetheless support in practice. A fairly mundane example of ideological fantasy is our attitude toward money. Although we know very well that a dollar bill is not indestructible abstract value, but just a perishable piece of paper, we behave on the assumption that it is the very embodiment of value (Žižek 31). This may look like mere contractual agreement, but the element of "consensual hallucination" (to adopt a phrase from William Gibson) appears more strongly in the more telling and relevant example of racism. We know very well that the racial other is a human being just like ourselves, but we behave under the assumption that the other is a grotesque parody of humankind. In the period of science fiction's emergence, this kind of racism extended into scientific discourse with the controversies concerning monogenetic versus polygenetic theories of the origins of the human race, that is, the question of whether white people and non-whites were really distinct species. There is no better example of science fiction portraying "the *mise en scène of the fantasy which is at work in the production of social reality itself*" (Žižek 36, Žižek's emphasis) than Wells's exploration of racist ideology in *The Island of Dr. Moreau*.

Three other powerful ideological fantasies also set the collective characters of progress into action on the terrain of science fiction. The first can be called the discoverer's fantasy: We know very well that there are people living in this land, but we act as if it were empty before our arrival. Mary Louise Pratt emphasizes this recurrent fantasy in the works of explorers from Columbus, Vespucci, and Raleigh to the monumental early-nineteenth-century natural histories of Alexander von Humboldt, all of which represent "America as a primal world of nature, an unclaimed and timeless space occupied by plants and creatures (some of them human), but not organized by societies and economies; a world whose history was the one about to begin" (126). The same fantasy informs arguments for the legal appropriation of native land for use by settlers. The keynote of legal justification of colonial seizure of land in the work of thinkers from Thomas More to John Locke is the idea that natives leave the land itself empty, that is, nonproductive—or, as Hugo Grotius argued, that "if usable things were left unused, there was no property in them, and hence people could appropriate land left unused by others" (Wood 72 and 68–101).

Another pervasive ideological formation is the missionary fantasy: Although we know that our arrival disrupts and destroys the traditional way of life here, we believe that it fulfills the deep needs and desires of all right-thinking natives. Here, disavowal of the obvious consequences of colonial invasion is so powerful as to often quite overpower any conscious recognition of it. The narrative of progress dictates that the old ways must give way to the new ones with the inevitability of the past becoming the present. The missionary's fantasy posits as a matter of faith that the goodness of this change is ultimately self-evident even to those who may appear to suffer from the process, and, keeping step with racist ideology, finds confirmation of their humanity itself in their recognition of the superiority of the colonizers' truth over their native falsehood. The whole process of the Westernization and Christianization of colonial elites attests to the power of this assumption. The corollary to this understanding of assimilation and conversion is that native resistance to colonization has to be considered alternatively as childlike perversity, evidence of sub-humanity, and entrenched self-interest. In any case, the defenders of native culture are understood to be the true enemies of the people. In the terms worked out earlier in relation to the colonial gaze, native resistance clings to the anachronism of the natives' past in the face of the universality of the colonizers' present. The way that the missionary's fantasy and the discoverer's fantasy are played out in the formulas of lost-race fiction will be discussed at length in chapter two.

Finally, there is the anthropologist's fantasy: Although we know that these people exist here and now, we also consider them to exist in the past—in fact, to be our own past. The point that bears repeating here about this already familiar ideological formation is that, especially in science fiction, technology is the primary way of representing this confrontation of past and present or of projecting it into a confrontation of present and future. The key element linking colonial ideology to science fiction's fascination with new technology is the new technology's scarcity. The thrill of the technological breakthrough is not that it benefits everyone but that it produces a singular, drastic difference between those who possess the new invention or power source and those who do not. Speculations about technology itself may be of significant interest to the technically oriented readership of early science fiction, but the relevance of colonialism to stories about technology shows up in the social relations that form around the technology's uneven distribution.

Consider, for example, the combination of wonderful gadgetry and headlong travel in the novels of Jules Verne. The accuracy or inaccuracy of Verne's predictions about technological innovation or the fascination exercised by the hardware itself are all finally less important in Verne's narratives than settings and place and especially access to place. Verne's marvelous journeys do not simply penetrate unmarked space. Often the travel gains its interest by defying political boundaries and threatening to render them meaningless. The opposition of the unbounded, anarchic sea to the national, political organization of the land is far more important to *Twenty Thousand Leagues Under the Sea* than is the design or practicality of Captain Nemo's submarine. What Nemo or similar figures introduce is not merely a new form of locomotion but a new unevenness of technological development that potentially destabilizes the contemporary distribution of political, economic, and military power, as indicated by the great powers' frantic attempts to locate the "master of the world" in the later novel of that name and buy his secret from him.

Thus the advent of the spectacular invention inevitably invokes that embracing pattern of uneven economic and cultural distribution, colonialism, and with it arises the specter of those encounters between cultures with wildly different technological capabilities that produced during this period some of the most one-sided armed conflicts in human history (see Headrick ch. 7). Behind the anxieties of competition between capitalist corporations and imperialist governments in stories of marvelous invention, lurks the possibility of finding oneself reduced by someone else's progress to the helplessness of those who are unable to inhabit the present fully, and whose continued existence on any terms other than those of the conquerors has been rendered an archaism and anomaly. Colonial invasion is the dark counter-image of technological revolution. In relation to technology, as in other contexts, the history, ideology, and discourses of colonialism dovetail with the crucial, double perspective that runs throughout the genre: on one hand, the wondrous exploration of the new and the marvelous encounter with the strange, but on the other, the post-apocalyptic vision of a world gone disastrously wrong.

chapter two

Fantasies of Appropriation
Lost Races and Discovered Wealth

The remarkable popularity of Jules Verne's *voyages extraordinaires* in English translations from the late 1860s on is one of the publishing phenomena that began to rearrange the genre system of popular fiction so as eventually to create that niche within it that we now recognize as science fiction. Only recently has English language criticism begun to catch up with the French in seriously assessing Verne's achievement, separating his English reception as a juvenile writer, often in highly unsatisfactory translations, from the scope and complexity of his entire project.[1] Another such publishing phenomenon, one that has received far less critical attention than even Verne's under-appreciated corpus, is the late-nineteenth-century burgeoning of lost-race fiction. Everett Bleiler's massive bibliography of science fiction up to 1930, *Science-Fiction: The Early Years*, includes more than three hundred examples of lost-race fiction in its three thousand entries, and the number rises to about three hundred fifty if one counts entries from the overlapping years in *Science-Fiction: The Gernsback Years*.[2] The transient efflorescence of this largely neglected body of narratives constitutes an important moment in the emergence of science fiction.

Bleiler comments in the preface to *The Early Years* that, in comparison to Verne and his imitators, the lost-race novel "is inherently a more romantic form, with reflections of deeper cultural currents and a closer figurative relation to the conflicts of the nineteenth century" (xx). Although the comparison to Verne does not stand up well in the light of recent scholarship, Bleiler's comment about "romantic form" is quite suggestive. The form of romance that characterizes lost-race fiction is not the Romanticism of Friederich Schiller or William Wordsworth, but rather that of the neomedieval "romance revival" of the late nineteenth century. In this context, the ancient forms of quest romance and the marvelous journey inevitably referred to contemporary colonial and imperial situations. Lost-race fiction shares this romantic reference to colonialism with a larger and far better studied class of narratives, best referred to simply as tales of adventure, a genre that Martin Green, in *Dreams of Adventure, Deeds of Empire*, calls the "energizing myth of English imperialism" (3). Although some historians of science fiction have been eager to emphasize the relation of science fiction to classic and Enlightenment-era imaginary voyages like those of Lucian and Swift, while downplaying or sometimes outright denying the affinity of science fiction to the work of H. Rider Haggard and his legion of imitators, the lingering presence of the conventions of colonial-imperial adventure fiction has a lot to do with the "xenophobia and colonialism" that Bleiler finds an overwhelming presence in pulp science fiction during the Gernsback era (*Gernsback Years* xv), elements of which certainly persist in late-twentieth-century mass-market products such as the *Star Wars* saga. But lost-race fiction is not merely a source of chauvinistic fantasy. The blending of the imaginary voyage and the imperial tale of adventure in such narratives also brings into view some of the central formal and aesthetic problems of science fiction. Lost-race fiction has much to tell us about how the intersection of imaginary voyages, tales of adventure, and colonial discourses affected the shape of emergent science fiction.

Satire and Quest Romance in the Imaginary Voyage

The imaginary voyage in the eighteenth century was primarily a vehicle for satire. The fantastic destination, whether located on an island, underground, or on the moon, was in eighteenth-century satire a tellingly distorted reflection of the readers' culture and a platform for philosophical debate. The main function of the imaginary land's marvelous features was to provide critical, subversive analogies with the norm, the plot's point of departure in both a geographical and axiological sense; and the central effect of the voyager's journey and return was the transformation of his values. The paradigmatic and most influential example is Lemuel Gulliver's estrangement from his fellow Englishmen upon his return home in Jonathan Swift's *Gulliver's Travels*. But a rival pattern also was established in the early eighteenth century. When Paul Baines, in an essay on eighteenth-century fantastic voyages, comments on the experience of Daniel Defoe's Robinson Crusoe that "the colonial voyage into alien culture actually serves to revalue one's own. . . . The ordinary becomes strange and rare, the familiar weapon a devastating Promethean device" (8–9), he is talking about the dominance of Crusoe's labor and technology over the island rather than the island's effect upon him (cf. Green 76–78). The keynote of Crusoe's voyage is acquisition, not reorientation. This, according to Green, is the difference that makes *Robinson Crusoe* (1719), not *Gulliver's Travels*, stand at the beginning of eighteenth- and nineteenth-century adventure fiction.

There is always a certain overlapping of adventure and satire in the eighteenth- and nineteenth-century imaginary voyage. Take for example two influential hollow-earth journeys, Ludwig Holberg's *Nicolai Klimii Iter Subterraneum*, translated into English in 1742 as *Journey to the World Under-Ground, by Nicholas Klimius*, and "Adam Seaborn's" 1820 *Symzonia*.[3] Nicholas Klimius, an impoverished Norwegian philosopher, enters the underworld by accident while exploring an oracular hole in Norway. There he meets a series of strange races—first a race of intelligent and conservative trees, then a nation of fashion-obsessed monkeys, and finally a race of negroid primitives who eventually make him their emperor. In the first land, Klimius is lectured to by sober philosophers, but in the second he becomes an entrepreneurial success by introducing periwigs, and in the third he gains power by introducing guns. The plot is a series of adventures in strange lands with marvelously fanciful inhabitants and customs, and its overall trajectory looks something like a series of acquisitions—of wisdom, wealth, and power—that we will find repeated throughout lost-race fiction. But the emphasis is clearly satirical. Klimius's success rises as his surroundings become more debased. His cultural assumptions are first undercut by the rational and virtuous arguments of the tree-philosophers, but then his commercial vanity is acted out in ridiculous fashion among the monkeys. His sojourn among the savages exposes the dependence of the new mercantile economy on military adventure in an even more grotesque and violent way. Klimius finally returns home not enriched but rather, in Swiftian fashion, embittered and quasi-insane.

Symzonia, too, is predominantly satirical, but with closer ties to the tale of adventure than Holberg's *Journey*. Rather than an accidental tourist, Adam Seaborn is a mercantile capitalist as well as an explorer, and the annexation and exploitation of the lands he discovers is his major concern. Ultimately, as in Holberg, commercialism and militarism are the central targets of the satire. The anticapitalist utopia, Symzonia, represents a moral and ethical critique of European society similar to that found in Holberg's land of the trees. Reason and moderation are the key to a good society. Luxury and superfluity can be traced back to cupidity. What is crucial, however, is that the drive for exploration that sends Seaborn sailing off the map and into the polar crevice is provided by the combined fact of the depletion of resources by rapacious exploitation—as in the harvesting of seal-skins undertaken by Seaborn's crew—and the fantasy that the resources are in fact limitless. As Žižek would say, Seaborn knows very well that the natural world is a finite source of wealth, but in the pursuit of profit he behaves on the belief that natural resources are infinite. The most interesting and indicative moment in this connection is when Seaborn decides that his discoveries should remain secret in order to protect them from mercantile competitors; otherwise the world will be used up and explorers will be forced to look for new resources on the moon and the planets. The fantastic geography of the hollow earth is not, as in Holberg, merely a way of opening up an analogical space for the satire. It is also an enormous expansion of the capacity of the planet to provide exploitable resources for capitalist expansion and colonialist annexation.

James De Mille's *A Strange Manuscript Found in a Copper Cylinder*, a lost-race fiction published in 1888 but written as much as twenty years earlier (De Mille died in 1880), is positioned even more tenuously between satire and adventure, but with the dominant element still definitely satire. This delightful novel is largely parodic, and one of its main targets is the plot of acquiring wealth in foreign lands that is the staple of adventure fiction. Adam More, the narrator of the strange manuscript, accidentally enters an Antarctic subtropical realm inhabited by a people, the Kosekin, whose values are radically the reverse of European: Their entire system is built on the desirability of death and the preference of darkness over light. But they are not demonic or satanic. They are instead hyperbolically self-denying, striving only to elevate their neighbors over themselves. This is a telling reversal of the principles of hierarchy and competition that structure Adam More's values, who at one point longs to find someone selfish and greedy among the Kosekin with whom he could establish some basis of sympathetic communication. At the end, in a delicious send-up of the white man's burden, More takes over rulership of the land by accepting the enormous wealth, large contingent of slaves, and resplendent palace that the Kosekin, in their quest for social prestige, willingly cast upon him. The narrator's name, combining allusions to the biblical Eden and Thomas More's *Utopia*, emphasizes the general, social character of the fantasy he embodies that the world lies all before the white male adventurer, waiting to give itself to him. More's enrichment by the Kosekin exposes, decidedly more sharply and rigorously than *Symzonia*, the colonial and capitalist ideological fantasy of the inexhaustible natural abundance of the "new world" in the face of the apparent impoverishment of its inhabitants. But where folly and vanity stand in the earlier satires of Holberg and Seaborn, the conventions of the tale of adventure come into play in De Mille.

By the time *A Strange Manuscript Found in a Copper Cylinder* was published, the lost-race novel had been transformed decisively into a vehicle of adventure, a change that made its pressure felt on all versions of the imaginary voyage. The watershed is without any doubt the astounding commercial success of H. Rider Haggard's *King Solomon's Mines* in 1885, followed by the equally phenomenal success of *She* in 1887.[4] The best emblem of the transformation of conventions involved is not either of these two novels, however, but the way that Haggard begins his sequel to *King Solomon's Mines*, also published in 1887, *Allan Quatermain*. Both *King Solomon's Mines* and *She* are quests instigated by ancient, mysterious maps, in the acquisitive, adventure-fiction mode of the treasure hunt. The trip into the heart of Africa in *Allan Quatermain* is instead motivated by Quatermain's grief after the death of his beloved and only son. Mourning is only part of the problem, however. Quatermain and his fellow travelers also suffer from a more general malaise following upon the wealth and ease they acquired at King Solomon's diamond mines. As Sir Henry Curtis puts it, "I'm tired of it too, dead tired of doing nothing except play the squire in a country that is sick of squires. . . . I am sick of shooting pheasants and partridges, and want to have a go at some large game again. There, you know the feeling—when once one has tasted brandy and water, milk becomes insipid to the palate" (424). Quatermain, Curtis, and Captain Good trek into Africa in order to reawaken their joy of living from the stupor it has fallen into in suburban England.

This motive is significant because it echoes the polemics of the debate between romance and realism in the contemporary romance revival, whose most effective spokesperson was Haggard's friend and supporter Andrew Lang. In the same year, 1887, Lang argued for the merits of romance in terms that parallel Quatermain's prefatory debate with himself over the comparative merits of civilization and savagery in the opening pages of *Allan Quatermain*, with its "depressing conclusion" that "in all essentials the savage and the child of civilisation are identical" (419). According to Lang in his essay on "Realism and Romance," "Modern romances of adventure . . . may be 'savage survivals,' but so is the whole of the poetic way of regarding Nature" (690). Romances appeal to "the natural man within me, the survival of some blue-painted Briton or of some gipsy" as opposed to the "bald, toothless, highly 'cultured'" audience "addicted to tales of introspective analysis" (689).[5] Thus, when Quatermain seizes upon the trip to Africa to deal with his grief, Haggard is also laying before us his generic program for romance: "When the heart is stricken, and the head is humbled in the dust, civilisation fails us utterly. Back, back we creep, and lay us like children on the great breast of Nature" (421). The quest in *Allan Quatermain* is a self-conscious repetition, not just an adventure but a return to the scene of adventure.

Allan Quatermain and "Realism and Romance" signal the emergence of a self-conscious, ideologically charged alliance between romance and the imaginary voyage. In an introduction to the American William Bradshaw's lost-race novel *The Goddess of Atvatabar* in 1892, Julian Hawthorne pumps the novel as part of "a reaction from the depression of the realistic school," associating it with a new school of writers that includes Haggard, Stevenson, and Kipling, and constructing a genealogy for "the intending historian of an ideal, social, or political community" that includes Plato, Sir Philip Sidney, and Swift along with Bradshaw's contemporaries Haggard, Percy Greg (*Across the Zodiac* [1880]), Ignatius Donnelly (theorist of Atlantis), and Edward Bellamy (Bradshaw 9–10; quoted in Clareson *Some Kind of Paradise* 168–69). But perhaps more telling than Hawthorne's critical position is the motive confessed by Bradshaw's narrator for seeking adventure abroad:

I used to dream of exploring tropic islands, of visiting the lands of Europe and the Orient, and of haunting temples and tombs, palaces and pagodas. I wished to discover all that was weird and wonderful on the earth, so that my experiences would be a description of earth's girdle of gold, bringing within reach of the enslaved multitudes of all nations ideas and experiences of surpassing novelty and grandeur that would refresh their parched souls. I longed to whisper in the ear of the laborer at the wheel that the world was not wholly a blasted place, but that here and there oases made green its barrenness. If he could not actually in person mingle with its joys, his soul, that neither despot nor monopolist could chain, might spread its wings and feast on such delights as my journeyings might furnish. (20)

Any hint of the exotic destination as a satirical or critical metaphor for the home culture, or of the possibility of radical cultural difference, is drowned in the project of setting the laborer's soul free to feast on the delights gathered in the earth's "girdle of gold" and sent home for consumption.

The obvious gendering of the natural, simple, other place in Haggard's image of the mother's breast and Bradshaw's girdle of gold is important, and recent critical work on adventure fiction—especially Anne McClintock's impressive study, *Imperial Leather*—has been most attentive to the way its gender ideology dovetails with the political and economic acquisitiveness of imperialism. Taking a clue from De Mille, however, I want to emphasize first of all that turning the tropical land and the "savage" other into the fountain of mother's milk depends upon an equivocation of the explorer's agency. The fundamental ideological trope—the one that the gendering of the foreign land rationalizes—is the one that disguises taking as receiving, from which follow the reversals of invasive penetration into return, and of gathering the fruits of conquest into recovering the gifts of nature. How does the lost-race motif plot this set of misrepresentations?

Lost-Race Fiction and the Civil War

The plots of "romantic" lost-race fiction can be summarized on the whole as fantasies of appropriation in (and sometimes of) the "virgin territory" of previously inaccessible foreign lands.[6] At the end of their ordeals, battles, scrapes, and escapes, the adventurers reap political, economic, sexual, and cognitive rewards. If we read the formulaic repetitions of lost-race fiction as anonymous myth on the model provided by Lévi-Strauss, we find that the social contradiction that the stories repeatedly "solve" ultimately lies between colonial claims to the territory's resources and land, and the competing claims of the indigenous people. Within imperial society, this contradiction made itself felt in political debates between the supporters and opponents of imperialist policy; in ethical indecision between condemning the colonial enterprise as conquest of the weak and vulnerable versus embracing it as benevolent modernization of the primitive and salvation of the heathen; and in the ideological dichotomy between glorification of progress and nostalgia for primitive joy and simplicity. Lost-race fiction, while registering the whole range of internal debate, derives its fundamental "mythic" power from the way it negotiates the basic problem of ownership by simultaneously reveling in the discovery of uncharted territory and representing the journey as a *return* to a lost legacy, a place where the travelers find a fragment of their own history lodged in the midst of a native population that usually has forgotten the connection.

The plot motif that most clearly expresses the ambivalence generated by sharing the wealth and benefits gained by "discovering" and taking possession of land already occupied by others is one whereby the newly discovered land both resists the protagonists as invaders and welcomes them as benefactors—the motif of the civil war. The adventurers' participation in a civil war dominates the middle of *King Solomon's Mines* and most of the second half of *Allan Quatermain*, and it is among the plot features of Haggard's novels most widely and often imitated in the explosion of lost-race fiction in the 1890s and on through to its final gasps in the pulp milieu of the 1930s. In fact, for reasons that should become clear in what follows, the presence or absence of civil war is one of the better indicators of the dividing line between "romantic" lost-race fiction and the older satirical and utopian traditions that continue unabated during the same period, if anything drawing new strength from the popularity of their adventure-oriented counterparts.

One can account for the prevalence of civil wars in lost-race fiction partly on the basis of the general militarism and masculinism of adventure fiction in this era. Robert H. MacDonald, in *The Language of Empire*, summarizes the dominant myths and metaphors of British popular culture during the high imperialist decades as "a poetics of war" (19–47), and in lost-race fiction, at least, the main contours of MacDonald's analysis extend across the Atlantic. As MacDonald puts it, war is "the game." One learns how to play it, and whom to play it with, among the "old boys" at public school (20–21). In the imperial context, "the ur-plot, was that of conquest: first came the traders and the missionaries; the 'natives' resisted or 'rebelled'; then came the army to conquer and pacify" (26). War becomes a mode of pacification and education: It restores order and teaches the natives a lesson. The lesson, ultimately, is the superiority of the whites over the non-whites, a belief corroborated by the endemic racism of popular culture, which alternately feminized and infantilized the natives (32–39).[7] The civil war in lost-race fiction most often enacts this "poetics of war" by portraying the society the explorers enter as one already riven by internal conflicts that the adventurers then play a decisive role in helping to solve. Thus the civil war equivocates the adventurers' agency by turning invasion and conquest into alliance and rescue.

These dynamics sometimes are established immediately in the scene of first contact between the adventurers and the locals. Three examples can illustrate the persistence of a certain version of the first-contact scene from the Haggard-inspired novels of the 1890s, to the caveman fantasies of which Edgar Rice Burroughs became the most successful exponent, to the naïve bloodthirstiness of the dime novel and pulp writing at its least sophisticated level. In Frank Aubrey's 1897 *The Devil-Tree of El Dorado*, the first humans the protagonists encounter in El Dorado are a white girl and a darker-skinned man pursuing her. The explorers shoot the man, thereby incurring both the lasting gratitude of Uluma, the girl, who turns out to be a princess, and the enmity of the vicious high priest whose son they have slain. The pattern of saving the princess from a vicious enemy and simultaneously establishing the explorers' superiority through the use of deadly force recurs in Robert Ames Bennet's 1901 *Thyra: A Romance of the Polar Pit*, a novel that employs a number of the devices that Burroughs later used most successfully. The first native the explorers see is Thyra herself, "a creature beautiful as a Norse goddess . . . tall and fair, in the costume of a huntress" (32), being pursued by a giant bear, "Ursus Spelaeus, the terror of early man" (35). She defends herself pluckily, but not entirely successfully, with an axe. The explorers finish the bear off with their guns, thereby establishing a romantic attachment between one of them and Thyra that later becomes a key issue in a political struggle. Finally, in "Submicroscopic," Captain S. P. Meek's contribution to the August 1931 issue of *Amazing Stories* (in Asimov 66–92), the same scene is still being echoed: "I heard a sound of running footsteps . . . Imagine my surprise when a girl, a white girl, came into view, running at top speed. Not fifty yards behind her came a group of men, or beasts, for I couldn't tell at first glance which they were" (Asimov 73). Our hero leaps to the rescue: "with a shout I stepped from my hiding place and threw my rifle to my shoulder. . . . I had four shells in my rifle and four of the blacks went down as fast as I could work the bolt" (74). By the time the scene is done, he has killed fourteen. In all three cases, the key point is that the explorers establish an alliance with a good native, who looks and thinks the way they do, against her local enemies—and they do so by shooting the enemies with a gun.

The explanation (or rationalization) for this spontaneous alliance often lies in the genealogy that links the explorers and the lost race to one another. One version of this trope is the return of the native, as in *King Solomon's Mines*, where Quatermain's rather haughty native helper Umbopa really turns out to be Ignosi, the rightful heir to the throne of Kukuanaland. Again, in *The Devil-Tree of El Dorado*, the mysterious guide, Monella, is the returning heir, and one of the white adventurers discovers that he too is descended from the El Doradans, which is why he has had visions of the place in his dreams before arriving there. Sometimes common ancestry is established indirectly by some kind of historical, cultural, or linguistic evidence. Considerable, but inconclusive, speculation is devoted to the possible Phoenician or Persian origins of the white race found in central Africa in *Allan Quatermain*—all of course motivated by the need to explain the primary sign of consanguinity, their skin color. Mr. Stranger, who visits Mars in Hugh MacColl's 1889 *Mr. Stranger's Sealed Packet* (where on first contact he uses his cigar-shaped spaceship to save a boy from drowning, and then falls in love with the boy's beautiful older sister), discovers that the blue-skinned natives speak a language with Indo-European roots. After a few months on Mars, Mr. Stranger's skin turns blue, confirming his racial commonality with the Martians. In *Thyra*, the explorers are able to complete the fragmentary sacred text, the Sermon on the Mount, that is presented as the key to the harmonious socialist democracy in Thyra's obviously Nordic community. The good natives, in one way or another, are always already members of the explorers' party.

The bad natives need to be accounted for as well. There are two major, often overlapping, strategies. One is racial or species differentiation. Thyra's socialist Christians find themselves struggling not only with a racially proximate but monarchic and idolatrous group called the Thorlings, but also with the subhuman "dwergers" and other survivals of prehistory like the *Ursus spelaeus* on the polar surface and the giant reptiles who dwell in the lowest level of the polar pit. Edgar Rice Burroughs codes the civil wars of Barsoom in racial terms—the green Martians versus the red—in *A Princess of Mars* (1912) and its sequels, and proliferates humans, apelike "missing links," mammoths, dinosaurs, and a super-intelligent race of reptiles in *At the Earth's Core* (1914). From one angle, such ensembles proceed from the same kind of missionary fantasy that *Thyra* acts out in the explorers' completion of the Updalers' sacred text. They dramatize the struggle of the local humans to separate their essential whiteness and modernity from its anachronistic surroundings. In the first novel of Arthur Conan Doyle's Professor Challenger series, *The Lost World*, the explorers actually help a group of stone-age humans to bring their long-standing struggle with a more apelike group to a genocidal conclusion. Their triumph prompts Professor Challenger to declare that they "have been privileged . . . to be present at one of the typical decisive battles of history— the battles which have determined the fate of the world. . . . Now upon this plateau the future must ever be for man" (182).

The Lost World is not simply advancing this obviously self-serving version of survival of the fittest, however. Malone, the narrator, comments on Challenger's speech, "It needed a robust faith in the end to justify such tragic means" (182). Challenger's marked physical resemblance to the king of the ape-men already has clued the reader that the brilliant professor's evolutionary theory may be the target of satire rather than an article of faith. Thus from another angle, the trope of species differentiation often critically estranges colonialism and racist ideology. For instance, the reptilian Mahars in *At the Earth's Core* recollect Wells's invading Martians in *War of the Worlds*, in the sense that both estrange anthropocentrism in order to disrupt ethnocentrism. Perry, the professorial inventor and paleontologist, explains to the standard adventurer narrator: "They look upon us as we look upon the beasts of the fields, and I learn from their written records that other races of Mahars feed upon men—they keep them in great droves, as we keep cattle. . . . They understand us no better than we understand the lower animals of the world. Why, I have come across here very learned discussions of the question as to whether the *gilaks*, that is, men, have any means of communication" (91). The fact that the reptiles, because they communicate telepathically, have no conception at all of speech is based on an anatomical difference, but it looks like a colonial master's cultural misunderstanding of a dominated race. (How, in spite of their inability to understand speech, they produce written records that Professor Perry can decipher is a problem Burroughs leaves to drown in the wake of the headlong movement of his plot.)

The second major strategy for explaining the bad natives speaks more directly to the theme of cultural difference. The enemies of the good natives are most often priests. MacDonald's poetics of war would explain, I think correctly, that the priests represent those who are used to teaching the natives their lessons, and therefore react jealously against those who want to teach them the new lesson of modernity and progress. Since the superiority of the modern is not in doubt, the priests are not representatives of some type of genuine native resistance. They are merely perverse. The most obvious indicator of their perversity is their grotesque attachment to rituals of human sacrifice, which they sometimes employ as a mask for political assassination and sometimes seem to indulge out of sheer sadistic delight. Gagool and her political front-man Twala set the pattern in *King Solomon's Mines* that is followed by the Dark Brotherhood of *The Devil-Tree of El Dorado*, who practice ritualized rape and sacrifice victims to the carnivorous devil-tree, and by the enemy priests in *Thyra*, who make their sacrifices to the worm-god Orm before an enormous, jewel-encrusted idol that they can sit secretly inside of to enjoy the show.

The combination of conspiracy, fetishism, and monstrosity in the evil priesthoods of lost-race fiction doesn't make for subtlety. The villains' uncomplicated evil is no doubt one of the supposedly refreshing simplicities of late-nineteenth-century adventure romance, yet the baroque extravagance of priestly perversity seems symptomatic of something more. It is as if the megalomania of imperial self-confidence were reversed systematically into an aesthetic of paranoia, and the semiotic burden borne by skin color or superficial anatomical features like thick lips or wooly hair were transformed hyperbolically into the fascinating abominations of priestly ritual. In fact, the lurid qualities of the priesthood are powerful enough to sustain a plot—almost a genre—all their own, the fiction of ancient, vampiric, extraterrestrial invasion, human idolization and cultic worship of the invaders, and conspiratorial anticipation of the monster-god's return that runs throughout H. P. Lovecraft's Cthulhu stories and those of his not inconsiderable band of imitators. The construction of the priestly cult out of a prior invasion, in the Lovecraftian variant, proceeds directly from the underlying logic of the lost-race priesthood, where the priests are also the uncanny doubles of imperialism. This is why they are so often allied to or conflated with another of the stock figures of the civil-war scenario, the spurned native lover of the princess. Just as the leading man and his rival share the same desire, but differ in their means of fulfilling it and their levels of success, the priests, with their religious authority and their bloody rituals, are both rivals and counterparts of the hero's supporting cast, with its Christianity, its science, and its guns.

The parallelism between the priests and the colonialists is both made explicit and characteristically disavowed in Thomas Janvier's *The Aztec Treasure House* (1890), in which an isolated survival of pre-Columbian Aztec civilization is ruled over by a priesthood who maintain secret contact with the outside world. The narrator comments: "The implication was unavoidable that this extraordinary man [the high priest] actually had a more or less complete knowledge of the powers and appliances of the nineteenth century, and that he was using his nineteenth century knowledge to maintain his supremacy over a people whose civilization was on a par with that of European communities of a thousand years ago. . . . The coincidence struck me as most curious that here among the Aztecs, wrought by themselves upon the men of their own race, should be found identically the same cruelties which the Spaniards practiced upon the Indians" (260, 293). But, of course, the present band of Europeans brings progress, not a return of the cruelties of the Spaniards. The anthropologist narrator appropriately is accompanied by a Catholic missionary, and the narrator tells the Aztecs, "the news which we bring you is not sorrowful, but glad" (199). His view of things is confirmed by the alliance that both the aristocratic elite and the general populace are eager to form with the adventurers against the priests.

The primary ideological significance of the evil priesthood, then, is that anticolonial resistance is really a species of oppression internal to the native culture. The general populace of the lost-race nations are usually little more than spear bearers or cannon fodder (as the technology dictates). Popular uprisings are no more than support for one of the elite factions or the other, and almost always for the princess, whom the populace, like the hero and his party, are wildly in love with. The rare combination of explicitly anticolonial sentiments with an internally unified native society signals one of two things, one coherent with adventure conventions and the other radically opposed to them.

The first is an aspect of "romantic" closure best exemplified by Haggard himself. As the adventurers prepare to depart from Kukuanaland at the end of *King Solomon's Mines*, Ignosi, who has as a result of the civil war regained his rightful place as king, warns them that his land will be closed to outsiders:

"But listen, and let all the white men know my words. No other white man shall cross the mountains, even if any may live to come so far. I will see no traders with their guns and rum. My people shall fight with the spear and drink water, like their forefathers before them. I will have no praying-men to put fear of death into men's hearts, to stir them up against the king, and make a path for the white men who follow to run on. If a white man comes to my gates I will send him back; if a hundred come, I will push them back; if an army comes, I will make war on them with all my strength, and they shall not prevail against me." (408)

The key point here is not native resistance to colonial invasion, however, but the separation of the adventurers themselves from the project of colonialism: "'But for ye three . . . the path is always open; for behold, ye are dearer to me than aught that breathes" (408). The anticolonial sentiment keeps open the romantic revival's path of return to a purer, simpler world, where the people fight with the spear and drink water. The same combination of anticolonialism and exceptionalism appears in *Allan Quatermain*, where Sir Henry Curtis's anticolonial speech at the end of the novel is once again an occasion to air the polemics of romantic revival—"I cannot see that gunpowder, telegraphs, steam, daily newspapers, universal suffrage, &c., &c., have made mankind one whit the happier than they used to be" (635)—and so is entirely coherent with Quatermain's earlier paean to the English spirit of adventure (490).[8] Full-scale colonial penetration and development is not a usual or comforting end to a lost-race novel. Most often the land remains the private secret of the adventurers.

When a lost race actually decides to protect itself against the adventurers themselves, the conventions of adventure fiction are not operating. Instead, we are dealing with utopian and satiric conventions, which often operate in self-conscious juxtaposition to adventure. A good example is the popular rebellion that resolves the plot of exploration in Albert

Bigelow Paine's pleasant and unassuming novel, *The Great White Way* (1901). Paine's explorers are met with open arms by the inhabitants of the Antarctic realm they discover, which is both utopian and lethean, a combination of social harmony and languid timelessness and forgetfulness. The crucial element of the social difference from elsewhere is telepathy, which makes lying and dishonesty and apparently even any prolonged disagreement impossible. In counterpoint to indigenous telepathy, an explorer's marvelous invention, the wireless telephone, plays a key role in the denouement. Chauncey Gale, a merry millionaire who has provided the ship and financial backing for the entire expedition, carries on an excited telephone conversation with the ship while in an Antarctic temple, not realizing (strange pre-vision of the cell phone era) that everyone there can hear his side of the conversation: "We'll make things hum. We'll get franchises from the government for electric lights and trolley lines, and steamboat traffic, and we'll build some factories, and I'll put a head-light on this temple, and we'll lay out additions in all directions. Vacant property here as far as you can see, and just going to waste" (274). News of Gale's plans transforms the customarily passive and tranquil Antarcticans into an angry, murderous mob. The travelers are forced to flee in haste, except for the wireless technician, Ferratoni, who instead procures "the pardon of love" by marrying the inevitable princess.

The Princess, the Treasure, and the Land

Although lost-race fiction's adventurers usually become embroiled in civil conflicts, taking political power is not their goal. If it comes to them, it is only as a supplement to possession of the princess, or as an expedient in the acquisition of treasure. The underlying projects, sexual possession of the princess and material possession of the land and its resources, tend to coalesce with one another, as anyone familiar with nineteenth-century imperialist ideology's feminized representations of "virgin territory" and exotic peoples would expect. The metaphor of land as woman is Anne McClintock's point of departure in *Imperial Leather*. McClintock begins her book with a reading of the map in *King Solomon's Mines* as the inverted figure of a woman, with the mountain range called "Sheba's Breasts" halfway between "Pan bad water," the sole marked feature of the desert below it—the devalued female head, according to McClintock—and, equally far above it, the "Mouth of treasure cave," the female genitalia and entrance to the mines or womb (1–4; cf. *King Solomon's Mines* 254). There are at least two ways to understand such coordination between the reification of woman and the personification of land and treasure. One is that the enjoyment of possession and the exercise of mastery comprise the tenor of the comparison between sexual and material objects. A second is that the translatability of woman into land into treasure rests on a systematic economic equivalency, the inherent exchangeability of forms of wealth. Marx explains how, in a generalized system of commodity exchange, the mediation of all of these exchanges by a universal equivalent, or money form, either translates or reduces all qualitative differences into quantitative ones. This disappearance of quality into quantity tends toward what Marx calls the fetishism of the commodity, the way that in commodity exchange "relations between persons take on the fantastic form of relations between things" (165). The question, however, is what kind of system, under the sign of what form of universal equivalent, we find at work in lost-race fiction's formulaic representations of sexual and economic acquisition.

Haggard's greatest embodiment of the feminine, "She Who Must Be Obeyed," proposes a version of systematic equivalency in one of the extended philosophical debates that she carries on with Henry Holly of Oxford University, the narrator of *She*. Ayesha contends that, "The world is a great mart, my Holly, where all things are for sale for him who bids the highest in the currency of our desires" (153). Although the fact that the domineering and ruthless Ayesha sounds like a *laissez-faire* economist is typical of Haggard's anticapitalism and anticolonialism (see note 8 above), Ayesha is talking about libidinal investments, not about gold or money, when she refers to "the currency of our desires." Bidding and selling refer to mastery and submission in sexual conquest, not to commodities. For Ayesha, wealth is only a subsidiary form of power, and power only the supreme form of enjoyment. What her quantification of desire in the "great mart" of the world primarily intends is the erasure of law, that is, of any barriers to the pursuit of mastery and sexual gratification. Hence the gift she offers her lover, Vincey, is removal of the ultimate barrier to unlimited gratification, death. Holly cannot understand the value of the gift of immortality Ayesha offers her lover. For him, immortality only offers an indefinitely prolonged opportunity to accumulate wealth, power, and wisdom. He cannot understand why, if Ayesha indeed possesses immortal life, she prefers "to remain in a cave amongst a society of cannibals" (91). But it is Holly, not Ayesha, whose concept of enjoyment is constrained by a measurement of value tied to quantities and things and therefore blind to quality. He does not understand the erotic "currency" by which Ayesha measures value because he does not know how to enjoy mastery for its own sake or how to embrace as a positive value Ayesha's transgression of the boundaries of law and death.

A parallel figure to Holly is Professor Goodwin, the narrator of A. Merritt's *The Moon Pool*, one of the most popular and influential narratives in the American pulp milieu from its appearance in *All-Story* in 1918 and 1919 through its reprintings in *Amazing Stories* in 1927, *Famous Fantastic Mysteries* in 1939, and *Fantastic Novels* in 1948 (*The Moon Pool* xxiv–xxv). The novel's erotic scheme is obvious enough in a passage like this one, where Goodwin is watching Yolara, the evil priestess, and Lakla, the Lemurian princess, fight it out for the love of Larry O'Keefe, the white adventurer hero:

> There they stood—Yolara with but the filmiest net of gauze about her wonderful body; gleaming flesh through it; serpent woman . . . hell-fire glowing from the purple eyes.
>
> And Lakla . . . translucent ivory lambent through the rents of her torn draperies, and in the wide, golden eyes flaming wrath, indeed—not the diabolical wrath of the priestess but the righteous wrath of some soul that looking out of paradise sees vile wrong in the doing. (216–17)

Dr. Goodwin repeatedly, reassuringly chastens his desire for Yolara by his admiration for the more proper Lakla, but it is hard not to see that Lakla is only the legitimate fragment of the more comprehensive and powerful erotic object, the "Aphrodite and the Virgin" (139) figure of Yolara. Yet Yolara, in her turn, is only a synecdoche for the ultimate allure of the Dweller, the "unearthly and androgynous" (33) god-monster worshipped by Yolara's cult as The Shining One. Merritt's purple prose goes absolutely ultraviolet in spinning out the irresolvable contradictions that characterize the vampiric creature made of light and music. It is

> neither woman nor man; human and unhuman, seraphic and sinister, benign and malefic—and still no more of these than is flame, which is beautiful whether it warms or devours. . . . Subtly, undefinably it was of our world and of one not ours. Its lineaments flowed from another sphere, took fleeting familiar form—and as swiftly withdrew whence they had come; something amorphous, unearthly—as of unknown unheeding, unseen gods rushing through the depths of star-hung space; and still of our own earth, with the very soul of earth staring out from it, caught within it—and in some—unholy—way debased. (226)

Merritt's descriptions of the Dweller raise the principle of transgression to the level of a mystical experience. Merritt's repeated formula, that the Dweller is "neither a nor b," does not erase boundaries between man and woman, angel and devil, and so on, but rather depends on the violation of them to define its unholy enjoyment. Ultimately, the formula means "both a and b," as in the simultaneous "ecstasy insupportable and horror unimaginable" (27) that contorts the Dweller's victims as it grasps them. The irresolvable contradictions are not paradoxes but rather the very form of enjoyment. In *The Moon Pool*, transgressive indulgence of erotic ambivalence is the "currency of our desires."

The principle of transgression embodied in Ayesha and the Dweller operates throughout lost-race fiction insofar as the entire situation always depends on penetration of the lost land's geographical isolation, and always involves the consequences of initiating commerce across the boundaries separating radically different systems of exchange. Nadia Khouri argues that the spectacular displays of gold and jewels that are almost as inevitable in this body of narrative as the princess herself represent the unimaginable accumulations of wealth enjoyed by the moguls and robber barons of late-nineteenth-century monopoly capitalism. According to Khouri, these images of conspicuous consumption cohere with an overall reversal of ascetic utopian values into fantasies of private satisfaction, where social planning and regulation have yielded their ground to an envious, fetishistic vision of individual success. But these figures of display are by no means peculiar to American lost-race fiction or to the 1890s, the field of material Khouri puts under consideration, so that what she says about the vision of wealth is not sufficient despite its being locally valid. The enormous mineral wealth common to lost-race settings is first of all based on the trope of inexhaustible natural abundance that is so basic to colonial ideology and comprises a common feature of lost-race fiction from before *Symzonia* to beyond *The Lost World*. But it is indeed more than that. Haggard's diamond mines and their myriad progeny represent not just natural abundance and unused, available resources, but also the peculiar colonial opportunity to get something for virtually nothing. That opportunity exists because the colonial territories, or rather the indigenous people, have not yet been integrated into the European system of commodity exchange. Trade between the first colonialists and the indigenous economy crosses between systems of exchange, skewing the measurement of value so that Manhattan can be bought for a string of beads.[9] The fantasy of appropriation that operates in adventure-oriented lost-race fiction indeed depends on the "currency of our desires" replacing or substituting for a rational universal equivalent like money.

The ambivalence that attaches itself to this fantasy of trade across the boundaries of systems of exchange partly derives from its being a guilty pleasure, a vicarious and nostalgic enjoyment of something that will not bear strict ethical scrutiny. It is a rather unusual moment in the genre when in an otherwise unremarkable novel, *The Aztec Treasure House* by Thomas Janvier, one of the characters says as they finally gaze upon the enormous treasure, "It's true for a fact, Professor, that never until this blessed minute, when we've really struck it, has th' notion come into my fool head that when we did ketch up with it the folks it rightly b'longed to might want to keep it for theirselves!" (379). There is the same hint of guilt and misgivings, but also something more at work in an odd moment in *King Solomon's Mines* that gets picked up often in the next few decades, Quatermain's assertion that if the entire treasure from King Solomon's diamond mine were to be brought to market the result would be a catastrophic devaluation of diamonds. This no doubt conforms to the logic of supply and demand, but it also seems to echo the nagging suspicion that—as both the usurper and the rightful restored monarch of Kukuanaland say—the diamonds are really *not* worth anything. The Kukuanans think them worthless, and who are the adventurers, who have neither mined the diamonds, nor earned them, nor paid for them, to say otherwise? The overabundance of gold and other precious metals in the lost-race locales, the common figure of gold being as common as iron, a metal absolutely commonplace and taken for granted by the isolated inhabitants, speaks for the same anxiety. The transgressive commerce between radically different systems threatens to destabilize the systems themselves, so that rational measurement and fetishization, or legitimate appropriation and illicit enjoyment, might become impossible to tell apart. It is once again *The Moon Pool* that gives a kind of metaphysical or at least mystical embodiment to the characteristic form of the treasure's value being suspended between radically incongruent systems of exchange, in Merritt's rendition of the Dweller's "loot" as a horde of zombies, the multitude of the dead-alive victims of the Dweller (224).

Other features of the lost-race setting, including the feminization of the land, also participate in and reinforce the economy of trangressive commerce. The torturous passages through mountain ranges, polar ice, and underground tunnels by which the explorers enter the lost land resemble the trauma of birth—that is, the symbolic rebirth and rejuvenation projected by the romance revival. But this return to origins ("Back, back we creep, and lay us like children on the great breast of Nature") is also a passage into radical difference. The ordeal of entry registers the discontinuity between the adventurers' world system and the isolated territory they have penetrated. Thus the ordeal of entry is often matched by a cataclysmic departure that seals the place off from return, emphasizing that the singularity of the opportunity that presents itself to those who can cross the boundary between the two realms depends on maintaining their separation. The lost-race scheme also frequently projects this discontinuity between systems onto the locale itself, so that the womblike fertility of the hollow earth, the enclosed valley, or the underground cavern produces remarkably heterogeneous fruits. This accounts for one of the features of lost-race fiction that exerts the strongest influence on the emergence of science fiction, the prevalence of anachronism in the lost-race setting—the side by side coexistence of dinosaurs and mammals, or of stone age, feudal, modern, and futuristic communities and technologies.

Such anachronism functions ambivalently in congress with the economic possibilities that the lost-race setting offers the explorers, producing a fanciful proliferation of possibilities on the one hand, but on the other the danger of incoherence. To argue that this tension is one of the major formal problems faced by writers of science fiction, one only need allude to the tremendous influence and power of Darko Suvin's definition of the genre as the literature of cognitive estrangement, a definition that focuses primarily on the logical rigor with which writers maintain the coherence of the *novum*, the story's departure from the empirical norm. This formal tension has strong roots in the historical realities of colonialism and imperialism. The penetration of colonizers and capitalism into the colonial territories results in the circulation and distribution of the extracted resources and displaced people in the newly articulated system of core and peripheral economies, and what can be vaunted as the assimilation of those territories, products, and people into modernity also can be decried as contagion. The colonial narrative of progress always threatens to reverse itself into the threats of racial miscegenation and cultural degeneration. Satirical lost-race fictions like A *Strange Manuscript Found in a Copper Cylinder* or Inez Gillmore's fine 1914 feminist allegory, *Angel Island*, tend to place such problems at the center of their concerns. In adventure-oriented lost-race fiction, anachronistic proliferation has to be read as a symptom of colonial discord, the same clash of cultural and economic values whose structure of abyssal difference and fantastic opportunity underlies Haggard's and Merritt's economy of transgression.

Owning the Narrative

The coexistence of dinosaurs and humans in lost-race settings also enacts a crossing over or contagion in which the living anthropological traces of the past that are thought to remain visible in colonial settings bring to life the geological ones as well. The fossil record is just as present in England or the United States as in the interior of Africa or the Amazon valley, but the fictional coexistence of humans with prehistoric animals is reserved for areas where human communities are considered to be in a primitive stage of development, that is, where the past of European civilization anachronistically persists in the present. The subtitle of Janvier's *The Aztec Treasure House* charmingly names the object of this anthropological perspective "contemporaneous antiquity," and Janvier's novel shows all too well how the Western scientist's narrative of the past is connected to colonial mastery of the present. Janvier's narrator, Professor Palgrave, is an anthropologist whose life ambition is to write a book, *Pre-Columbian Conditions on the Continent of North America*. The burden of Janvier's fable is to disavow the continuity between the bad colonial invasion of the conquistadors and the contemporary colonial ensemble represented by the adventurers—an engineer, a soldier, an anthropologist, and a Catholic priest. The keynote is Palgrave's assumption that it is up to him to interpret history for the natives, that is, that their past is a story that he alone knows how to tell correctly. Brandishing a token mistakenly given to him in an earlier scene by a dying Aztec priest, Palgrave proclaims to the natives, "Here is the token of summons left behind by Chaltzantzin; but we come not to call you forth to battle, but to bring tidings that the fate which that wise king and prophet foresaw for his people, long since was fulfilled" (199). That is, the residents of the isolated valley have been trapped in the past by a conspiratorial priesthood, and Palgrave and his associates now have come to liberate them into the present. Thus the Aztec prophecy of Chaltzantzin requires the anthropologist from the University of Michigan to explain it. Alongside the political, economic, and sexual modes of appropriation in the lost-race motif, this represents a cognitive appropriation by which the scientist takes ownership of the narrative and of history itself.

On their way through the nearly impassable wastelands that cut off Ayesha and the Amahaggers from the rest of the world in *She*, Holly and Vincey are confronted by a monumental sculpture of an Ethiopian head (chapter five). Holly speculates as to whether the sculpture's origins are Phoenician, Persian, or perhaps Jewish. The point is that it must be the product of white civilization. Well into the later twentieth century, the white minority regime of Rhodesia encouraged the idea that all stone ruins in sub-Saharan Africa were the remnants of non-African settlement colonies (*The Annotated She* 216, n. 4). The entire logic of Haggard's African lost-race tales is that settlement colonies of ancient white civilization have left fragments of themselves behind, while the surrounding non-white savages have no history of their own. The inability of the Kukuanans to read the writing on the walls built by King Solomon is of a piece with their valuation—that is, their nonvaluing—of the diamonds. The Western eye that reads the writing on the wall also sees the meaning and value the natives unknowingly live in the midst of—not only their "unused" land and resources, but also their uninterpreted fossil record and their inadequately understood flora and fauna. The acquisition of knowledge goes hand in hand with other modes of acquisition, then. However, the prize in this case is not the princess, but the narrative itself.

One of the strongest common elements that lost-race fiction shares with 1930s science fiction in general is the prevalence of scientist narrators, a feature one also finds in the broader category of imaginary voyages, particularly those that combine the voyage with the tale of invention, such as often happens in the works of Jules Verne. Within lost-race fiction, even Allan Quatermain has his ethnographic and archaeological moments. Professor Goodwin of *The Moon Pool* is an archaeologist, and the entire narrative is generated by the project of research in the ruins of Ponape in the Solomon Islands. *The Moon Pool* is also typical in its use of an editorial apparatus that includes scholarly footnotes discussing such topics as the customs and technology of the Murian underworld, some of which (we are told) have had to be suppressed for reasons of national security. Sometimes the scientist character is not the narrator, but still provides vital information about the background and history of the situation, as in Professor Perry's research in the archives of the Mahar in *At the Earth's Core*. What is important to the argument here is not merely the presence of the scientists or the quasi-scientific scholarly apparatus, but rather the way that they make clear the relevance of colonialism and imperialism to the science in science fiction. Consider three of the scientific features that pervade lost-race fiction: maps, ethnographies, and the gathering of specimens.

The map in *King Solomon's Mines* already has been brought up for discussion twice, but it is not Haggard's most impressive working out of this convention. What José da Silvestra's map does for gender ideology in *King Solomon's Mines*, the "sherd of Amenartas" does for imperial scholarship in *She*. Even more than da Silvestra's map, the sherd of Amenartas functions as a deed of property, a legacy that legitimates the explorers' foreign adventure. But instead of the pirates' map in *Treasure Island*, the model for the sherd of Amenartas is probably the encrypted revelation of the way into the underground that Professor Lidenbrock must decipher in order to begin his journey of scientific exploration in Verne's *Journey to the Center of the Earth* (1864). What Holly and Vincey have to decipher in *She* is not an encrypted message, however, but rather the lapidary inscription on a quasi-archaeological fragment, the potsherd, which comes accompanied by a body of documents attesting to its authenticity and commenting upon its significance. In a web of language and translation that calls to mind the Rosetta Stone, the uncial Greek of the inscription is translated into medieval Latin and commented upon in Elizabethan English, all of this authenticated in part by a medallion bearing an inscription in Egyptian hieroglyphics. The potsherd's provenance turns out to constitute a veritable "progress of empire," as its documentation attests to its having traveled from ancient Egypt by way of Athens, Rome, and Charlemagne's Lombardy to England, where the history of its owners passes from military conquest to mercantile adventure. Holly's scholarly footnote on the source of the misquotation of *Hamlet* in one of the English documents completes Haggard's *tour de force* interweaving of gentlemanly erudition, archaeology, and imperial genealogy. Thus Vincey's personal legacy coalesces with his class privilege and with imperial England's construction as the destination of history.

Ethnographic chapters abound in lost-race novels. In the chapter "About the Zu-Vendi People" in *Allan Quatermain*, Quatermain discusses in quick order the meaning and derivation of the name of Zu-Vendi (which he translates as "the yellow country"), the country's mineral resources (its extraordinary abundance of gold, perhaps explaining the name), its climate, the racial characteristics of the people and their possible place of origin, the current political situation, the religion, the legal system, marriage customs, the language, and their calligraphy. In chapters on "The Seeds of Revolt" and "The Gold-Miners of Huitzilan," Professor Palgrave of *The Aztec Treasure House* explores the historical determinants of the current political situation and the long-term opposition of interests between the priesthood and the people. He also mentions gathering data for his chapters on "House Life and Domestic Customs of the Aztecs" and "Mining and Metal-Working among the Aztecs" for his opus on *Pre-Columbian Conditions on the Continent of North America*. In a chapter on "The Marvels of Manoa" in *The Devil-Tree of El Dorado*, the narrator discusses the Manoans' herbal medicine, technology, and racial background as well as the historical roots of the religious conflict in which the adventurers have become embroiled. One finds similar material scattered throughout these volumes and in almost every example of the lost-race novel. As a whole, such features exhibit a habit or discipline of surveying and explaining that gestures back towards the popularity of travel writing, and that, like travel writing, installs the reader in a position of command over the history and expanse of the territory being explored. As ideology, these surveys allude to and cohere with what Thomas Richards calls the imperial archive: "The great Victorian projects of knowledge all had at their center the dream of knowledge driven into the present. The new disciplines of geography, biology, and thermodynamics all took as their imperium the world as a whole, and worked out paradigms of knowledge which seemed to solve the problem of imperial control at a distance" (6). In formal terms, lost-race fiction's ethnographic impulse is one of the principal means of giving substance and coherence to the *novum*. In later science fiction, when the *novum* tends no longer to be a strange land the characters enter by venturing out of the empirical norm, but instead is a full-blown reality that the reader has to learn about from details of behavior and background, the persistence of this impulse becomes such a major measure of aesthetic success that Samuel R. Delany can say, flamboyantly but without irony, that the setting always has been the real hero of the science fiction novel (*Trouble on Triton* 282).

The observation and gathering of curious biological specimens is one of the ubiquitous and most delightful features of lost-race and lost-world fictions. In addition to the standard fare of dinosaurs and extinct mammalian predators, the narrator of *At the Earth's Core* observes "the gorgeous flowering grass of the inner world, each particular blade of which is tipped with a tiny, five-pointed blossom" (112). The narrator of *Thyra* admires the phosphorescent flowers of the underworld. The princess-goddess of *The Goddess of Atvatabar* shows her visitor from the surface around a marvelous garden "wherein were treasured strange and beautiful flowers and zoophytes illustrative of the gradual evolution of animals from plants, a scientific faith that held sway in Atvatabar" (120). The parody of evolutionary theory, if one is intended, is quite feeble, but the fancifully illustrated cataloguing of the lilasure, laburnul, green gazzle, jeerloon, lillipotum, jugdul, yarphappy, jalloast, gasternowl, crocosus, jardil or lovepouch, blocus, clowngrass, glerosal, and eaglon comprises perhaps the best moment in this rather pretentious novel (117–31).

Gathering knowledge of exotic species is serious business, however. The paradigmatic instance of the "rich symbiosis between scientific exploration and political and economic expansion" in the Victorian era, as a responsible historian puts it, is the discipline of biogeography, the mapping of the geographical range of animal and plant species throughout the world, which forms the data base on which Darwin and Wallace were able to erect the theory of evolution by natural selection (Fichman 87, 26–28). In the best section of *The Queen of Atlantis* (1899), Frank Aubrey's prequel to *The Devil-Tree of El Dorado*, the adolescent George, who is the focus of the narrative only in this episode, goes sailing (off the coast of Atlantis, in the middle of the Sargasso Sea) and gets out of his usual range by following a beautiful, heretofore unknown marine butterfly. Having learned his lessons well from the scientist of the piece, George's curiosity leads him on to an island where he lands in order to observe more specimens of plants and animals that he does not recognize. He soon sees a winged girl—along with a new species of snake and a peculiarly fascinating variety of orchid—and is led by her into the inner realm of the island, the land of the Flower-Dwellers. Here botany and zoology give way to ethnography, as George learns not only about the Flower-Dwellers' mode of flight (which turns out to be artificial), but also about their advanced methods of agriculture and herbology. When he returns to the main plot, he takes with him an herbal concoction that proves crucial in the victory of the good princess and her party over the evil priesthood. Throughout the episode, this young scientist hero, whose assiduous application to his lessons saves the day, could be a model expressly written to support Hugo Gernsback's vision of science fiction as an educational genre offering "charming romance intermingled with scientific fact and prophetic vision" (3).

The centrality to fully emergent science fiction of this strain of zoological and ethnological acquisitiveness is not at all a matter of conformity to Gernsback's didactic project, however. We can gauge it better by noting its impact on Stanley Weinbaum's acclaimed classic of the 1930s pulp milieu, "A Martian Odyssey." Weinbaum's story is a marvelous journey of exploration with an entrapment and escape climax in which a native ally plays a key role in the escape, so that at a fairly high level of abstraction it does resemble much lost-race fiction of the adventure type. The strength of the story, however, lies in its specimen gathering, its representation of the aliens encountered on the surface of Mars by the explorer, Jarvis. The five extraterrestrial species cover an impressive range of possibilities: earthlike plant-animals; a dangerous and exotic carnivore; radically unearthlike, silicate, mechanically repetitive nonplant nonanimals; a stubbornly mysterious and finally hostile form of intelligent life; and a manlike friendly alien. The most important are the last two. Tweel, the ally, an ostrich-like being who is highly intelligent, carries a chemically powered gun, and manages to communicate with the human in English, is finally the protagonist of the story. The most threatening and mysterious life form is a fascinating counterpart to Tweel. Like Tweel, these creatures possess advanced technology. But their linguistic behavior is as different from

Tweel's as the princess's love for the hero is from the priesthood's incurable perversity. The members of the species look like drums and imitate speech, apparently communicating the imitative sounds instantaneously to their entire group, but without any sign of understanding their meaning. When Tweel exhibits his heroic loyalty by saving Jarvis from the barrel creatures, Jarvis exhibits his human cleverness by stealing a possibly cancer-curing device from them in the process of escaping from their lair. One of the marks of colonial-racist ideology on the narrative is the fact that for some unexplained reason Tweel seems to be as much an isolated stranger in this environment as the human narrator does, as if for the good Martian, like the good natives of lost-race fiction, the planet is a wilderness waiting to be humanized. Another, more crucial point is that the plot's resolution ultimately turns not on recognizing otherness or even gathering knowledge but rather on the narrator's transgressively reaping a kind of windfall profit, valorizing the colonial investment in the venture of exploration by his theft of the cancer cure from the barrel people.

Specimen gathering also occupies the center of interest in the novel that gives lost-world fiction its name, Arthur Conan Doyle's *The Lost World*. Conan Doyle's novel deliberately employs one after another of the conventions found in Haggard and the romance revival—the perilous journey to the isolated locale, the crucial role played there by the adventurers and their guns in a civil war, the discovery of diamonds, the crucial role of map-making and map-reading, and not least of all the Edenic moments of "good comradeship" among the four male adventurers: "We lay in good comradeship amongst the long grasses by the wood and marvelled at the strange fowl that swept over us and the quaint new creatures which crept from their burrows to watch us, while above us the boughs of the bushes were heavy with luscious fruit, and below us strange and lovely flowers peeped at us from among the herbage" (190). The attraction that draws the adventurers to the nearly inaccessible plateau in the remote Amazon valley, however, is not the discovery of new species or of mineral wealth. It is the presence there of "our contemporary ancestors," as Professor Challenger puts it (50). The scientific journey of Challenger and his companions makes explicit the paradigmatic basis of colonial expeditionary science in general by viewing the plateau primarily as a living record of "our" own past.

What is at stake in *The Lost World* is not the paradigm, as Thomas Kuhn would call it, of contemporary anthropology or evolutionary theory, however, but rather the popularization and public reception of science. That is why the expedition itself is framed by two riotous public lectures.

In the first, Challenger disrupts the lecture being given by an exponent of standard evolutionary theory by claiming that many of the species the lecturer calls extinct still survive, and the expedition is set up to confirm or deny Challenger's claims. In the second, Challenger's triumphant return is disrupted by a large group who still refuse to believe the explorers' accounts of what they have seen, and Challenger secures his ultimate triumph by the spectacular unveiling of a live specimen, a pterodactyl, that escapes through a window high in the Queen's Hall. (Unlike the escaped specimen in *King Kong*, the pterodactyl flies off over the ocean and is never heard of again.) Conan Doyle's focus on popularization is also evident in the ongoing quarrels between Professor Challenger and his intellectual opponent, Professor Summerlee. Instead of realistically portrayed scientific debate over the interpretation of evidence, the novel parodies such controversy in the pair's pedantic squabbling, for instance as they argue over the racial type and language classification of the cannibals whose drums are beating the message, "We will kill you if we can," as they make their way up the river to the forbidden plateau (79). Conan Doyle is not dramatizing the problem of elaborating scientific theory on the basis of empirical evidence, but rather the enclosure of science in a specialized vocabulary and an apparent divorce between its concerns and those of common sense.

The overarching problem is mediation. It enters the novel in the sceptical reception of Challenger's photographic evidence from his first visit to the plateau. It becomes a more drastic problem when the adventurers manage to reach the plateau but find their means of return blocked. Malone, the journalist narrator, writes, "We had been natives of the world; now we were natives of the plateau. The two things were separate and apart. . . . The link between was missing" (106). The figure of the "missing link" then culminates in the species of ape-men who inhabit the plateau. The main joke here, of course, is the stunning resemblance between the king of the ape-men and Professor Challenger, the point of which is not merely to mock the scientist's contentious and aggressive manner, to deflate his comically immense egotism, or even to suggest that his defense of scientific truth acts out primitive instinctual drives. Challenger's resemblance to the missing link condenses the play of identity and difference between the observer and the observed that permeates colonial discourse. Challenger is never less authorial than in his boisterous conviction that "Truth is truth, and nothing which you [Malone] can report can affect it in any way, though it may excite the emotions and allay the curiosity of a number of very ineffectual people" (63). On the contrary, the novel makes it clear that truth is an elaborately constructed representational practice poised with inescapable uncertainty between knowledge of the real and projection of desire.

The tone of *The Lost World* is by no means so philosophically heavy as I have been making it sound. It is a very funny book, and if Conan Doyle throws the shadow of racist ideology over the enterprises of scientific exploration and the popularization of evolutionary theory, he also suspends his entire narrative from didacticism or overbearing polemical engagement by means of the very device that most obviously plays with the suspicion that truth is a construction: the hoax. Conan Doyle burlesques the unreliability of Challenger's photographs of dinosaurs within the novel in the faked photograph of the four adventurers, with Conan Doyle himself posing as Challenger, in the novel's frontispiece. In this, as in so many other ways, he takes his clue from Haggard, whose frontispiece to *She* is a photograph of a carefully constructed facsimile of the sherd of Amenartas. Such devices procure an unusually self-conscious version of the willing suspension of disbelief, one that delights in and indulges the illusion as a form of mastery over the manipulability of appearances.

Haggard's and Conan Doyle's hoaxes are fitting emblems of these two writers' canny ability to deliver the exotic and sensational contents demanded of adventure fiction while simultaneously distancing themselves from immersion in their commercial milieu. The play of appearance and reality in these hoaxes achieves this double purpose by dramatizing the tension between cognitive appropriation and epistemological destabilization, involving the display of specimens or the interpretation of evidence in a blending together of satire and romance that in turn alludes to the more troubling permeability of the border separating science and ideology. Lost-race fiction's forays along these troubled boundaries ultimately constitute its most important contribution to shaping the generic contours of science fiction.

chapter three

Dramas of Interpretation

Haggard's and Conan Doyle's self-conscious delight in trumping up quasi-scientific evidence is typical enough of the emerging genre of science fiction that Hugo Gernsback, not someone who normally would be counted as a proponent of irony, included Edgar Allan Poe's pseudo-journalistic hoax, "The Facts in the Case of M. Valdemar," in the first issue of *Amazing Stories*. The possibility or even probability that Gernsback did not think of the story as satirical or as partaking in Poe's penchant for hoaxes only makes the generic edginess of Poe's story all the more striking. As the discussion of cognitive appropriation in lost-race fiction in the preceding chapter began to show, playing with the equivocal nature of "facts," and the corollary problem of comprehensibility, of bringing the exotic and alien into the realm of the representable, are central to the formation of science fiction. The facts raise both discursive and ideological problems by implying entire fictional worlds whose assembly depends in varying measures on rational cognition and ideological fantasy, and these scientific and ideological energies engage the stories, or entangle them, in the discourses and ideologies of colonialism. The protagonists' confrontations with enigmatic others and the reader's confrontation with generic borders—the riddles posed by early science fiction's impossible facts—are the main topics of this chapter. Since we are dealing with facts, let us proceed, like the narrator of Poe's "The Facts in the Case of M. Valdemar," along good journalistic lines. After a preliminary exposition of the status of the factual and the impossible in critical discussions of science fiction, we will proceed to ask who, where, when, and what are the interpretive dilemmas or dramas of interpretation produced by the impossibilities of early science fiction.

Impossible Facts and Science Fiction

The status of "facts" in science fiction is a crux in much of what has been written about the genre because one of science fiction's givens is that some of a story's facts must be not only counterfactual—which is true of realist fiction as well—but not currently possible, producing a category that ranges from plausible extrapolations of current technology or social conditions, like the submarine in Verne's *Twenty Thousand Leagues Under the Sea* or the class warfare in Jack London's near-future *The Iron Heel* (1907), to far more extravagant but theoretically possible developments like the post-human species in the distant future of Wells's *The Time Machine*, to flat-out impossibilities like the time-travel device itself. The contrasting views of Darko Suvin and Mark Bould should clarify the dimensions and consequences of this problem. One of Suvin's most emphatic positions in *Metamorphoses of Science Fiction* is that, in order to succeed as a "literature of cognitive estrangement," science fiction has to order its impossibilities (or not-yet-possibilities) with rigorous and coherent scientific rationality.[1] Bould, in a recent essay articulating a broad theory of literary fantasy that includes science fiction as a special instance, emphasizes ideology rather than rationality in the construction of science fiction. Bould suggests that the totalizing rigor with which science fiction and fantastic narratives integrate impossible facts into a coherent version of the world resembles the psychic mechanism of paranoia. His purpose is not to pathologize such narratives, but rather to connect fantasy with literary realism by way of the French psychoanalyst, Jacques Lacan's, thesis that paranoia's insatiable drive for coherence makes it the appropriate paradigm for the construction of personal identity and social reality as such.[2] Since conventional reality itself is fundamentally fantastic, Bould argues, fantasy as a genre is not distinguished from realism by its world-building but by its deliberate foregrounding of its untruth: "what sets fantasy apart from much mimetic art is a frankly self-referential consciousness . . . of the impossibility of 'real life'" (83). That is, the way that science fiction handles the impossible introduces a self-consciously "paranoid" construction of the world that tends to expose the unself-consciously fantastic nature of socially accepted reality.

Although Suvin stresses discursive articulation and Bould focuses on ideological disclosure, both critics argue that science fiction's aesthetic success and critical power turn on the relation the story achieves between the impossibilities it posits and conventionally accepted, normal reality.

They agree not only that science fiction's impossible "facts" must be pieces of a coherently imagined world that differs significantly from the one agreed upon by contemporaries as the real, but also that the organizing principle behind this coherent divergence from reality is absolutely crucial. Thus one of the pleasures that readers of science fiction expect from a well-written piece is that they will find themselves caught up in a kind of epistemological riddle by the gradual unfolding of the interpretive paradigm, cultural assumptions, or analogical principle governing the coherence of the impossible world in which the story is taking place. Following the lead of Samuel R. Delany's essential essay "About 5,750 Words," Carl Freedman has analyzed lucidly how this epistemological drama unfolds stylistically, at the level of the sentence, in good science fiction, his main examples being drawn from the work of Philip K. Dick (*Critical Theory and Science Fiction* 30–43).

In the present context, however, we have to observe an important distinction between the emergent and mature phases of science fiction. Mark Rose explains the distinction between generic emergence and maturity thus:

Any genre appears to develop in at least two phases. First, by combining and transforming earlier forms, the genre complex assembles and the idea of the genre's existence gradually appears. Later, a generically self-conscious phase occurs, one in which texts are based on the now explicit form. (10)

The epistemological riddles that confront the readers of mature or second-phase science fiction at the level of style and the sentence usually appear in the earliest approaches toward science fiction as elements of the plot, in the form of alarming, enigmatic situations that confront protagonists who start out in a conventionally realistic setting. The riddle of the landscape had become a self-conscious generic feature for at least some writers, but not for all readers, by 1930, when Sydney Fowler Wright wrote, in a preface to the American edition of his time travel story *The World Below*:

It is observed [by some critics] that there is much that is expressed or implied in the course of the narrative which is left without adequate explanation, and is, in some instances, inexplicable; and it is suggested that this is a defect, such as is unusual in books that attempt a vision of other days than ours.

The observation is accurate enough; but my reply must be that that is exactly how such a book should be written—how, indeed, it *must* be written, if it is to maintain a realistic atmosphere, and to be a tale, not a treatise. (v, Wright's emphasis)

The stylistic problem of maintaining a realistic atmosphere displaces the earlier, more straightforward procedure of disrupting one. But the generic constitution of science fiction in its emergent phase is not for that reason less complex. The reader's problem of how to put things together involves, as Rose says, the way the story combines and transforms earlier forms. Realism, adventure, utopia, satire, and the discourses of travel and science all may be operating to produce an effect distinct from any of them—that is, to produce a kind of coherence among a set of impossible facts that is not simply utopian or satirical or adventure-romantic, but something else that we now can recognize as early science fiction.

Who: The Dislocated Subject

What can we say, then, about the facts in "The Facts in the Case of M. Valdemar?" The narrator presents the story as a sober corrective to certain sensationalistic versions of the case that have been put into circulation:

> a garbled or exaggerated account made its way into society, and became the source of many unpleasant misrepresentations, and, very naturally, of a great deal of disbelief.
>   It is now rendered necessary that I give the *facts*—as far as I comprehend them myself. (194, Poe's emphasis)

Thus Poe highlights from the beginning questions about reliability and accuracy, problems that the narrator's elaborate attention to medical terminology, transcription of eyewitness accounts, and descriptions of mesmeric technique keep in the foreground throughout. The point of all this concern for truth-telling is to produce M. Valdemar's impossible utterance, "I am dead." Thus the story carefully sets up both the situation, the mesmeric experiment, in which the utterance can be made, and the subject who can make it, the mesmerized consciousness arrested in the process of dying. But Valdemar—or more precisely the "I" in the sentence "I am dead"—is a profoundly dislocated subject, one that can enunciate his/its own absence, whose voice "seemed to reach our ears—at least mine—from a vast distance, or from some deep cavern within the earth" (200), so that subject and utterance alike hover between embodiment and disembodiment, and between personal voice and autonomous language (Barthes 153–54).

All of this puts the entire story into a similarly ambiguous generic situation, hovering between satire and supernatural horror. Are we to take

M. Valdemar's utterance as a titillating communication from the land of the dead or as a parody of impersonal scientific truth? Is the story a cannily crafted vehicle for occult visitation or a lampoon of sensationalized accounts of scientific experiments? Is the final, instantaneous dissolution of Valdemar's corpse into "a nearly liquid mass of loathsome—of detestable putridity" (203) the horrific resolution of a tale of terror or a confession of the impossibility of sustaining the extravagant lie? Poe's distinction, of course, is that he achieves both hoax and horror story at the same time, so that his initial gestures concerning the believability of his story and the rationality of the medical and mesmeric science can never be simply dismissed. If the effect were merely ludicrous, the story would be merely satirical, but the sublime or incomprehensible status of the subject who/that announces his/its own death moves the story into a generic borderland that, between the initial publication of "The Facts in the Case of M. Valdemar" and its reprinting in *Amazing Stories*, connects its combination of hoax and horror to emergent science fiction.

The way to understand "The Facts in the Case of M. Valdemar" that is most pertinent to the status given it by its inclusion in the first issue of *Amazing Stories*, I suggest, is to read it as an imaginary voyage that tests the limits of communicability across the transforming effects of the voyage itself. The subject who knows the impossible must either be produced by a more or less traumatic transformation (like the ordeal endured by the travelers in lost-race fictions on their way into the lost land) or supplied whole from a culture or world with an alternative epistemological frame (like the utopian societies of Venus and Mars that the title character, a visitor from outer space, explains to his earthly hosts in Wladislaw Lach-Szyrma's *Aleriel* [1883]). Thus the narrative of the impossible implies a narrator or protagonist who, like M. Valdemar, has been profoundly dislocated, and the narrative sometimes becomes the story not only of that dislocation but also of the difficulty of communicating its effects.

Edwin A. Abbott's brilliant intellectual satire, *Flatland* (1884), handles the dislocation of the subject and the difficulty of communicating the traumatic experience of confronting the impossibly other with, if you will forgive my putting it this way, geometric precision. When the two-dimensional narrator, A. Square, converses in a vision with the one-dimensional Monarch of Lineland, he finds himself utterly unable to communicate to him the notion of recognizing a person by sight, since to the inhabitants of Lineland all that can be seen in either direction is a point. The linear Monarch, meanwhile, is unable to believe that the Square does not already know and understand the Linelanders' natural and inevitable modes of marriage and reproduction, which take place entirely through the medium of auditory harmony, since inhabitants of Lineland can touch only the persons next to them. A. Square complains, "I had the greatest possible difficulty in obtaining information on points that really interested me; for the Monarch could not refrain from constantly assuming that whatever was familiar to him must also be known to me and that I was simulating ignorance in jest" (43–44). Later, A. Square finds himself in much the same position relative to a Sphere who visits him to preach the Gospel of Three Dimensions. When the Sphere, unable to communicate the meaning of space or to make the figure of a cube intelligible to the Square, finally pulls the Square out of his Flatland plane into Spaceland, the Square's initial experience is one of "unspeakable horror":

There was a darkness; then a dizzy, sickening sensation of sight that was not like seeing; I saw a Line that was no Line; Space that was not Space; I was myself, and not myself. When I could find voice, I shrieked aloud in agony, "Either this is madness or it is Hell." "It is neither," calmly replied the voice of the Sphere, "it is Knowledge." (64)

The main target of Abbott's satire is religious intolerance, as the Square eventually ends up being imprisoned for heresy when he attempts to preach the Gospel of Three Dimensions in Flatland. But perhaps more poignant is the gradual disappearance of A. Square's ability to remember or comprehend his own three-dimensional experience, as his mnemonic mantra, "upwards but not Northwards," becomes unintelligible to him. Thus Abbott's metaphor of transdimensional experience not only parodies ethnocentrism and skewers religious dogmatism and intolerance but also explores the limits of empiricism. Although A. Square's rational convictions about multi-dimensionality outlast the intuitive grasp of three-dimensional reality he is able to base on sensory experience, the perceptual limits of his two-dimensional common sense defeat any attempt to rationally persuade others of the concrete reality of a third dimension.

H. G. Wells engages the same set of problems as *Flatland* in a cross-cultural setting that also more explicitly targets colonial-imperial ideology in his satirical treatment of the lost race motif, "The Country of the Blind."[3] The protagonist, a mountain climber named Nunez, is a would-be conqueror who, when he literally falls into the isolated Andean mountain valley where everyone has been congenitally blind for fifteen generations, assumes that "In the country of the blind the one-eyed man is king." But his illusions of intrinsic superiority are rudely shaken when he finds his vision of little use in negotiating the social spaces that the blind community has crafted for itself. Furthermore, he has no more success explaining the world outside the valley or the wonders of sight than A. Square has in propagating the Gospel of Three Dimensions. In fact, he finds himself in much the same dilemma, accused of speaking nonsense when he uses words like "sight" and "blindness" and of heresy when, denying the blindmen's firm and pious belief in the world's smooth stone roof, he tries to describe the sky. Both the incommunicability of his radically different sensory experience to the blind community and the defeat of his ambitions of conquest come together in the name the blind give Nunez, "Bogota," thereby degrading the civilized origin that he initially thinks the guarantor of his superiority into a nonsense word that they fasten upon him to designate his mental inferiority.

Wells does not stop at merely ridiculing Nunez's chauvinism any more than Poe's "Facts" merely constitute a hoax. Once Nunez's aggressive ambitions have been foiled, the story turns its focus to the dogmatism and enforced conformity of the country of the blind. The climax comes when "Bogota" has been assimilated sufficiently into the society that he wants to marry, but the bride's family objects because he is still considered mentally deficient and unstable. A wise man of the community proposes at last the definitive cure:

"Those queer things that are called the eyes, and which exist in order to make an agreeable soft depression in the face, are diseased, in the case of Bogota, in such a way as to affect his brain. They are greatly distended, he has eyelashes, and his eyelids move, and consequently his brain is in a state of constant irritation and distraction. . . . I may say with reasonable certainty that, in order to cure him completely, all that we need do is a simple and easy surgical operation — namely, to remove these irritant bodies." (563)

"Thank Heaven for Science!" proclaim the citizens. Thus the dislocation or suspension of the subject Nunez/Bogota between the realms of sight and blindness, like A. Square's suspension between dimensions and M. Valdemar's between life and death, registers with devastating force the shock of redefining oneself in the face of the exotic. Nunez finds himself at last in a double bind. He cannot have the woman he desires without sacrificing the very faculty that attracts him to her in the first place. Forced to choose between blindness within the society or vision without it, he opts for the latter, but the last lines of the story show Nunez frozen on the mountainside enclosing the valley, arrested between the world he cannot fully enter and the one to which he cannot return: "The little details of the rocks near at hand were drenched with subtle beauty — a vein of green mineral piercing the grey, the flash of crystal faces here and there, a minute, minutely beautiful orange lichen close beside his face. . . . But he heeded these things no longer, but lay quite inactive, smiling as if he were satisfied merely to have escaped the valley of the Blind where he had thought to be King" (568). The beauty of the lichen-covered rocks registers the pathos of Nunez's dislocation as a kind of success, but, like M. Valdemar's achievement of announcing his own death, and like A. Square's terrible induction into three-dimensional knowledge, it comes with a severe price. These three explorers pay for their extravagant experiences by the transformation it works upon them, turning them into dislocated subjects who can no longer occupy the epistemological position that holds conventional reality in place.

Where: Generic Borders and the Permutations of Analogy

Nunez's situation, like Valdemar's, draws energy from the play of different generic possibilities. On the one hand, the entire story's satirical strategy depends on its reference to and avoidance of the conventions of romantic adventure. On the other, the status of the valley of the blind itself is poised between a straightforward satirical analogy to social conformity and an internally self-consistent development of the science fiction premise of an entire culture being founded on a radically different perceptual basis from our own. The complex generic possibilities directly produce the story's complex thematic success. Beyond that, the tension between satirical analogy and science fiction premise engages one of the central problems of colonial discourse, the problem of whether the exotic other is being understood only as a distorted projection of the observer, and if this is the case, of how the observer can come to occupy a more appropriate, less ego- and ethnocentric perspective. Colonial discourse and the drama of interpretation in early science fiction are tied together closely by such generic and epistemological tensions, and the artistic success of early science fiction often depends on whether it thrives or falters in handling them.

William Bradshaw's *The Goddess of Atvatabar* provides an example of satirical topicality spoiling the integrity of an imaginary culture. At one point, the travelers in Atvatabar hear a manifesto on art pronounced at a religious procession: "Art is a green oasis in an arid and mechanical civilization. It creates an earthly home for the soul, for those wounded by the riot of trade, the weariness of labor, the fierce struggle for gold, and the deadly environment of rushing travel, blasted pavements and the withering disappointment of life" (91). The problem is that Atvatabar is not described as arid or mechanical, and there is definitely no fierce struggle for gold, which is as common as iron there. The Atvatabarese aesthetic manifesto is a weak cover for authorial polemic, and here (as elsewhere in this poorly written novel) the cultural *novum* proves to be merely a projective fantasy with little internal integrity, so that the exotic other takes whatever shape it suits Bradshaw to give it for his momentary purposes.

A more interesting example of an imaginary other's form being dictated by an external logic is the straightforward and thoroughgoing satirical reversal crafted by Samuel Butler in *Erewhon*. Erewhon's inhabitants consider crime a disease and disease a crime. One of the highlights of the book is an Erewhonian judge's speech to a man convicted of a pulmonary disorder, in which Butler quotes an English judge's speech to a convicted thief and merely substitutes the disease for the crime (Butler 114; 116, n.3). Butler's strategy succeeds strikingly in making the point that what passes for moral superiority is often mere self-congratulation for our good luck at being born and raised in the right circumstances, not only because of the bizarre aptness of the English judge's speech for Butler's purpose but also because of the strict self-consistency of Butler's Erewhonian legal system.

Elsewhere in the book, oddly, it is precisely where Butler's satirical intention fails that the book begins to look something like later science fiction. Butler's "Book of the Machines" is at one level an attempt to parody Darwin by substituting machines for organisms. What remains of interest is not the satirical irony of the attack at all, but rather the unintended plausibility of the premise, taken up many times by later science fiction writers, of machines becoming so lifelike as to subvert profoundly the distinction between the natural and the artificial. The impossible starts to look like science fiction when outrageous analogy crosses from the ludicrous to the plausible. A look at two major achievements of early science fiction, James De Mille's *A Strange Manuscript Found in a Copper Cylinder* and "Godfrey Sweven's," that is, John MacMillan Brown's *Riallaro: The Archipelago of Exiles* (1897) and *Limanora: The Island of Progess* (1903), can illustrate some of the permutations of analogy, plausibility, and the ludicrous in more detail.

James De Mille stages a remarkable dialogue about generic ambiguity in the frame story of *A Strange Manuscript Found in a Copper Cylinder*. The four characters, who have found the copper cylinder while cruising the southern Pacific in a yacht, and read it to one another to pass the time, engage in an ongoing argument about the generic status of Adam More's story of his adventures in the land of the Kosekin. While one character insists that the story is fiction, the others insist that "it is a plain narrative of facts" (246), allowing De Mille to explore the story's literary ancestry and affiliations on the one hand, while on the other describing the devices that he has used to lend it plausibility. Melick, "a *littérateur* from London" (65), initially classifies More's narrative as a "sensation novel" (66), using a term that was current and a bit controversial in the 1860s (the novels of Wilkie Collins and Mary Elizabeth Braddon are the major examples of the category). But Melick also compares More's narrative to the Arabian nights' stories of Sinbad the sailor, and finally settles on identifying it as "satirical romance"—not, he is quick to add, "scientific romance . . . because there is precious little science in it, but a good deal of quiet satire" (245). While Melick's description of the satirical intentions of More's story sounds a good deal like authorial ventriloquism, his contention that there is "precious little science" in the story meets with the strong objections of young Oxenden, "late of Trinity College, Cambridge" (65), and the professorial Dr. Congreve. (The fourth character, Lord Featherstone, owner of the yacht, finds the whole discussion a bore.) By means of Oxenden's and Congreve's insistence that the manuscript is genuine, De Mille rehearses his use of various scientific discourses—geology, philology, and anthropology—to generate the plausible and coherent subtropical land of the Kosekin lying beyond the polar ice.

Dr. Congreve, the biologist and geologist, defends the plausibility of the survival of otherwise extinct flora and fauna in this isolated realm, and identifies several of the dinosaur species by their scientific names. But Oxenden delivers the more important philological and anthropological material. He insists that the "monsters and marvels of nature" are less interesting than the bizarre culture of the Kosekin themselves (254). Invoking contemporary debates regarding the origins of racial difference (that is of monogenetic versus polygenetic theories of the origins of humankind), Oxenden surmises that the Kosekin are not autocthonous but rather descended from ancient Hebrews, citing as his evidence the fact that many of the Kosekins' words seem to be simple transformations of ancient Hebraic by the mechanism of Grimm's Law. Their love of death, therefore, is not the difference of a radically separate species, but must, like the language, be cognate with that of the readers of the manuscript. Rather than considering the Kosekin as unnatural or merely degenerate, Oxenden contends that their culture expresses their adaptation to their environment—"Their eyes and their morals have become affected by this way of life" (166–67)—and then speculates that "the connecting link between the Kosekin and their Semitic brethren" is provided by the "Troglodytes" or cave-dwellers of Arabian and Egyptian antiquity (167). Oxenden goes on to cite accounts of Troglodyte customs that lend plausibility to the value given to death and darkness among the Kosekin:

"In their burials they were accustomed to fasten the corpse to a stake, and then gathering round, to pelt it with stones amid shouts of laughter and wild merriment. They also used to strangle the old and infirm, so as to deliver them from the evils of life." (168)

Later in his disquisitions, Oxenden bolsters his defense of the plausibility of the Kosekin culture by comparing their love of death to the Buddhist doctrine of "the bliss of Nirvana, or annihilation," and finally to the tragic wisdom of Sophocles in *Oedipus at Colonus*: "Not to be born surpasses every lot" (256).

A paraphrase of the frame dialogue of De Mille's *Strange Manuscript* would boil it down to something like this: Don't take this too seriously (Featherstone), because it is a fantastic, make-believe story (Melick); nonetheless, the fantasy is crafted in such a way as to retain a certain degree of scientific plausibility (Congreve), and more importantly, the culture depicted here is no mere fantasy but a satirical analogy to our own (Melick); above all, this analogy bears within it, in estranged form, a deep-lying pessimism and a ritual embrace of death that, far from lying beyond the realm of human possibility, are central to human culture's greatest achievements (Oxenden). De Mille's frame commentary is certainly one of the most complex and perspicacious attempts to theorize "scientific romance"—a.k.a. science fiction—before Wells. Two features of De Mille's commentary are especially relevant to the present discussion. First, De Mille makes no attempt to enforce strict generic definitions or boundaries, but rather emphasizes the intersections of fictional and discursive genres within his text, and the interplay among them. The frame's dialogue form itself models the proximity and interdependence of these various genres. Second, these generic intersections include colonial discourses and refer to colonial ideology with a certain inevitability. As Said's thesis about the novel in general would predict, colonialism provides a structure of power and knowledge that De Mille's fictive elaboration of an imaginary culture cannot help but articulate. The various elements of what I earlier called the colonial gaze come together strikingly in Oxenden's contribution to the dialogue. His juxtaposition of Troglodytic ritual, Buddhist philosophy, and Sophoclean tragedy is typical of anthropology in the developmental model insofar as it draws upon primitive, Asian, and antique sources as parallel exhibits. What is unusual is that the point he makes using this panoply of evidence tends to subvert the ideology of progress, as he instead draws upon the universalizing humanism that assumes its coherence to argue for the profound relevance of the apparently bizarre Kosekin beliefs to the reader's own.

In John MacMillan Brown's *Riallaro: The Archipelago of Exiles* and *Limanora: The Island of Progress*, the relation between satire and science fiction once again proves crucial, but in this case, the generic complexity produces a more double-edged, almost self-contradictory relationship to colonial ideology. The two volumes actually comprise a single, rather daunting piece of fiction that crosses from being predominantly an allegorical satire in the first volume to a science fiction utopia in the second. The unnamed narrator sets out on a voyage in search of a cure for the "inborn sickness of the human spirit," surmising that it is most likely to be found "in primitive conditions of life, perhaps in some obscure tribe that lived close to nature and had never heard an echo of our western world" (*Riallaro* 10–11). What he finds, in an immense fog-shrouded region of the southern Pacific, is the archipelago of exiles, in which a group of larger islands use the smaller islands near them as asylums, each relegated to a different type of aberrant personality. It turns out that the populations of the larger islands are in their turn the descendants of exiled criminals, deviants, and misfits from the central island, Limanora, regarded with fear and loathing as the "island of devils" by the outer islanders. The narrator manages to penetrate the defenses the Limanorans have set up to prevent visitors to their island, and finds that it is a highly advanced society. *Limanora* then describes this utopian society in immense detail.

The difference between the satirical first volume and the utopian second volume conforms precisely to the difference between the ludicrous and the plausible. The societies—or rather populations—described in Brown's anatomy of folly in *Riallaro* share the "daemonic" quality that, as Angus Fletcher says, is typical of allegorical personages in general (Fletcher 25–69). That is, it is as if they are possessed by a single quality that dictates their appearance, and directs all of their behavior in one narrow channel. Believability is the last quality one would expect or desire from such figures. Their comic and critical effectiveness arises from their hyperbolic display of the vice or folly that inhabits them, and from the cleverness and abundance of invention with which Brown elaborates their maniacal ways. But once the narrator enters Limanora, the generic situation changes drastically. Now that the society is supposed to represent the upper limits of human possibility, its plausibility becomes crucial. Brown's vehicle for making Limanora believable for the reader is a standard mechanism of utopian literature, the process of the narrator's education in the customs and philosophy of Limanora. But this education is not the usual guided tour and lecture series. Instead, the narrator has to be refashioned from the inside out, starting with dream therapy and extending finally to his acquiring an entirely new perceptual capability, the "firla," which senses electromagnetic fields. The narrator of the science fiction utopia has to become the transformed, dislocated subject of impossible knowledge.

Colonial ideology and evolutionary discourse inevitably come into play in Brown's fashioning of this utopian "island of progress." Brown's disdain for certain aspects of the history of colonialism, such as military conquest and slavery, is readily apparent. The collection of religious fanatics in the "theopathic" islands of the archipelago of exiles distances him about as far as it is possible to be from any sympathy with Christian missionaries. Ultimately, however, the question of the bearing of colonial ideology on the construction of Limanora has to focus upon the relation of the central island to the other islands. Here the refashioning of the narrator is very much to the point, because it is a microcosmic recapitulation of the historical transformation of Limanora. Both are processes of purgation, expulsion of the animal past in pursuit of a human (or post-human) future. The narrator learns from the dream therapists or "somnologists" that, "Into the making of our bodies and our brain-tissues go elements of our human and animal past, ages buried beyond the reach of history or speculation.... There are a hundred brains in every man ... composed out of the elements of all his ancestry, even his far-back animal ancestry" (*Limanora* 20–21). One could not easily imagine a more invasive, manipulative, and prescriptive science than the one practiced by these somnologists, who scan their subjects' brains in search of atavistic animal or savage tendencies, and attempt to eliminate them. The rationale for this practice is a severe form of Social-Darwinian ideology that also justifies the expulsion of misfits, and the progressive island's dedication to eugenic discipline:

The Limanoran sages explain this reappearance of animal natures in human civilisations and individuals by showing how the elements of all exist in infinitesimal germ in the most primitive form of animal life; as this crept up the scale, certain elements grew stronger and led to new species still retaining the others in subordination.... And the only means of ridding these of their retrogressive influence is to make the newer and higher spiritual qualities more dominant. The first rule of a civilisation that means to advance in reality and not in mere appearance is to monasticise all atavistic natures and prevent them from handing on their retrogression to a posterity; the second is to encourage only the higher and more spiritual features of those that remain. (22–23)

Thus, when the generic difference between satirical and science fiction analogy turns the Spenserian device of the archipelago of exiles into the Limanoran program of therapeutic discipline, the effect within Brown's fiction is alarming. His powerful, explicit anticolonialism and antiracism cannot disentangle themselves from the colonialist and racist implications of an ideology of progress so ruthlessly sure of its identification of the higher, more advanced human that it is ready to subject the less advanced to incarceration, exile, or oblivion.

What makes the category of the "retrogressive" in Social Darwinism of the type we see in Brown so pernicious is in large part its foolish self-confidence that it fully understands the savage or barbarian other. Such self-confidence is among H. G. Wells's primary targets in *First Men in the Moon*, where Wells employs another form of generic dialogue in order to stage the problem of understanding the exotic other in the context of scientific exploration and colonialist appropriation. The alien ethnography in the final section of *First Men in the Moon* is one of the most influential such pieces in early science fiction. Wells constructs the underground lunar society of the Selenites on the model of an insect hive, producing not just a set of ancestors for the infamous bug-eyed monsters of the pulp illustrators, but also a version of the social organization of labor that resonates with dystopian fictions like Aldous Huxley's *Brave New World* (1932) or Yevgeny Zamyatin's *We* (1924), because of the Selenites' complete disregard for the rights or fulfillment of the individual as compared to the achievement of organized social aims. But Wells's depiction of Selenite specialization is not clearly dystopian, hovering instead on the boundary between coherent realization of the science fiction premise—that hive insects could evolve into a highly intelligent species with a complex industrial society—and satirical commentary on early-twentieth-century England. Consider the description and comments of Cavor, the scientist observer, on the way the Selenites literally shape their young for specific jobs:

> Quite recently I came upon a number of young Selenites confined in jars from which only the fore limbs protruded, who were being compressed to become machine-minders of a special sort. The extended "hand" in this highly developed system of technical education is stimulated by irritants and nourished by injections, while the rest of the body is starved.... That wretched-looking hand sticking out of its jar seemed to have a sort of limp appeal for lost possibilities; it haunts me still, although, of course, it is really in the end a far more humane proceeding than our earthly method of leaving children to grow into human beings, and then making machines of them. (200–201)

The description of the mutilated Selenite children sets up the satirical thrust at the end of the passage, but alongside the shock of recognition produced by the comparison of Selenite education to class destiny, Cavor's more conscious intention of chastising himself for his ethnocentrism keeps it own force. Cavor's savaging of earthly civilization works so well because he is willing to admit that he is himself in the position of an ignorant outsider trying to understand the inner logic of a complex society: "I have as yet scarcely learnt as much about these things [Selenite food production and delivery] as a Zulu in London would learn about the British corn supplies in the same time" (186).

The generic complexity of Cavor's ethnography plays itself out in the larger narrative against the adventure-fiction conventions and jingoistic assumptions of the other narrator, the journalist Bedford. The escape sequence that Bedford narrates as exciting adventure appears in the later comments of Cavor as a series of rash, senselessly violent, self-destructive blunders. Bedford, echoing imperialist politicians of the day, envisions the moon as a receptacle for earth's "surplus population" (84). For Bedford, the most interesting thing about the lunar underground is the apparent abundance of gold there, and the Selenites are merely obstacles in the way of getting at it. The first thing that leaps to Bedford's mind when he learns of Cavor's invention of the means of space flight is a vision of "the whole solar system threaded with Cavorite liners . . . 'Rights of preemption,' came floating into my head—planetary rights of pre-emption. I recalled the old Spanish monopoly in American gold" (31). Nonetheless it is Bedford who puts his finger on a key difference between Cavor and himself when he says that not one man in a million has the same "twist" as Cavor, the desire for knowledge for its own sake rather than for some practical material advantage (123). This sets Bedford's fantasies of appropriation in stark opposition to Cavor's disinterested attempt to comprehend Selenite society, and it corresponds to the formal opposition between the careful elaboration of the science fiction premise in Cavor's fragmented ethnography, and the plot-driven forward energy of Bedford's tale of adventure. The opposition in *First Men in the Moon* between knowledge for its own sake and cognition as appropriation points toward one of the enduring dichotomies in the developing genre of science fiction, the difference between attempting to imagine radical difference as an intellectual and philosophical exercise and exploiting the exotic as a spectacular opportunity for wish fulfillment. If Bedford is right, the latter is always going to be the more popular choice. But who would remember Bedford if it were not for Cavor?

When: The Nature-Culture Opposition and Time Travel

Unlike a voyage to the moon, the plot of time travel remains scientifically impossible both in practice and in theory.[4] Its importance in early science fiction is nonetheless firmly grounded in evolutionary science, on the one hand, and colonial geography, on the other. Time travel stories in the later nineteenth and early twentieth centuries are variations on the imaginary voyage—rather than being, as they often became in the 1930s and after, preoccupied with paradoxes of circular causality[5]—largely because in the ascendance of imperialism, travel into the non-Western world was widely understood as travel into the past (see Stafford 313–15). But the status of the past itself was made into a highly charged issue by evolutionary theory's contention that species themselves—above all the human species—are not stable, unchanging entities. Thus interpretation of primitive societies put at stake the question of where cultural difference ends and where natural, biologically ordained species difference begins, particularly in the context of ongoing scientific debate about whether and how much racial differences resemble species differences. Stories of time travel often explore the abstract scientific question of the limits of human cultural malleability; and, even more than that, ideas about progress and its dark opposite, degeneration, pervade these stories. Both for scientific and for ideological reasons, then, the problems of interpretation that confront time travelers are entangled with Western understanding of non-Western cultures, and constitute one more way that colonialism is woven into the texture of early science fiction.

That colonial geography sets up an understanding of travel in space as travel in time is quite clear in Joseph Conrad's *Heart of Darkness* (1895), and so are the interpretive quandaries it raises. In the novel's framing conversation, Marlow posits an analogy between traveling into colonial Africa and traveling back in time to the Roman colonization of the area that became London. The question Marlow means to pose by means of this analogy is whether London's primitive past has been superceded or not. Is the spectacle of African savagery merely an anachronism for contemporary Europeans, or does it represent the unchanging truth of human nature? The options become both more explicit and more drastic later, as he remembers looking upon the interior of the Belgian Congo from his riverboat. Marlow says he believed in the shore's inhabitants and their business "in the same way one of you might believe there are inhabitants in the planet Mars.... We were wanderers on a prehistoric earth, on an earth that wore the aspect of an unknown planet" (129, 138). The sense of disconnection and unreality Marlow voices when he ascribes to Africa "the aspect of an unknown planet" registers his anxious desire to disavow the status he gives it in the same breath, that of his own prehistory.

Like Marlow contemplating Africans who may or may not stand for London's past, William Morris's visitor to London's future in *News from Nowhere* (1890) finds himself feeling like "a being from another planet" (16: 54, 135), for reasons that are more similar to Marlow's than they might at first appear to be. It is not just that both narrators find themselves confronting and, in mirror-like fashion, transformed into anachronisms. More importantly, for each of them questions of cultural relativism and humanistic universality are crucial. One story asks how much difference there is between the civilized European and the savage African, while the other asks to what extent the limitations and weaknesses of contemporary humankind are effects of social organization rather than qualities intrinsic to the species. The sense of estrangement that Morris's narrator feels before the incredibly youthful, vigorous citizens of the future in *News from Nowhere* has beneath it the same doubts about his own possible similarity to them that Marlow feels before the spectacle of Africa in *Heart of Darkness*, but with an exactly opposite emotional charge. The two situations follow opposite vectors leading from the same set of ideas—and doubts—about progress, with the present of 1890s London as the center of reference where questions meet about what we have been, what we are, and what we could become.

The plot of time travel is an excellent vehicle for exploring the nature-culture opposition because the isolation of the traveler and the instantaneous or discontinuous mode of the travel itself tend to heighten the usual difficulties of the stranger in a strange land. Before Wells invented the time machine, time travelers usually fell into a trance or deep sleep from which they awoke, after the fashion of Rip Van Winkle, in another age. (Wells himself used this form of time travel again after *The Time Machine* in *When the Sleeper Awakes* [1899].) The bewilderment of the traveler and his difficulties in understanding and negotiating the past or future into which he awakes are standard developments.[6] For example, two of the most influential and popular stories of time travel before *The Time Machine*, Edward Bellamy's *Looking Backward* and Morris's *News from Nowhere*, both employ the device of the mutual incomprehensibility of the narrator and his future utopian interlocutors, and for both of them this is a strategy for exposing the artificiality of contemporary social arrangements. For example, when Bellamy's narrator marvels that he has woken up "among a people of whom a cartload of gold would not procure a loaf of bread," his friend from the future can only reply, "Why in the world should it?" (235) Similarly, Morris's traveler finds himself quite unable to explain why a very elaborately carved pipe should strike him as "too valuable for its use, perhaps" (16: 45).

As a corollary of this denaturalization of contemporary society, both narrators experience their return to the present as a nightmarish unmasking of the arbitrary injustice that pervades it. Bellamy's narrator attains an impressive intensity in this situation:

The squalor and malodourousness of the town struck me, from the moment I stood upon the street, as facts I had never before observed. But yesterday, moreover, it had seemed quite a matter of course that some of my fellow-citizens should wear silks, and others rags, that some should look well fed, and others hungry. Now on the contrary the glaring disparities in the dress and condition of the men and women who brushed against each other on the sidewalks shocked me at every step, and yet more the entire indifference which the prosperous showed to the plight of the unfortunate. Were these human beings, who could behold the wretchedness of their fellows without so much as a change of countenance? (297–98)

The estrangement of the returning traveler from his homeland is a familiar satiric convention, of course. But unlike Gulliver, whose inability to re-enter society with the humans whom he now recognizes as Yahoos signifies a fundamental disillusionment with human nature, these utopian travelers see their contemporaries as potentially noble creatures degraded and perverted by their social arrangements. Thus the question, "Were these human beings," is clearly meant to be a rhetorical one. But does it not also pose itself reflexively against the future society? The shocking discontinuity between present and future makes it impossible *not* to ask whether this society can ever change into that one. The gap separating them inspires in Bellamy's returning traveler something all too close to the play of self-recognition and disavowal in Marlow's vacillating identification of Africa as prehistoric Earth or another planet. The dilemma of both travelers exposes a stubborn antagonism between the notion of universal human nature, whether asserted pessimistically or optimistically, and the division of human societies into civilization and savagery; but their dilemma is comprised in the fact that they cannot let go of either side of the antagonism.

In contrast to the play of human universality against cultural difference in these texts, Grant Allen's *The British Barbarians* (1895) and John Davys

Beresford's *The Hampdenshire Wonder* (1911) pursue a more explicit strategy of turning contemporary anthropological discourse about savage societies back on England itself. In Allen's novel, an anthropologist from the future visits contemporary England to study the taboos of the primitive people who live there, allowing Allen to use the vocabulary of contemporary anthropology and the equation of indigenous cultures with the past to produce the straightforward satirical effect of transposing England into the place of the savage other. The superiority of the cosmopolitan visitor from the future over the boorish Englishmen of the present merely switches the roles Englishmen usually occupy in the scheme of anthropological discourse, however, so that the novel's protest against the savagery of Allen's contemporaries leaves intact the ideology inhering in its framework of assumptions about civilization and progress. Far more impressive is Allen's ability to articulate the subversive implications of Darwinian science in relation to ethnocentric and even anthropocentric ideology—as when the future anthropologist ridicules the notion that anything remotely resembling humanity would ever be found on another planet, emphasizing instead the peculiar and surely unique combination of circumstances that produces any given species. Unfortunately, this stripping away of any hint of progressive teleology from nature seems quite forgotten in the realm of culture.

John Davys Beresford pursues a closely related rendering of the English present as the savage past in a generic neighbor to the time-travel story, the evolutionary fantasy *The Hampdenshire Wonder*. Beresford's avatar of the future is not a time traveler but instead a child, the prodigious Victor Stott, who at the age of five reads books at page-turning speed, remembers everything, and sees through Hegel at a glance. Young Stott—like many a future human in the pulp milieu of the following decades—has an extraordinarily large head and a hypnotic power in his gaze. Also like many pulp hyper-encephalic humans, Victor Stott embodies a vision of modernity as soulless rationality: "His mind is a magnificent, terrible machine. He has the imagination of a mathematician and a logician developed beyond all conception, he has not one spark of the imagination of a poet. And so he cannot deal with men" (193). Indeed, the clear implication is that Victor Stott represents an evolutionary break with contemporary humanity, so that, if he is not quite a being from another planet, he is probably one from another species.[7]

Victor Stott deals with others so little that the story is less about him—certainly not about his actions, which are minimal—than it is about the small rural community's reactions to the frightening, enigmatic child.

Stott's main protector is an anthropologist named Challis who is also studying totemism "among the Polynesians of Tikopia and Ontong Java" and seeking "to correct some inferences with regard to the origins of exogamy made by Dr. J. G. Frazer" (113). But Challis's science simply articulates an ideology of progress when he interprets the child prodigy as the next "stage" of human development. The conflict between Challis and the dull-witted cleric Crashaw, who becomes the child's major enemy and possibly his murderer, pits scientific rationality against insular superstition. In his attacks on Stott, according to the narrator, Crashaw "was seeking to crush, not some paralyzed rabbit on the road, but an elusive spirit of swiftness which has no name, but may be figured as the genius of modernity" (212). The narrator's sympathies clearly lie with Challis and with Victor Stott in this struggle, so much so that Crashaw's stupidity and brutality end up serving as a kind of apology for "the genius of modernity" in spite of Victor Stott's obvious shortcomings. The ideology supporting such advocacy shows up most clearly in the way the novel adamantly makes the opposition between civilization and savagery into something dictated by nature rather than culture. As Challis says, "Think of the gap which separates your intellectual powers from those of the Polynesian savage. Why, after all, should it be impossible that this child's powers should equally transcend your own?" (156). What, then, are we to infer about "the intellectual powers . . . of the Polynesian savage?" The implication is clearly that the cultural and racial differences of Polynesians from Europeans are actually tantamount to a difference between species. Rather than exposing and playing out the tensions within anthropological discourse and progressive ideology, then, *The Hampdenshire Wonder* simply presents us with a contradiction—a polemic for rational toleration of difference that at the same time closes down the possibility of positive social change along racial lines.

Rather than mistaking cultural differences for biological ones, as Challis does, the best early science fiction treatments of post-human species dramatize the opposite error, that of mistaking biological adaptations for merely cultural practices. William Henry Hudson's *A Crystal Age* (1887) and H. G. Wells's *The Time Machine* (1895) both narrate the difficulties that a man from the present encounters in understanding the workings of a far future society. In each story, the narrator misrecognizes what seem to him to be arbitrary and unjust social arrangements, but are in fact species differences between the men of his world and the inhabitants of the future. Wells's accomplishment is well known and has been written about and studied as thoroughly as any other piece of science fiction, early or late. Nonetheless, there is room to say a few words about the bearing of colonialism and colonial ideology on *The Time Machine*. Hudson's *A Crystal Age*, in sharp contrast to *The Time Machine*, is not widely acknowledged as an important piece of early science fiction, and his decidedly quirkier invention has not been nearly as widely studied nor, I think, as well understood.

Critics and scholars of *A Crystal Age* usually have assumed that the future society represented in it is meant to be a pastoral utopia, encouraged by Hudson's allusion to *News from Nowhere* in his 1906 preface following the comment that "romances of the future . . . are born of a very common feeling—a sense of dissatisfaction with the existing order of things, combined with a vague faith in or hope of a better one to come" (v–vi). But Everett Bleiler complains that the novel portrays "one of the most horrible ideal cultures ever imagined" (*Early Years* 377). David Miller observes the "sublimated, crystalline, neuter purity" of the future citizens, and judges that "at this point in his writing Hudson is not able to create successfully a definite image for spirituality in terms of personhood" (121, 123). And Felipe Arocena takes the next step, arguing that Hudson's "exasperatingly asexual novel" is a counter-utopian satire: "what Hudson is presenting is a cruel caricature of Victorian society, and he does this by inventing a community where Victorian ideals have been taken to extremes" (75–76). But one ought to hesitate before concluding that a communistic future society without war, poverty, pollution, or disease, where people live in harmony with nature and enjoy healthy life spans of several centuries, is meant as a "cruel caricature of Victorian society" merely because the protagonist is frustrated by his ignorance of its sexual mores. The social organization depicted in *A Crystal Age* is a more fully realized, complex, and ambiguous one than any of these critics gives it credit for being, and, while some satirical mockery of Victorian prudery may well be intended, the main thrust of the novel is its drama of mutual miscommunication and misrecognition between a stranger in a strange land and its inhabitants.

Like Richard Jefferies in the remarkable opening chapters of *After London* (1885), and perhaps in direct debt to Jefferies, Hudson at many of his best moments in *A Crystal Age* lets the landscape tell the story. Before Smith, the Rip-Van-Winkle-style time traveler, sees any humans in the far future where he has awakened, he encounters apparently wild sheep, horses, and birds that seem oddly unafraid of him. Even more strange is the later scene where he is sent out to plough a field and the horses come to him unbidden, put themselves into the plough, and literally lead him through the task. Near the end of the story, as the lovesick Smith wanders forlorn through the forest, he finds comfort in its abundant natural beauty, in a passage that shows why Hudson the naturalist's several books on birds continued to be in print in the second half of the twentieth century:

> I came on a great company of storks, half a thousand of them at least, apparently resting on their travels, for they were all standing motionless, with necks drawn in, as if dozing. They were very stately, handsome birds, clear grey in colour, with a black collar on the neck, and red beak and legs. My approach did not disturb them until I was within twenty yards of the nearest—for they were scattered over an acre of ground; then they rose with a loud, rustling noise of wings, only to settle again at a short distance off. (286)

The storks are not symbolic of anything. They are just storks. What is significant is that they react to Smith as if he, too, were just another animal. The abundance and the behavior of the wild animals, particularly the birds, in *A Crystal Age* shows first of all that humans have stopped hunting. But the behavior of the horses goes beyond that, and the fact that Hudson carefully describes new species of flowers and birds hints that the change is not merely one of social organization. Somehow the lines between nature and culture have been redrawn, so that horses join without restraint or compulsion into agricultural labor. A few pages after the description of the storks, Smith stops and talks to one of the extremely intelligent dogs that, like the horses, have become something a little more than domestic animals:

> "When I speak to you, you don't wag that beautiful bushy tail which serves you for ornament. This reminds me that you are not like the dogs that I used to know.... Where are they now—collies, rat-worrying terriers, hounds, spaniels, retrievers—dogs rough and dogs smooth; big brute boarhounds, St Bernard's, mastiffs, nearly or quite as big as you are, but not so slender, silky-haired, and sharp-nosed, and without your refined expression of keenness without cunning." (292)

Clearly the relations between humans and dogs have changed, breeding practices must have changed, and canine appearance and behavior have changed. The question is, what gives coherence to the unfrightened wild animals, the strangely intelligent domestic ones, and the human society in which Smith finds himself? Are these humans any more like Smith than the dogs and horses are like the ones in the past he has left behind?

The extraordinary rapprochement between the humans and the dogs and horses signals a more radical and original form of harmony with nature than pastoral utopia. Instead, the human society of *A Crystal Age* is simply no longer entirely human. The difference in their sexual behavior and reproductive system amounts almost, but perhaps not quite, to a species change—not quite, because apparently it would still be possible for Smith and Yoletta, the woman he falls in love with, to produce offspring. But this possibility, which remains untested, does not diminish the key role of the change that is at the heart of all the miscommunication and problems that Smith suffers in the future society. In the first exchange between Smith and the old man known as the father, the spokesperson and ruler of the local community, they run afoul of one another over the meaning of "house." When Smith comments that the large house they lead him to "must have cost a pot of money, and taken a long time to build," the father's reply that he does not know the meaning of the phrase "a pot of money" is a commonplace of utopian literature. But he goes on, "When you add *a long time to build*, I am also puzzled to understand you. For are not all houses, like the forest of trees, the human race, the world we live in, eternal?" (37, Hudson's emphasis) What is a cultural artifact for Smith is a natural phenomenon for the father, and this initial misunderstanding extends to the meaning of family and love. Smith comes to understand only at the end of the novel that those several hundreds of people who live in any one of the world's seven thousand independent, self-sufficient, quasi-eternal houses are literally all members of one family, and that there is only one sexually active couple per house. In other words, the organization of sexual reproduction is that of a hive, not of a human community as Smith would recognize one. When Smith falls in love with the beautiful Yoletta, his flirtation and hope for reciprocity quite literally can not be returned in kind, because she is no more sexually active than a dog or a horse that is not in heat. The utopian harmony with nature of Hudson's future society entails the erasure of the largest physiological difference between human and animal sexuality, the extension of human sexual activity beyond the period of fertility and the purpose of reproduction.

The most serious flaw in *A Crystal Age* is the narrowness of Smith, the narrator, whose obsession with Yoletta is matched by his unbelievable lack of curiosity about everything else. During his initial encounter with the people of the future, rather than being alarmed and struck with wonder at having somehow been transported into an entirely different society, he admires the lovely young girl and wonders how he can get to know her better. When the father, reading from a sacred text after dinner, divulges the story of the great plague that brought Smith's civilization to an end and of the subsequent reorganization of society by the survivors, it goes in one ear and out the other because he is more busy thinking about Yoletta. In short, Smith is reduced in almost allegorical fashion to an emblem of passionate, lovesick desire. His final, rash decision to drink a potion promising to cure him of his desire, but that turns out to be poison granting the cure of death, is entirely typical and appropriate. The strange intolerance of the members of the future society that so disturbs Bleiler and befuddles Arocena is not a flaw, however. The members of the house simply do not understand the possibility of a cultural difference like the one Smith brings with him, because for them the organization of the house and the family is a matter of nature, not of culture. The father's attempts to account for Smith's bizarre behavior are always attempts to explain it away, to see him as injured or damaged rather than as really, profoundly different. The strange rules and laws that the father administers cohere with Hudson's vision of a society with a level of conformity and narrowness of routine that is certainly more like animal behavior than like human culture, but to complain about this is to miss entirely the operation of Hudson's science fiction premise. A *Crystal Age* is a deliberately ambiguous utopia and, probably not intentionally, a somewhat opaque satire on the difficulty an almost manically, if narrowly, acquisitive English traveler suffers in understanding what a radically foreign culture does, and does not, offer him. But this opacity is the price it pays for its remarkably inventive and difficult accomplishment as science fiction.

Unlike A *Crystal Age*, *The Time Machine* is not in need of fundamental elucidation.[8] This is not simply due to the amount of critical attention it has commanded. It is more a result of the superior clarity and explicitness with which Wells presents and realizes his premise. The biggest difference is in the character of the Time Traveller himself. By making the Time Traveller a scientist taking an exploratory expedition into the future, rather than an everyman subjected to Rip-Van-Winkle-style transport, Wells turns the drama of interpretation into the protagonist's dominant motive and the novel's conceptual skeleton. *The Time Machine* explains itself at almost every step, from the opening lecture about time as the fourth dimension, through the traveler's successive, shifting hypotheses about the origins of the Eloi and the Morlocks, to the astronomical theories that help explain the grim setting of the traveler's final, bleak glimpse into the last days of life on Earth. When Hillyer, the frame narrator, comments at the end that "the story was so fantastic and incredible, the telling so credible and sober" (89), this self-reflexive, meta-generic statement culminates and sums up the entire novel's success at commenting upon, explaining, and defending its integration of psychological realism, scientific plausibility, and the impossible facts of the Time Traveller's expedition.[9]

Wells also made it quite clear that *The Time Machine* was written against "the placid assumption of that time that Evolution was a pro-human force making things better and better for mankind" (*Seven Famous Novels* x). But the novel's response to Social Darwinism does not consist merely in the idea that the future of humanity might involve degeneration into subhuman species like the Eloi and the Morlocks, rather than a rise toward perfection à la Herbert Spencer. When the first sight that greets the eye of the Time Traveller in the future is a sphinx, Wells may well be alluding to an essay by his teacher T. H. Huxley, "The Struggle for Existence in Human Society," in which Huxley says that "the true riddle of the Sphinx" is how to escape the "eternal competition of man against man" that produces "the accumulation of misery at the negative pole of society, in contrast with . . . monstrous wealth at the positive pole" (212; quoted in *The Time Machine*, ed. Ruddick, 199). The hypotheses the Time Traveller proposes in order to explain the Eloi's and the Morlocks' descent from humanity then appear as so many allegorical readings of Wells's future society in terms of contemporary class relations, climaxing in the understanding that the Morlocks' feeding upon the Eloi represents a kind of long-term justice that reverses the exploitative relation of Capitalist to Labourer. But this is the point where things cease being entirely clear, because when the Time Traveller reaches this stage of his interpretation of the Morlocks' dietary practices he confesses to an entirely unscientific motive: "I tried to preserve myself from the horror that was coming upon me, by regarding it as a rigorous punishment for human selfishness" (71). The absolutely bleak planetary teleology revealed by his trip into the far future should be enough to squelch any serious consideration that the Morlocks' relation to the Eloi has to do with some kind of providential or moral process. And indeed the Time Traveller retreats from this brief bout of moralizing in his final reflection on the Eloi's fate, when he concludes that it results from the "law of nature . . . that intellectual versatility is the compensation for change, danger, and trouble" (81).

What causes the Time Traveller to resort to moral comfort rather than scientific explanation is also clear, however: the visceral repulsion inspired in him by the Morlocks, whom he compares to sloths, spiders, ants, and rats. The same disgust causes him, some commentators think, to underestimate the intelligence of the Morlocks and to misinterpret as cannibalism what is in fact a symbiotic relation between two separate species: "The Morlocks gather Eloi like cattle, devour them periodically, but allow for the replenishment of the captive population; the Eloi's contentment and biological comfort are, therefore, in the Morlocks' long-range interest as a species.... For the Eloi, extinction would be inescapable, without the carnivorous paternalism of the Morlocks" (DePaolo 72). In his 1895 essay "Bio-Optimism," Wells argues against the notion that symbiotic relations between natural species invalidate Darwin's thesis of natural selection based on the struggle for existence: "Because some species have abandoned fighting in open order, each family for itself, as some of the larger carnivora do, for a fight in masses after the fashion of the ants, . . . because man instead of killing his cattle at sight preserves them against his convenience, . . . is life any the less a battle-field?" (*Early Writings* 208). Wells does not refer explicitly to the Morlocks in "Bio-Optimism," but the reference to ants and cattle certainly points us to *The Time Machine*, and not only to the Morlocks. As has often been remarked, almost the first thing the Time Traveller says on his return is to ask his dinner guests to "Save me some of that mutton. I'm starving for a bit of meat" (39). It is no accident that the Time Traveller's own "carnivorous paternalism" confesses its basis in the struggle for existence with that banal exaggeration, "I'm starving." The Time Traveller is more like the Morlocks than he is willing to admit, and Wells makes a point of alerting his readers to this fact.

If the Time Traveller's loathing for the Morlocks has in it some element of disavowed self-recognition, the way it disrupts his scientific discipline suggests further that, in addition to the interpretive difficulties he suffers because of insufficient evidence, he also is running up against ideological limitations that have to do with his sense of identity. Part of the point of the Time Traveller's prejudice against the Morlocks may be to satirize anthropocentrism. It is clear that Wells carefully crafts the Eloi and the Morlocks to undermine the opposition between human and animal, for the Eloi look more like humans, but only the Morlocks use tools or exhibit any signs of rational foresight. Thus the Time Traveller's prejudice against their appearance muddles his attempts to explain the divergence of humanity into Eloi and Morlock in terms of evolutionary theory, for that explanation has to treat humans as an animal species like any other. But the Time Traveller's interpretations of the future call just as prominently on a class analysis of society as on an evolutionary analysis of the struggle for existence, and thus his gut reactions call his own class identification into the discussion as well. Here, I think, is where the entanglement of both evolutionary discourse and class analysis with colonialism comes into the picture. I want to suggest that the complex identification and repulsion that the Time Traveller feels toward the post-human inhabitants of the future has a basis, not only in the conflicted class position of Wells himself, which John Huntington has described as uncomfortably poised between the below-stairs servant class of his mother and the complacent dinner guests above ("*The Time Machine* and Wells's Social Trajectory"), but of the British working class as a whole, poised between the upper classes at home and the colonized nations abroad.

The Time Traveller's initial encounter with the Eloi alludes throughout to colonial settings. The Time Traveller proposes the same analogy that Cavor later will use in *First Men in the Moon* to describe his attempts to understand the Selenites: that in their midst he finds himself as baffled as a "negro, fresh from Central Africa" would be in contemporary London (57); but in his dealings with the Eloi he seems more like a European confronting the enigmatic inhabitants of savage Africa. The child-like, flower-wearing Eloi's belief that the Time Traveller has arrived from the sun during a thunderstorm might have reminded some contemporary readers of the Kukuanans in *King Solomon's Mines*, and it certainly marks them as primitives. When the Time Traveller communicates to the Eloi his wish to enter the sphinx in order to retrieve his machine, their response seems to signal that he has violated a local taboo: "They behaved very oddly. . . . Suppose you were to use a grossly improper gesture to a delicate-minded woman—it is how she would look" (55). The inexplicability of their reactions makes it look like mere superstition. Although the Time Traveller accounts for the extreme heat of the days in astronomical terms—"It may be that the sun was hotter, or the earth nearer the sun . . . [for] the planets must ultimately fall back one by one into the parent body" (60)—Wells is clearly also evoking a tropical climate, as if to suggest, in the context of the imperial geography that Marlow articulates in seeing Africa as "prehistoric earth," that in the Eloi we see human culture, like the Earth itself, falling back into its origin. Finally, the sphinx itself alludes to a setting that is both ancient and colonial, and if the riddle of the sphinx may refer us to Huxley's essay on class inequity, this does not cancel out its more usual role of posing the questions of human nature, origins, and destiny. In fact, in the context of evolutionary theory, the part-human, part-animal form of the sphinx makes these questions all the more pertinent.[10]

All of this changes once we discover the Morlocks, of course. Now the surface acquires depth, and such mysteries as the manufacture of the Eloi's clothing and the absence of cemeteries resolve themselves into aspects of the Eloi's and Morlocks' economic interdependence. The Time Traveller's new understanding transposes the Eloi from the position of childlike primitives to that of a degenerate, parasitic aristocracy supported by an ultra-civilized technology, a reversal whose force is emphasized by the earlier colonial allusions. And the Morlocks, who are both less and more human than the Eloi, and whom the traveler assigns first the position of slave, then of master, also, like the Eloi, seem to conflate human origins and post-human destiny. Rather than tropical primitives, they resemble cave men, a likeness that Harry Geduld, in his introduction to *The Definitive Time Machine*, links to a childhood incident in which Wells was terrified by an illustration of a gorilla in J. G. Wood's *Illustrated Natural History* (1872), whose caption, "*Troglodytes Gorilla*," makes, as Geduld tells us, "a manifest association of underground (or cave) man and ape" (28). Indeed, the way the Time Traveller's interpretation of the Eloi and Morlocks oscillates between the opposites of savagery and civilization, natural arrangement and cultural artifice, or mastery and slavery is perhaps more important than the Time Traveller's final, admittedly tentative, explanation of their divergence. Darko Suvin argues that Wells's schematic inversion of evolutionary history is a generic paradigm for converting scientific material to artistic use (*Metamorphoses of Science Fiction* 223–33), but perhaps John Huntington gets at the power of Wells's achievement better when he describes Wells's ability to "see contradiction clearly in all its appalling and irresolvable conflict, and then to try by whatever means possible to mediate that disjunction" (*Logic of Fantasy* 52).

An appallingly resolved class conflict is the central example of such mediation in *The Time Machine*, and the Time Traveller's aversion to the Morlocks and the mixture of sympathy and contempt he feels toward the Eloi surely have some biographical basis in Wells's own conflicted class identification. But this remarkably fertile text puts more into play than just Wells's position in English society, or even class relations in the domestic economy. The canny combination of class analysis and questions of economy, on the one hand, with evolutionary anthropology's oppositions between civilization and savagery, human and animal, ancient and modern, and origin and destiny, on the other, also puts into play England's position in the world. For doesn't the initial association of the Eloi with tropical primitives suggest that the extremely resonant opposition between surface and underworld in *The Time Machine* includes a geographical reading of the underground, as well, as nontropical and industrial? If so, the oscillation of the roles of master and slave implies a corresponding instability in this geographical metaphor, such that we must include, among the contemporary social contradictions registered and mediated in Wells's post-human future, the one that makes the English public look like the industrious Morlocks in domestic class relations but like the parasitic Eloi in the global economy—or, finally, in the kind of self-recognition that repulses the Time Traveller, like the enslaved Morlocks in the domestic context but like the predatory Morlocks in the global one. The horror that comes upon the Time Traveller when he realizes the substance of the Morlocks' diet shares a structural similarity to the horror that confronts Marlow in *Heart of Darkness*, in that both vacillate irresolvably between constituting a recognition of human nature and a recognition of the subject's own position ("starving for a bit of meat") in a brutally exploitative economy. What I am suggesting is that the conscious allegory of class in *The Time Machine* overlaps, inevitably perhaps but also deliberately and artfully, with a less explicit representation of the contradictions of the colonial economy, and that Wells's drama of interpretation places the Time Traveller squarely at the heart of those contradictions.

What: Confronting Radical Difference

One way to describe the immense influence of *The Time Machine* on later science fiction is to say that Wells's example made the problem of absorbing and coming to terms with the story's impossible facts into one of the genre's firmest conventions, at the least, and arguably its definitive concern. By the 1930s, a certain play of disorientation and explanation had become a conventional expectation operating in the background of science fiction, especially in a story's opening sentences. For example, Charles R. Tanner's "Tumithak of the Corridors," from the January 1932 issue of *Amazing Stories* (in Asimov 229–83), begins, "It is only within the last few years that archaeological science has reached a point where we may begin to appreciate the astonishing advances that our ancestors had achieved before the Great Invasion"—thus setting forth several unexplained implications. A little exposition soon makes clear that the story is set in the distant future; that somewhere in the distant past of that imaginary future the Earth has been invaded, its surface occupied by extraterrestrials, and humanity driven underground; and that by the time the story is being told humanity has reclaimed the world's surface for itself. This exercise in disorientation and readjustment thrusts itself back into the foreground during the ensuing adventures of Tumithak, the leader of the human rebellion against the alien occupiers, when the hero emerges from the underground world and sees the surface for the first time:

It seemed that he had emerged into a mighty room or hall, so tremendous that he could not even comprehend its immensity. The ceiling and the walls of this room merged into one another to form a stupendous vault like an inverted bowl . . . of a beautiful blue, the color of a woman's eyes. This blue glowed like a jewel, and was mottled with great billowy areas of white and rose, and as Tumithak looked he had a vague feeling that those enormous billowy spots were slowly moving and changing shape. . . . Sick and terrified at the enormity of the scene before him, he darted back into the passageway and cowered against the wall. (275–76)

In this moment of estranged cognition, the science fiction setting suddenly pays off, unexpectedly disrupting what is for the most part an entertaining, competent piece of adventure fiction with an epistemological crisis that momentarily calls upon and puts to use the philosophical authority of Plato's allegory of the cave. Tumithak proves his heroic stature nowhere more cogently than when he overcomes his initial, panicky reaction and steps out of the corridor to confront the immensity of the sky.

Tumithak manages to make provisional sense of what he sees on the surface by recoding it in the vocabulary of the underground, seeing grass as "a strange carpet consisting of long green hairs thickly matted together" and trees as "tall, irregular pillars whose tops were covered with a great bunch of green stuff, of the same color and appearance as the hairs of the carpet" (276). But this is a strategy that can go wrong when that moment of perceptual vertigo in the face of the unknown turns into a more sustained encounter, especially in a colonial context. In one of the great vignettes of 1930s science fiction, Olaf Stapledon's *Last and First Men* (1930) dramatizes the potentially catastrophic consequences of understanding the exotic other in terms of one's own experience. In the ninth chapter of Stapledon's future history, the intelligent inhabitants of Mars decide to colonize the Earth in order to make use of its abundant natural resources. Stapledon's Martians consist of clouds of micro-organisms that bind themselves into an intelligent aggregate through electromagnetic communication, but have no consciousness or identity other than the ones they attain in these ephemeral group formations. The report that the Martian scouting expedition gives of humans on their first foray to the Earth is an exercise in misrecognition based on their anatomical and cultural assumptions:

There were solid animals, of the type of the prehistoric Martian fauna, but mostly two-legged and erect. Experiment had shown that these creatures died when pulled to pieces, and that though the sun's radiation affected them by setting up action in their visual organs, they had no really direct sensitivity to radiation. Obviously, therefore, they must be unconscious. (128)

The Martians decide that the primitive, two-legged, erect animals must be under the control of some hidden intelligence, an assumption that eventually produces the looked-for object:

> Presently the Martians discovered the sources of terrestrial radiation in the innumerable wireless transmitting stations. Here at last was the physical basis of the terrestrial intelligence! But what a lowly creature! What a caricature of life! . . . Their only feat seemed to be that they had managed to get control of the unconscious bipeds who tended them. (129)

This comedy of errors both encourages the Martians' colonial project, by allowing them to see the Earth as empty territory, and sets their plans awry, since they are unable to understand the continued resistance and hostility they encounter from terrestrial broadcasting stations and their animal servants. The humans, on their own part, are equally slow to realize that the mysterious cloud formations are intelligent life forms rather than some weird sort of weather phenomena. It is no doubt with an eye to the imperialist roots and chauvinist ideologies of the First World War that Stapledon goes on to narrate how this drama of misinterpretation plunges the two planets into a horribly extended and destructive conflict that ends with the collapse of human civilization and near extinction of the species.

No early science fiction story more effectively engages the problem of understanding the exotic other in the intricacies of colonial history, ideology, and science than Jack London's "The Red One" (1918), and so a reading of "The Red One" can serve to conclude this chapter and summarize much of what has been said in the first two chapters as well. The story (composed in Honolulu in 1916, six months before London's death) tells of a scientist named Bassett who ventures into the previously unexplored interior of Guadalcanal, in the Solomon Islands, in search of the origin of a tremendous, otherworldly sound. There he finds an enormous, metallic, artificial red sphere of extraterrestrial origin that has been buried in the mountainside for perhaps thousands of years, and that has been excavated by the cannibalistic villagers in the neighborhood, who worship it as a god and perform grisly human sacrifices before it. The sound that has attracted Bassett is produced during the villagers' rituals by striking the sphere with a great, elaborately carved log. On his way to the Red One, Bassett is attacked by headhunters who kill his bearer; he contracts malaria after mosquitoes have "literally pumped his body full of poison" (2299); and he is saved and aided by a native woman, Balatta, who out of love for him betrays the religion of her tribe in order to show Bassett the way to the Red One.[11] Thus a summary of the story can make it look like an adventure romance based on the plot of the treasure hunt, complete with ordeal of entry, native lover, evil priest, ghastly rituals, and the tremendously misunderstood and undervalued treasure itself. But these romantic elements are undercut not only by the ending, when Bassett is decapitated ritually before the Red One by Ngurn, the head priest, but at every step of the way by London's naturalist realism. There is nothing romantic about the jungle setting, "a monstrous, parasitic dripping of decadent life-forms that rooted in death and lived on death" (2300); filth and disease prevail over any hint of exoticism in the interior village; and because Bassett finds Balatta hideously ugly, he treats her brutally and exploits her mercilessly. Add to this that Ngurn, far from being the perversely evil priest of lost-race fiction, ultimately may command more philosophical authority than Bassett in a story where the search for meaning—of the Red One, first of all, but ultimately of death—partly displaces and partly overlaps the motif of the treasure hunt. Adventure, quest romance (London includes a pointed, prominent allusion to Browning's "Childe Roland to the Dark Tower Came" in the opening sequence), science fiction, and philosophical allegory all vie for space in this generically complex fable.

One of London's major strategies for subverting the romantic possibilities in the plot is his grounding of the story in colonial history. London casually mentions that Bassett arrives on the island in the first place by way of a "blackbirder" (2297), that is, "a vessel employed in kidnapping natives for what was in effect slave labor" (López 396). When Bassett reaches the location of the Red One, he finds himself "on the rim of an excavation for all the world like the diamond mines of South Africa," and recalls from "old history, the South Seas Sailing Directions" that "it was Mendana who had discovered the islands and named them Solomon's, believing that he had found that monarch's fabled mines" (2309). That this unmistakable allusion to *King Solomon's Mines* is ironic, not a tribute, becomes entirely clear in an equally deliberate echo of *Heart of Darkness* when London describes Bassett's ambition, once he has discovered the Red One, to "lead an expedition back, and, although the entire population of Guadalcanal be destroyed, extract from the heart of the Red One the message of the world from other worlds" (2314). By casting the shadows of slavery, mineral extraction, and genocide across Bassett's path, London emphasizes that he is writing this quest romance over—without erasing—the horrors of colonial history.

Bassett is a scientist engaged in a quest for knowledge, not wealth, and the way he understands and negotiates with the exotic others on the island makes admirably explicit the relation of colonial setting, discourse, and ideology with science fiction. Bassett's perceptions become a kind of hinge for the play of anachronism between the "grinning and chattering monkey-men" (2302) of the village and the super-civilized "intelligences, remote and unguessable" (2311) who must have made the spaceship. Bassett stands between these two poles not only as the representative of the present-day norm, occupying either pole of the civilized-savage opposition depending on which direction he looks, but also as the proponent of several versions of universality that might command a stable perspective on the vertiginous glimpses into past and future. The first is the scientific principle that local events should be assumed to be average and representative on an astronomical scale of comparison. While "speculating as to the dwellers on the unseen worlds of those incredibly remote suns," Bassett thinks that "surely, in that cosmic ferment, all must be comparatively alike, comparatively of the same substance, or substances" (2313). His attitude towards Balatta introduces a second, ideological form of universality. Reasoning that "eternal female she was, capable of any treason for the sake of love," Bassett decides to use her attraction to him as a means of getting her to lead him to the Red One: "He put the affair to the test, as in a laboratory he would have put to the test any chemical reaction" (2308). Bassett's sexist assumptions may be intended to ring falsely (and certainly do nowadays, whatever London's intentions in 1916), but a third version of universality represented by Bassett's practice, rather than his rationalization of it, is the exercise of power and domination of one organism by another. The Darwinian principle of the struggle for life figures prominently into Bassett's speculations about the aliens as a figure for the possibilities open to humanity:

To be able to send such a message across the pit of space, surely they had reached those heights to which man, in tears and travail and bloody sweat, in darkness and confusion of many counsels, was so slowly struggling. And what were they on their heights? Had they won Brotherhood? Or had they learned that the law of love imposed the penalty of weakness and decay? Was strife, life? Was the rule of all the universe the pitiless rule of natural selection? (2313-14)

One way to explain the motives prompting this group of questions is that they arise from Bassett's (or London's) awareness that, given Bassett's relations with the villagers and the colonial history operating in the background of the story, cosmological uniformity would yield anything but comforting expectations about contact with the aliens who made the Red One. In its attempt to articulate the question posed by the Red One's sublimely mysterious "message," this passage weaves together the scientific discourse, ideology of progress, and colonial history that are the basic fabric of the story.

The strongest mark of colonial ideology on "The Red One" is the overriding ambivalence that makes itself felt at every level at which one attempts to approach the text. The general configuration of London's fictional Pacific, which is polarized between the earthly paradise of Hawai'i and the inferno of the Solomon Islands, matches both the generic polarization of "The Red One" between naturalist realism and quest romance, and its schematic contrast between the grotesque islanders and the idealized aliens. Perhaps the most viscerally effective instance of colonial ambivalence is Bassett's making love to Balatta despite the repulsion she inspires in him. Bassett's contempt for Balatta has much more to do with racism than misogyny: "Her face . . . [was a] twisted and wizened complex of apish features, perforated by upturned, sky-open Mongolian nostrils, by a mouth that sagged from a huge upper-lip and faded precipitately into a retreating chin, and by peering querulous eyes that blinked as blink the eyes of denizens of monkey-cages" (2302). So it is not mere hypocrisy that fuses together his brutality toward her—"as she had been a dog, he kicked the ugly little bushwoman to her feet" (2311)—and his sense of noble purpose before the Red One—"he felt his soul go forth in kinship with that august company, that multitude whose gaze was forever upon the arras of infinity" (2313). His hatred of Balatta stems at least in part from the polluting fact that she is the means to his noble ends.

The same ambivalence structures Bassett's attempts to understand the riddle of the Red One itself. When Bassett first hears the Red One's enormous, resonant sound, he likens it to "the trump of an archangel" or "the mighty cry of some Titan of the Elder World," but in striving to analyze it confesses that "there were no words nor semblances in his vocabulary and experience with which to describe the totality of that sound" (2296). To this paradoxical combination of apocalyptic portent with the absence of any comprehensible content, Bassett's ideology answers with a corresponding debasement of the language of the villagers, "if by *language* might be dignified the uncouth sounds they made to represent ideas" (2303, London's emphasis). The grotesque islanders communicate meaning without significance, while the idealized alien "message" is full of significance but devoid of meaning, allowing Bassett to fill its empty volume with his own fantasies. This dichotomous structure pays off when Bassett finally reaches the Red One, finds it surrounded by the corpses of human sacrifices, and thinks, "Truly had the bush-folk named themselves into the name of the

Red One, seeing in him their own image which they strove to placate and please with such red offerings" (2312). Such a pronouncement on Bassett's part is heavily laden with irony, because Bassett himself is quite willing to offer human sacrifice before the Red One. He knows perfectly well when he forces Balatta to lead him to the idol that she is breaking a taboo and risking the punishment of torture and death. Ultimately he offers himself as a sacrifice, allowing Ngurn to decapitate him ritually, not in order to save Balatta, but in order to spend his last moments looking upon the Red One as the villagers strike it and call forth its "message."[12] That message, if there is one at all and not just an extraordinary, mechanically produced ringing, is inextricably confused in his perception with his own theological vocabulary: "Archangels spoke in it; it was magnificently beautiful before all other sounds; it was invested with the intelligence of supermen of planets of other suns; it was the voice of God, seducing and commanding to be heard" (2317). Thus the irony that Bassett himself understands, that for "this wonderful messenger, winged with intelligence across space, to fall into a bushman stronghold . . . was as if Jehovah's Commandments had been presented on carved stone to the monkeys of the monkey cage at the Zoo" (2312), is clearly intended to cut against both Bassett's own idolatry and his racism.[13]

The generic, thematic, and ideological complexity of "The Red One" all contribute to the power of its extraordinary final sentences. As Bassett bends his neck to receive the blow of the ritual axe,

for that instant, ere the end, there fell upon Bassett the shadow of the Unknown, a sense of impending marvel of the rending of walls before the imaginable. Almost, when he knew the blow had started and just ere the edge of steel bit the flesh and nerves, it seemed that he gazed upon the serene face of the Medusa, Truth—And, simultaneous with the bite of the steel on the onrush of the dark, in a flashing instant of fancy, he saw the vision of his head turning slowly, always turning, in the devil-devil house beside the breadfruit tree. (2317–18)

The science fiction "sense of impending marvel" gives way to the philosophical allegory of "the serene face of the Medusa, Truth" only to have it yield to "a flashing instant of fancy" that combines exoticism and naturalist realism, the vision of his decapitated head being shrunk—cured—in Ngurn's devil-devil house. The figures of finality and truth finally and truly can do nothing but turn, slowly and always, between the poles of colonial ambivalence, between the super-civilized alien and the grotesque savage, between revelation and absurdity. The status of the impossible fact that makes "The Red One" into science fiction, the alien artifact with its unearthly sound, is that of radical, incomprehensible difference—perhaps. But one cannot even know that, because every attempt to understand its mystery is based on asserting a fundamental identity, whether it be the universality of the cosmological principle or of the struggle for life or of the opposition between the civilized and the savage that structures the power dynamics of colonialism. Thus every meaning attributed to the Red One is paranoid, as Bould would say, because it is based on the construction of an inescapably self-centered construction of a coherent reality. The Red One is, as the final sentences precisely put it, as unknowable as death, because it is impossible to construct a subject who could know it without placing him or her outside the possibility of communicating the knowledge.

Thus the priest, Ngurn, ends up being the antithetical counterpart of the Red One, and his wisdom mirrors and reproduces the limits of knowing and communicating with the alien. When Bassett negotiates his final contract with Ngurn—to be allowed to see and hear the Red One, and to pay for the vision with his death—Ngurn makes him another promise: "And I promise you, in the long days to come . . . I will tell you many secrets, for I am an old man and very wise, and I shall be adding wisdom to wisdom as I turn your head in the smoke" (2316). This is an image that turns and turns as well. On the one hand, imparting Ngurn's wisdom to the oblivious head of the dead Bassett is the ironic counterpart of the process of projecting tremendous meanings into the incomprehensible sound of the Red One. On the other, the dead Bassett's very obliviousness to Ngurn's wisdom is an all-too-appropriate metaphor for his contempt of the villagers' language, customs, and humanity in life, as well as for the impossibility of either Bassett or the villagers ever understanding the Red One. The way Ngurn's secrets oscillate between disclosure and opacity therefore both delivers science fiction's generic promise of wondrous cognition—"adding wisdom to wisdom"—and forecloses the possibility of its inevitably paranoid construction of "facts" ever reaching beyond a fantasy of radical difference.

chapter four

Artificial Humans and the Construction of Race

If this study has succeeded at all in demonstrating how early science fiction articulates the structures of knowledge and power provided by colonialism, then it also will have indicated along the way—for example, in the discussion of lost-race fiction or of London's "The Red One"—that some of the racism endemic to colonialist discourses is woven into the texture of science fiction. The interdependence and permeability between the fictional narratives and the social discourses and circumstances in which they circulate makes the presence of racism in early science fiction inevitable. In focusing on that presence more directly in this chapter, however, I do not mean to draw up a catalogue of notoriously racist works, nor to describe in greater detail the more or less casual contamination of the fiction by the ideological spirit of the age. Instead, I want to ask how science fiction handles the discourse of race and its attendant contradictions in one of science fiction's most prominent motifs, the construction of the artificial human.

The prominence during the period from the 1870s to the 1930s of a scientific discourse about race and of powerful, widespread racist ideologies has much to do with colonialism. Historians of modern racist theories usually locate their origins in the colonial slave trade and the massive use of African slaves in colonial agriculture, practices that differed from classical European and earlier African slavery in that the slaves bore the mark of their inferiority permanently and "naturally" on their skins. But as Nancy Stepan remarks at the outset of her study of the idea of race in the nineteenth and twentieth centuries, the puzzle is why "just as the battle against slavery was being won by abolitionists, the war against racism in European thought was being lost" (1). The growing virulence of racism after British abolition and American emancipation implies that the concept of race played an ongoing ideological and political role that caused it to outlast its affiliation with slavery in America, in dealing with the effects of the Civil War and in relation to national expansion into the American West, and in Britain, in colonial and imperial management.

Nor did the paradigm shift in early-twentieth-century anthropology — away from accounts of savage societies that integrated them into a universal developmental history, and towards an attempt to understand instead their radical cultural difference — have much immediate effect on undermining racist theories. Although the mitochondrial DNA studies that today show that "there is more genetic variability in one tribe of East African chimpanzees than in the entire human species" (Graves 9) were the eventual outcome of the neo-Darwinian synthesis of evolutionary theory and genetics that began to take shape in the first decades of the twentieth century, the first fruits of the rediscovery of genetics included the eugenicist projects of involuntary sterilization that affected tens of thousands of the racially, mentally, and socially "unfit" in the United States and elsewhere. The Nazi holocaust was unparalleled in its ferocity and its grimly bureaucratic thoroughness, but its quasi-scientific rationalization of its project was far from an isolated phenomenon.[1]

In fact, it would be difficult to name a concept that troubles the boundaries between science and ideology more stubbornly from the mid-nineteenth century to the Second World War than race. By the same token, no discursive nexus more powerfully interweaves colonialism, scientific discourse, and science fiction than racism, for one of the best reasons to emphasize the importance of evolutionary theory and anthropology to the emergence of science fiction is that early science fiction, at its best, often explores the challenges that those scientific discourses posed to established notions of what was natural and what was human. As the reading of time-travel narratives offered in the previous chapter begins to indicate, the opposition between biological determination and cultural construction is as central to much science fiction as it is to anthropology itself. Pursuing the implications of this reading further will involve spending some time at the *locus classicus* of the problem of nature versus culture in Wells's novel, *The Island of Dr. Moreau*. But Moreau's colony, while it is one of Wells's most powerful fictional achievements, is also an unusually striking articulation of an often-repeated pattern that can be discerned, not only in *The Time Machine* and *The War of the Worlds*, but also in the fiction of Mary Shelley, J. MacMillan Brown, Olaf Stapledon, and many others. I want to argue, in what follows, that such repetition is based not just on literary imitation, but also on the anonymous, "mythic" operation of the concept of race.

Frankenstein's Monster Meets the Missing Link

The classic and most influential example of the plot of constructing an artificial human being is Mary Shelley's *Frankenstein*. Currently one of the most frequently reprinted and critically discussed novels of the early nineteenth century, *Frankenstein* enjoys a canonical status in literary studies comparable to that of Jane Austen's *Pride and Prejudice* (1813) or Sir Walter Scott's *Waverly* (1814). A great deal of the critical discussion of *Frankenstein* has concerned its treatment of gender, or what one influential essay calls Victor Frankenstein's "circumvention of the maternal" (Homans). In fact, it has become a kind of nodal point connecting biblical, classical, Miltonic, and popular versions of the story of the fabrication of human life by a male creator. Moreover, Shelley's novel both connects these widely diverse texts and marks a crucial break between the earlier and the post-Shelleyan ones, because Shelley's fable alters the relation between the natural and the paternal that is central to the most culturally authoritative earlier versions. Once the divine male fabrication of human life in *Genesis* and *Paradise Lost* becomes an all-too-human, and sexually perverse, accomplishment in the workshop of Victor Frankenstein, the boundary between nature and culture thereafter remains one of the main stakes in its interpretation. The many stage, cinematic, and literary adaptations and offshoots of Shelley's novel, for example, sometimes reassert the primacy of "natural" reproduction by turning Frankenstein's act into a self-destructive attempt to transgress fatally determined boundaries, and at other times make it increasingly difficult to untangle the "natural"-born human from the manmade one (Rieder, "Patriarchal Fantasy").

What is important for our present purpose is the considerable common ground shared by the dynamics of gender and of racial identification. Both gender and racial identity turn on the crucial pivot that articulates biological determination and cultural construction. Both involve the expression of identity in anatomy, on the one hand, and the performance of identity according to culturally and historically variable scripts, on the other. Race, like gender, poses the dual questions of the boundary that separates nature from artifice and of the limits of human control over one's place and destiny in the world. Particularly in the milieu of the late nineteenth century, when, as has been mentioned earlier, *Frankenstein* was released from restrictive copyright and sold many times more copies than it had in the rest of the century till then, the novel's difficult articulation of biological determination and cultural construction may well have invoked ideas of race in a way that might have surprised Shelley.

Frankenstein has a certain amount of explicit colonial content—Robert Walton's exploratory voyage in quest of the North pole, in the context of which Frankenstein's creature is first recognized as "a savage inhabitant of some undiscovered island" (24)[2]; the ambitions of Victor Frankenstein's friend Henry Clerval, who wants to become an Orientalist and make his career in the colonies; the entire incident of the Turkish girl Safie's engagement to Felix DeLacey; and, not least of all, the inclusion of Volney's *The Ruins of Empire* (1791) in the eclectic reading list that provides Frankenstein's creature his education in human affairs. But Shelley poses the problem of nature versus culture most directly in the autobiographical narrative of Frankenstein's creature that occupies the center of the novel. The creature begins as an uncorrupted, benevolently inclined natural man, who only turns murderous when he is rejected and attacked by every human who sees him. This progression serves the polemical function of arguing that criminality is not inherent, but rather is produced by political injustice, along lines that derive from the rationalist philosophy of Shelley's father, William Godwin's, *Political Justice* (1793). Within this context, the "strange multiplicity of sensations" (102) that form the creature's first memories are meant to be those of a Lockean *tabula rasa*, an empty slate ready for the world to write upon it.

In the context of the romance revival of the late nineteenth century, however, the creature's early confusion and wonder at the world would look less like individual psychology than racial, anthropological difference:

Soon a gentle light stole over the heavens, and gave me a sensation of pleasure. I started up, and beheld a radiant form rise among the trees.* [Shelley's note: "The moon."] I gazed with a kind of wonder. It moved slowly, but it enlightened my path; and I again went out in search of berries. (103)

Both the spontaneous animism with which the creature identifies the "radiant form" of the moon as gentle and pleasure-giving, and his food-gathering and simple diet, mark him as a primitive, still residing in the embrace of "the great breast of Nature," as Haggard might have said (*Allan Quatermain* 421). Later, after learning about the "manners, governments, and religions of the different nations of the earth" by listening to Felix DeLacey reading Volney's *Ruins of Empire* to Safie, where he hears of "the slothful Asiatics; of the stupendous genius and mental activity of the Grecians; . . . [and] of the discovery of the American hemisphere, and [weeps] with Safie over the hapless fate of its original inhabitants," the creature wishes "that I had forever remained in my native wood" (119–20). Thus, although the dominant vocabulary of the creature's account is that of Lockean empiricism, the typological vocabulary assigned to Asiatics and Greeks introduces him to a set of distinctions that hover ambiguously between national and racial, or cultural and natural, ones. More importantly, the creature's sympathetic identification with indigenous Americans offers a way of reading the opposition between his original, innocent savagery and the civilization he tries to enter through the portal of the DeLacey cottage that would tend to make the creature's narrative resonate, not just with the sentimental atmosphere of the romance revival, but also with anthropological and evolutionary discourses about the origins and development of humankind and European civilization. This last possibility is one that, for obvious reasons, Shelley's novel can only evoke and not explore, but the influence of *Frankenstein* in the early 1890s strongly suggests that the theme of the artificially constructed human did indeed evoke such evolutionary anthropological meditations in that milieu.

Consider two novels that anticipate some aspects of *The Island of Dr. Moreau*: J. Compton Rickett's *The Quickening of Caliban: A Modern Story of Evolution* (1893) and Frank Challice Constable's *The Curse of Intellect* (1895). In both novels, the place occupied by Frankenstein's creature in the passage just cited is given to a primitive, quasi-human *specimen* from Africa. Both can help us to further understand the questions about racial identity, evolutionary theory, and the workings of culture that Wells would make central to the plot of the artificial human.

In Rickett's *The Quickening of Caliban*, the Caliban character, Forest Bokrie, plays the part of the Missing Link in a carnival show, whose agent describes him as "a brownie who was caught young and brought up by the mission fellows. . . . The doctors, who have seen him, say that he is a bit unfinished; not got comfortably through his evolution" (21). Another, bettereducated character describes Bokrie in terms typical of "scientific racism" at the time, noting his "retreating facial angle. He has a somewhat long muzzle, like a dog's jaw. His eyes are large and brown, with a big animal's unconscious stare in them" (71). The major spokesman for science in the novel's prolonged debate between religion and science, Professor Racer, thinks that Bokrie "is a sort of Marble Faun and Frankenstein rolled into one" (90). Racer's interest in Bokrie has to do with the polygenist hypothesis, a position held by many respected and authoritative evolutionary anthropologists at the time, that "the evolution of mankind was not from a single stock, [and therefore] that it is quite possible there may be still men on earth who have not yet passed through the rudimentary stage" in which humans acquired "a share in the spirit life" (66). Eventually Racer, anticipating Dr. Moreau's methods, tries to provide Bokrie with a soul through hypnosis, prompting an accusation from the Miranda character that Racer is putting himself in the place of God. Racer replies that this is exactly right, because the civilized morality encapsulated in religious teaching is no more than a kind of hypnotic machinery (219). The crux of this novel's handling of the debate between nature and culture, in fact, is Racer's claim that "we are only automata, the best of us" (40). The novel is more complex, and more intelligently critical about racism, than this snippet of description has indicated, but it involves the construction of an artificial human only in the abstract, philosophical sense in which individual identities and cultural differences are products of scientific and ideological labor. Rickett does, however, explicitly and carefully insert Forest Bokrie into a scheme that both implies how Frankenstein's creature might be read in racial and evolutionary terms and constructs a version of the invasively manipulative scientist that resembles Wells's Dr. Moreau.

Constable's *The Curse of Intellect* is both more clearly indebted to Frankenstein and a more direct precursor of *The Island of Dr. Moreau*. It concerns a man named Reuben Power who brings into London society an ape whom he has taught to dress and speak like a human being, and who, in the mode of *Frankenstein*, eventually murders his keeper. The central portion of the book, the ape's narrative, clearly is modeled upon the autobiography of Frankenstein's creature. However, Power's Beast, unlike Frankenstein's creature but like Rickett's Bokrie, is a member of a pre-civilized African community. His transformation into an artificial human coincides with being cruelly separated from his kind by Power's civilizing project. The Beast begins:

I remember vaguely, and as a former life, the time before Reuben Power found and took me away. A life in the forest, of perfect health and virgin strength, with many of my kind; a life taking no thought for the morrow, a life above thought; free from the conscious restraint of any law, the daily sufficient food gained by daily labour; a life of perfect, of pure happiness—instinctive happiness from reasonable life and the unaffected intercourse of living creatures.... Then, looking back, comes a long sad time of some horrible striving—a striving of something in me, yet foreign to my instinct, to conquer nature. In all that time there stand out clearly but two things—a man and a whip. (95–96)

Self-consciousness is a disaster for Power's Beast, just as it is for Frankenstein's creature. But in Shelley, the creature's horrified reaction to his reflection in a pool of water is a calculated reversal of Eve's narcissistic response to her reflection in *Paradise Lost*, and the creature's reading of Frankenstein's notebooks detailing the process of his creation leads him to the conclusion that he is a "filthy type" of Adam (114, 130). In contrast to Shelley's Miltonic context, the terrain where Constable places the Beast's narrative is that of Andrew Lang's and H. Rider Haggard's romance revival, the same terrain that would later become the territory of Edgar Rice Burroughs's *Tarzan of the Apes* (1917). Here the Beast's coming into self-consciousness is nonetheless a Fall from quasi-Edenic, primal harmony with his fellow apes into "horrible striving . . . to conquer nature." Any hint of the Darwinian struggle for existence has been displaced entirely into the realm of a counter-instinctual human culture whose emblem is the whip that enforces the "conscious restraint" of law itself.

The goal of Reuben Power, the man with the whip, is actually alienation of a different sort. His project is explicitly an anthropological one, an attempt to answer the question "What is man?" It is almost as if Constable were intentionally enacting the reversal of positions within the framework of the colonial gaze that I earlier proposed as a paradigm for science fiction itself, as he asks the imaginary, exotic other to look back at the civilized, technologically dominant, invasive scientist and reveal, not the Beast's own truth, but the invader's: "We want a new standpoint of criticism. Man cannot criticise himself, it is impossible. . . . I should like to know from some independent source what I really am, what my fellows really are" (15–16). Constable may be taking his inspiration from Darwin himself here, who in *The Descent of Man* (1871) argues that previous naturalists have greatly overemphasized humankind's difference from other mammals: "If man had not been his own classifier, he would never have thought of founding a separate order for his own reception" (191). But Constable portrays Power's attempt to overcome such limitations as a failure.

Indeed, the conclusion the Beast draws from his experience, and with which he concludes his autobiography, is that no "independent source" of understanding is available in the natural world:

All I have written is before me, and I see, true as is the miserable state of the human beast, I have myself written from no truly independent standpoint. I have failed to accomplish what Power wished, expected from me. I am a monkey, and my clothing of hair, though from God, determines my judgment of all existence as certainly as the robes of a duke from Stultz, the rags of a beggar from the gutter, even as surely as the liver of a philosopher, determine their views of life and their fellows. No creature of God can see, can write truth: whatever the standpoint, the outlook is distorted and falsified by the glamour and deception of social circumstance. (155–56)

In an apparent contradiction of the Beast's earlier insistence upon the chasm separating ape life from human culture, he here erases the opposition between nature and culture by equating the limitations imposed by "the glamour and deception of social circumstance" with those of the monkey's anatomy. Perhaps this collapse of the distinction between nature and culture within the realm of human or quasi-human endeavor is a corollary to understanding human culture itself, in its entirety, as a violation of nature, in which the perversion of "conscious restraint" turns out to yield a wholly illusory version of autonomy from natural determination. Unfortunately, the Beast's equation of social and anatomical "clothing" also conforms all too well with a racist understanding of cultural difference and social inequality as the inevitable expressions of biological structures. In contrast to the entirely explicit debates on racial identity in *The Quickening of Caliban*, it seems that in *The Curse of Intellect* the threads of racist ideology become entangled with the nostalgic sentimentalism of the Beast's recollection of his animal life and the determinist cynicism of his final position accidentally but also inevitably, because the construction of the quasi-human Beast takes place, not in a laboratory, but in the contact zone formed by the European scientist's invasion of the African native's community.

The Island of Dr. Moreau

Although racial ideology inevitably is broached in *The Curse of Intellect*, the dominant note of the Beast's narrative and the clearest satirical intention of the entire novel remains its deflation of Power's intellectual pride. Intellectual pride is certainly one of the dominant characteristics of that more famous man with a whip, Wells's Dr. Moreau, as well. But the relevance of his pride to colonial ideology is more direct than in *The Curse of Intellect*, for where Power performs his experiment on a single individual whom he detaches from his natural community, Moreau's experimental subjects become members of a new and bizarre community that is itself of more interest than any individual within it. The scientific colony where Moreau performs his sadistic experiments is thus comprised of two quite different settings: the "House of Pain," the compound where Moreau relentlessly pursues his project; and the village of the Beast People nearby. The Beast People's physical reconstruction in the compound only begins to suggest what the cultural assimilation enacted in their ritual chanting of the Law (where the refrain, "Are we not Men?" pointedly alludes to the motto of the British abolition movement, "Am I not a man and a brother?" [38]) drives home forcefully: a sustained and deliberate resemblance of Moreau's experimental subjects to colonial ones.[3]

One of the challenges in interpreting *The Island of Dr. Moreau* is to assess the significance of this allegorical strategy with respect to the relation of nature and culture worked out literally and explicitly in the scientific plot, where the ultimate failure of Moreau's experiments, his inability to keep the Beast People from reverting to their original animality, would seem to assert a basic, inviolable boundary. Ultimately, their bodies are their destinies, and can only be manipulated so far, and no further, by the devices of culture. The way this natural order reasserts itself is a conclusive chastisement of Moreau's intellectual pride. But when taken as an element of the novel's colonial metaphor, where the boundaries between nature and culture and between animal and human are held in tension with the boundaries between civilization and savagery or between the colonizer and the colonized, its significance becomes more complex.

Although Moreau's subjects are animals, his inquiry into the plasticity of living forms certainly implies a related inquiry into the natural and proper shape of the human. In his essay, "Human Evolution, an Artificial Process," Wells proclaims that *The Island of Dr. Moreau* is about the process of civilization—the formation of "the artificial man, the highly plastic creature of tradition, suggestion, and reasoned thought." In this context, "what we call Morality becomes the padding of suggested emotional habits necessary to keep the round Paleolithic savage in the square hole of the civilised state." Readings of *Moreau* predominantly have followed Wells's lead in interpreting the formation of the Beast People as a metaphor for the conflict between "natural man, . . . the culminating ape" and the demands of "civilisation" (*Early Writings* 217). But Wells's fable is not so abstract in its terms that it resists a more pointed historical reading. Robert Philmus, in his variorum edition of *Moreau*, comments that the early manuscript draft of the novel, because it "describes the Beast People in terms suggestive of colonized races" and "by reason of its continual emphasis on the strict hierarchical division between Moreau and company," strengthens the case that *Moreau*, like *The War of the Worlds*, is intended as a satire on the colonial enterprise (xxiii).[4] More recently, critics increasingly have emphasized the topical references in *The Island of Dr. Moreau* to contemporary racial ideology, connecting the novel to ideas about hybridity, miscegenation, and degeneration as well as to the scientific debate rehearsed in *The Quickening of Caliban* between monogenist and polygenist theories of the origins of racial difference (Brody 130–69; and Christensen).

In order to weigh the satirical and topical dimensions of the colonial metaphor in *The Island of Dr. Moreau*, we need to look carefully at the generic relation the novel creates between its colonial metaphor and its science fiction premise. What kind of an allegory or analogy has Wells invented in Moreau's project? I think Philmus is right on the mark when he says that "Wells 'darwinizes' the Yahoos and Houyhnhnms" of *Gulliver's Travels* (xxvii). Wells also darwinizes Mary Shelley's *Frankenstein*, transposing Shelley's biblical allusions to a racialized evolutionary discourse when Moreau, in the central chapter "Doctor Moreau Explains," tells Prendick that he "moulded" his first man from a gorilla, producing "a fair specimen of the negroid type," and then "rested from work for some days" (49–50). This is not just a satirical thrust at Christian theology, however. What is crucial is rather Moreau's self-recognition, his conviction of his own godlike freedom to pursue his experiment "just the way it led [him]" (48). I propose that Moreau's colony is neither a vehicle for a satirical attack on any particular colony, nor merely a parody of the biblical Eden. Instead, the features of Moreau's colony—the facts that it is presided over by a man whose whiteness Wells emphasizes at every opportunity; that this white man irresponsibly and callously tortures his subjects into a pathetic semblance of his own rational, civilized ways; that the entire process is underwritten by the obvious, physiological gap between his own humanity and their animalism; and that the mutilated subjects both rebel against their transformation and inhabit an elaborate ritual apparatus for justifying it and accepting its results—all add up to something that, like Blettsworthy's delusionary island, is both phantasmagoric and a clarification of reality at the same time.

Let me repeat, then, the thesis about *The Island of Dr. Moreau* that I proposed in the introductory chapter. It is not so much a distorted, metaphorical representation of colonialism as it is a literalization of the racist ideological fantasy that guides much colonial practice: We know very well that non-whites are human beings, but we behave under the assumption that they are grotesque parodies of humankind. Moreau's practice actually unfolds the ideological terms in reverse: He knows very well that his experimental subjects are *not* humans, but by laboriously transforming them into grotesque parodies of humankind, he arrives—without any apparent intention of doing so—at the role of colonial master. Generically, this is more like Kafka's "In the Penal Colony" than Orwell's *Animal Farm*, because it is a bizarre enactment of the logic of racism rather than an extended metaphor for any actual social or historical situation. Moreau is, as Žižek puts it, "the *mise en scene of the fantasy which is at work in the production of social reality itself*" (36, Žižek's emphasis).

The perspective of Wells's Gulliver-like narrator, Prendick, is crucial. Before we know any details of Moreau's project, Prendick's perspective already has entangled the reader in the discourse of scientific racism. Prendick's account of his first encounter with one of the Beast People associates the "misshapen man" with the animalistic traits attributed to non-whites by the theorists of race in nineteenth-century physical anthropology: "He . . . had peculiarly thick, coarse black hair. . . . The facial part projected, forming something dimly suggestive of a muzzle, and the huge half-open mouth showed as big white teeth as I had ever seen in a human mouth" (8). The retreating facial angle and prominent lower jaw were among the favorite physiological marks that racial theorists used to illustrate the proximity between apes and non-white races, as many a diagram from nineteenth-century treatises on race can attest (see for example the diagrams from Robert Knox's *The Races of Men* [1869], John Jeffries's *The Natural History of the Human Races* [1869], and Alexander Winchell's *Preadamites* [1888] reproduced in Graves, 67 and 72; and Fichman, 116). The psychometrician Francis Galton, Darwin's cousin and the inventor of the term "eugenics," found the same overlapping of animal and human traits in his studies of intelligence, claiming that the average Australian aborigine was only a little more intelligent than the very smartest kind of dog (see the comparative table from Galton's *Hereditary Genius* [1892] reproduced by Graves, 95). Thus, while the revulsion Prendick feels before "the grotesque ugliness of this black-faced creature" is a mark of its monstrosity (one could compare Prendick's reaction to that inspired by the physiognomy of Frankenstein's creature, for example, or to the instinctive repulsion all spectators feel in the presence of the bestial Mr. Hyde in Stevenson's *Dr. Jekyll and Mr. Hyde* [1886]), it is at least as important that the uncanny sense of familiarity the figure inspires by its disturbing mixture of humanity and animalism evokes the vocabulary of racism.

More telling than this initial association that Prendick establishes between the Beast People and racialized humans, however, are the reversals of understanding Prendick goes through in the course of the novel. Using a narrative strategy that he already had employed in *The Time Machine*, Wells first draws the reader into Prendick's initial interpretation of

Moreau's project—that the scientist is turning humans into animals—then overturns this theory with Moreau's explanation that he actually is trying to turn animals into humans. According to Prendick's initial suspicion, then, Moreau resembles a colonial tyrant brutalizing his subjects, while according to Moreau's explanation, he is more like a missionary, a scientific prophet of progress, selflessly pursuing the task set him by his high calling. But rather than settling the allegory into a final shape, this strategy sets up another pair of reversible perspectives. The Beast People, who initially appear as grotesquely racialized others, become, in the Swiftian device of the novel's conclusion, a way of seeing Wells's readers, the inhabitants of London. In the terms Wells uses in "Human Evolution, an Artificial Process," the monstrous artificial man of the scientific colony now stands for the round Paleolithic savage in the square hole of contemporary European civilization. At the same time, the Beast People's quasi-racial ugliness also looks more and more like a disavowed self-recognition. The racialized other becomes the estranged self.

Both of these reversals of perspective are presented by Prendick as if they are progressive revelations in which falsehood gives way to truth, but the strength of Wells's narrative does not lie in unmasking falsehood. It lies in exposing the patterns and motives of misrecognition. No doubt Wells meant for us to draw from *Moreau* the lesson that humans are really animals, as his remark about the "culminating ape" says they are, but it is more to the point that Wells grasps and exposes an ideological attitude, in the relation between Moreau and the Beast People, that makes what appears to be irresponsible cruelty from one perspective look like the pursuit of a noble enterprise from another. The mise-en-scène of racist ideology in *The Island of Dr. Moreau* has more to do with the social relationship of Moreau to the Beast People, with the understanding, or lack of it, Moreau's position allows him to have of them, than with any sort of biological truth about human beings.

Wells's remark about the round savage in the square hole of civilization, in fact, employs an opposition between civilization and savagery that his fiction exposes as something just as unstable and collapsible as the one between animals and humans. The savagery of civilized humans in the novel is obvious enough, not just in Moreau's scientific sadism or in the affinity that Moreau's assistant, Montgomery, professes for the companionship of the Beast People, but also in the drunken cruelty of the captain of the *Ipecacuanha* who maroons Prendick, or in the cannibalism sequence "In the Dingey of the *Lady Vain*" in the opening chapter. If Prendick finds himself threatened with death on several occasions by his supposedly civilized companions acting like animals, the balancing threat from the Beast People is that of finding himself unwillingly dragged into their community, a threat most forcefully dramatized in the scene where he is forced to join them in chanting their Law and its refrain. In the aftermath of Moreau's death, Prendick manages with difficulty to keep himself apart from the Beast People by inheriting Moreau's whip and perpetuating a set of quasi-religious lies about Moreau's power and immortality, but he finds himself at last equalized with them by "the imperious voices of hunger and thirst" (77). This final collapse of the hierarchical difference between civilization and savagery into the monotony of the struggle for existence is no surprise at all, but rather culminates the coherent development of a pervasive theme.

Wells himself holds onto the opposition between savagery and civilization only by reliance on what he calls the "acquired factor," the accumulated effect of tradition and education upon the members of a civilized society. In his essay on "Morals and Civilisation," published in February 1897, he writes, "If, in a night, this artificial, this impalpable mental factor of every human being in the world could be destroyed, the day thereafter would dawn, indeed, upon our cities, our railways, our mighty weapons of warfare, and on our factories and machinery, but it would dawn no more upon a civilised world" (*Early Writings* 221). The way that savagery constantly threatens to intrude itself back into civilization in *The Island of Dr. Moreau*, like the scenario of a degenerate post-human society in *The Time Machine*, expresses Wells's antipathy toward a certain Social Darwinian version of the ideology of progress. Here is how Mike Hawkins describes the logical contradiction within the ideology of progress that Wells is attacking: "moral progress and the triumph of civilisation . . . could be shown to be the work of natural laws such as the struggle for existence," but "the complete realisation of these ideals implied a future state in which the laws of nature were no longer applicable to humans" (108). But Wells is only following the lead of a powerful bunch of Social Darwinian thinkers, including Alfred Russel Wallace, Charles Darwin, and Thomas Huxley, when he holds that natural selection is indeed effectively suspended for the members of a civilized society (Wallace 20; Darwin 168; Huxley 81). Wells's emphasis invariably lies on the fragility of this achievement, and his own ideology of progress in his later writings stresses both the difficulty and the necessity of supplanting the workings of mere natural process with rational social planning.

But the crux of racist ideology is not the opposition between civilization and savagery. It is rather the way scientific racism confuses cultural and natural phenomena. As Joseph Graves demonstrates repeatedly and persuasively, the fundamental error of scientific racism is that of mistaking a relationship for a substance, a cultural construction for a biological necessity, the posture of a slave for an expression of anatomy. Thus the crux of the racist ideological fantasy worked out in Moreau's project is Moreau's identification of his pitilessness as the way of nature itself. Although Moreau himself shows no signs of guilt, this identification is essentially an apologetic strategy that absolves him from responsibility for the atrocities he has produced. This is perhaps where Moreau's project dovetails most tellingly with racial ideology. Even the monogenist Darwin sees the extermination of "savage races" as an inevitable result of natural selection at a social level: "At some future period, not very distant as measured by centuries, the civilised races will almost certainly exterminate and replace throughout the world the savage races" (Darwin 201; cf. Wallace 21, quoted in chapter five). The racial other of polygenist theory remains, as in monogenist versions of evolutionary anthropology, an anachronistic remnant of the civilized observer's past, but one rendered static, trapped in a body that determines its inferiority, not a case of arrested development but rather an evolutionary dead end. The consequent ease of disavowing responsibility for the sometimes-catastrophic consequences of contact between civilized and savage cultures is, in retrospect, one of the most alarming features of colonialism's ideologies. Wells's portrait of Moreau's arrogant, irresponsible, and messianic employment of science is not just about science. Moreau's position as a white colonial master also embodies in horrific form the logic of racial ideology.[5]

Hybrids and Cyborgs

At one point in *The Descent of Man*, Darwin demonstrates the superficiality and consequent imprecision and untrustworthiness of racial categorization by pointing out that those who practice it divide humanity into as few as two races and as many as sixty-three (226). Perhaps if racism really were about scientific explanation, rather than science often merely being one more venue for explaining away racist practices, Darwin's argument would have had a far greater impact than it did. The apologetic function of the concept of race does not depend on precise categorization, however, but simply on division itself. As long as race naturalizes the division between civilization and savagery, its essential work is done. The troublingly savage behavior of civilized nations can henceforth be written off as an expression of natural law, when it comes to enslaving and exterminating inferior races, or degeneration, when racial discourse slides over into biologically determinist ways of understanding the presence within civilized societies of imbecility, criminality, pauperism, and other ways of proving oneself unfit for the survival of the fittest.

In the science fiction motif of the artificial human, the function of division is likewise paramount. There is first of all the tightly bound pair of the scientific genius and his monstrous creation, from Victor Frankenstein and his nameless fabrication to Dr. Jekyll and Mr. Hyde, Reuben Power and his Beast, and Dr. Moreau and his Beast People. Victor Frankenstein and his creature often have been interpreted as divided expressions of a single individual, and Jekyll and Hyde are explicitly so. But for all of these couples, within the horizon of expectations prevailing in the 1880s and 1890s, the ideologically powerful opposition of civilization and savagery is a clear-cut structuring principle governing the division of the scientist's aspirations from their ironic results. A similar governing principle appears to pertain to artificial or altered human beings throughout early science fiction, who tend to diverge or be forced in two directions away from normal human anatomy—one towards animals and the other towards machines. The logic that binds together these two groups is certainly that of evolutionary progress and degeneration. If the first, animalistic group obviously resembles the racialized, degenerate, savage other of colonialist ideology, doesn't the second stand forth in contrast as the product of the "acquired factor," the civilized human insulated from the vicissitudes of natural selection? And isn't the cyborg inevitably, therefore, also a racialized figure? I propose that one of the most striking ways early science fiction handles the discourse of race is in these two repetitive, complementary figures of anatomical distortion, the hybrid and the cyborg.

A survey of the hybrid-cyborg pair has to begin with the three great early novels of H. G. Wells that already have played such an important part in this analysis of colonialism and the emergence of science fiction, *The Time Machine*, *The Island of Dr. Moreau*, and *The War of the Worlds*. Wells's Martians are the prototypical cyborgs of early science fiction. Their combination of prosthetic supplementation and organic atrophy is one of the most influential, widely imitated inventions in the field. Alongside the Martian colonizers, the colonized humans find themselves relegated to the status of animals, not just in the many analogical comparisons of the Martian invasion to humans' unthinking destruction of animal lives and habitats, but literally, in their role as livestock feeding the Martians' thirst for blood, and as domestic pets for the triumphant conquerors, in the projected future imagined by the man on Putney Hill. *The Time Ma-*

chine and *The Island of Dr. Moreau* each anticipate different aspects of the relationship of the Martian cyborgs to the animal-like humans. The Eloi serve as cattle for the machine-tending Morlocks, and the narrator's identification with the Eloi plays against his carnivorous likeness to the Morlocks with quite similar critical effect to the play of identification and revulsion inspired by the Martians in *The War of the Worlds*. In *The Island of Dr. Moreau*, Moreau's arrogance and his lack of any sense of moral responsibility for the results of his experiments anticipate the soulless calculation with which the Martians destroy human lives. Moreau is no cyborg—his only prostheses are the scalpel and the whip—but his alienation of intellect from emotion and his instrumentalization of bodies earns him a place in the cyborg's genealogy. And once again, in *The Island of Dr. Moreau*, the play of identification and revulsion around the white colonial master and his beast-like subjects lies at the crux of Wells's satire.

Repetition of the cyborg-hybrid pair in other early science fiction is so widespread and prevalent that it cannot be attributed solely to the influence of H. G. Wells. Instead, it takes on the anonymous character of a collective fantasy. I want to propose that racial ideology provides the point of departure for the pattern of repetition that constitutes the generic convention, or in other words, that the hybrid-cyborg pair is a hyperbolic extrapolation of racial division. This does not mean that cyborgs represent white people and hybrids represent non-whites, but rather that the exaggerated separation between the anatomies and the evolutionary status of the two figures plays upon the imaginary differences produced by racist ideology to buttress racist practices. One finds the pattern worked out in a revealing way, for example, and without any apparent debt to Wells, in J. MacMillan Brown's *Riallaro, The Archipelago of Exiles* and *Limanora, The Island of Progress*. There the Limanoran scientists seek to purge humans of their inherited animal ancestry, and Limanoran society carefully insulates itself from the archipelago of exiles, which is dominated by the sub-human or pre-human traits of its inhabitants, so as to leave the Limanorans free to develop a post-human anatomy in their utopian center. One might argue that Brown's explicit antiracism provides evidence against the dependence of this pattern on racist ideology. The counterargument, however, is that the Limanorans' political arrangement takes the shape it does precisely because their eugenicist project cannot be disentangled from its intimacy with the mythic "solution" of racial division. Brown's example thus also serves as a reminder of the way that racist ideology overlaps with, borrows from, and in turn contaminates Social Darwinian ideas about class and criminality.

The hybrid-cyborg pair appears in monumental form in the careers of two of the greatest writers of science fiction in the 1920s and 1930s, Olaf Stapledon and the Czech Karel Čapek, who is certainly worth mentioning here because of his contribution, despite his not having written in English, of the word "robot" to the language. The hybrid counterparts to the cyborg robots of Čapek's *R.U.R.* (1921) are the salamander-like creatures who take over the world in his devastating satire on colonialism and racism, *War with the Newts* (1937).[6] Stapledon's great hybrid is the humanly intelligent dog who is the title character of *Sirius: A Fantasy of Love and Discord* (1944), where Stapledon explores, among other things, the ways that human anatomy has dictated and limited our cultural and philosophical assumptions. Stapledon's cyborg demands to be given more space here, however, because it is such a good example of the way the cerebral hypertrophy, organic atrophy, and prosthetic supplementation Wells invented in *The War of the Worlds* was elaborated upon in the interwar period.

In Book XI of *Last and First Men*, titled "Man Remakes Himself," Stapledon describes the making of the first of the "great brains":

> A human ovum had been carefully selected, fertilized in the laboratory, and largely reorganized by artificial means. By inhibiting the growth of the embryo's body, and the lower organs of the brain itself, and at the same time greatly stimulating the growth of the cerebral hemispheres, the dauntless experimenters succeeded at last in creating an organism which consisted of a brain twelve feet across, and a body most of which was reduced to a mere vestige upon the under-surface of the brain. (157)

The brain has to be supplied with an artificial circulatory and digestive apparatus in order to keep it alive, and its sensory equipment blends the natural and the artificial, so that, for instance, "the retina could be applied to any of a great diversity of optical instruments" (158). Eventually the scientists succeed in making a master brain that is apparently immortal, its artificial cranium grown to "a roomy turret of ferro-concrete some forty feet in diameter." It can no longer be called an organism but rather has become a "strange half-natural, half-artificial system, . . . [a] preposterous factory of mind" (159).

The anatomy of Stapledon's great brain partakes of a pattern that is repeated many times in American pulp science fiction. Anyone who does even casual reading in this milieu certainly will run across example after example. In G. Peyton Wertenbaker's "The Coming of the Ice," the first original story to appear in *Amazing* (June 1926), the time-traveling narrator describes the men he encounters in the future: "Strange men, these creatures of the hundredth century, men with huge brains and tiny shriveled bodies, atrophied limbs, and slow ponderous movements on their little conveyances" (Ashley 1:63). Francis Flagg's "The Machine Man of Ardathia," first published in *Amazing Stories* in November 1927, is a visitor from thirty thousand years in the future, putting him as far from the present as the present is from the early neolithic. He appears to the narrator encased in a cylinder, and "seemed to be a caricature of a man—or a child. . . . The head was very large and hairless; it had bulging brows, and no ears. . . . Its legs hung down, skinny, flabby; and the arms were more like short tentacles" (Ashley 1:70). Edmond Hamilton's "The Man Who Evolved," from *Wonder Stories* of April 1931, is a scientist who speeds up the process of evolution artificially, and becomes "a huge hairless head fully a yard in diameter, supported on tiny legs, the arms having dwindled to mere hands that projected just below the head" (Hamilton 28–29). Travelers into the far future in Clifford Simak's "The World of the Red Sun" in the December 1931 *Wonder Stories*, find it ruled over by a dictator named Golan-Kirt, who, "Hanging in the air, suspended without visible means of support, was a gigantic brain, approximately two feet in diameter. . . [with] two tiny, pig-like, lidless, close-set eyes and a curving beak which hung directly below the frontal portion of the brain, resting in what was apparently an atrophied face" (Asimov 214). And so on.

Not only do all of these imaginary beings share a similar anatomy, they also all seem to be acting out something like the same script. Stapledon's great brains, for whom "instinctive tenderness and instinctive group-feeling were not possible" because they are "without the bowels of mercy," eventually demand the extermination of all "useless animals," create a race of human slaves whom they control telepathically, and engage in genocidal warfare with the rest of humankind (160–66). Wertenbaker's future beings "put to death all the perverts, the criminals, and the insane, ridding the world of the scum for which they had no more need. . . . I was kept on exhibition as an archaic survival" (Ashley 1:63). Hamilton's evolved man announces his intention to "master without a struggle this man-swarming planet," and when the narrator objects, adds, "You think it terrible that I should rule your race! I will not rule them, I will *own* them and this planet as you might own a farm and animals" (30, Hamilton's emphasis). Golan-Kirt, a scientist who has attained near immortality by altering his anatomy, has enslaved mankind with his hypnotic powers and convinced them he "came out of the Cosmos to rule over the world" (Asimov 208). In Laurence Manning's "Master of the Brain," from *Wonder Stories*,

April 1933, the narrator wonders when the mechanical brain that controls all of society will realize that "the Brain did not really *need* human beings at all! . . . When it had evolved sufficient automatic devices to care for its own needs, would it destroy these servants of flesh and blood and live its own cold metallic life in solitary grandeur upon a lifeless world?" (Manning 56, Manning's emphasis)

What connects this anatomy and script with one another? Clearly, these figures embody ideas about progress, technology, and evolution, but above all they embody the ambivalence and contradictions that cluster around those ideas. The cyborgs stand for the dominant half of a number of hierarchical binary oppositions: the future as against the past, the mind as against the body, civilization as against savagery, the human as against the animal, the master as against the slave. But they also destabilize these hierarchies, because the anatomical enhancement of their brains and prosthetic supplementation of their senses that gives them their power is simultaneously a mutilation of their bodies. Thus another, less straightforwardly hierarchical opposition, the one between nature and culture, is at work undermining the quasi-natural determinism that connects their anatomies and their scripts by instead implying that they—and perhaps the entire set of hierarchical oppositions they seem to embody—represent a horrific divorce of culture from nature.

The way that the nature-culture opposition suspends the figure of the cyborg amidst the ideological contradictions and ambivalence surrounding notions of progress gets worked out in exemplary fashion in Hamilton's "The Man Who Evolved." The relationship between the ambition of the scientist Pollard and the effects of his cosmic-ray machine is tellingly ambiguous. As Pollard explains it to the two observers of his experiment, the machine speeds up the process of evolution, so that he steps into it a man of the present and emerges as a man of the future. On his second emergence from the machine, hairless and with an immense head and brain, he tells the two onlookers: "You see a man a hundred million years ahead of you in development. And I must confess that you appear to me as two brutish, hairy cave-men would appear to you" (27). When the observers plead with him to stop the experiment because of what seem to them its alarming effects, he answers their appeal to friendship with a threat to kill them: "I am millions of years past such irrational emotions as friendship. The only emotion you awake in me is contempt for your crudity. Turn on the rays!" (28) A reader might well ask whether the machine is really speeding up an inevitable natural process, or instead reproducing a logic that is Pollard's, or that of Pollard's theories, and not nature's at all.

The machine's effects thus can be taken either as a kind of time travel or as the embodiment, not just of Pollard's ambition, but of an ideology of the progress of civilization that imagines that the dominance of the technologically advanced cyborg over the animal-like humans of the present must inevitably take the "natural" form of chattel slavery: "I will not rule them, I will *own* them and this planet as you might own a farm and animals."

The merging of organism and machine in the figure of the cyborg thus resonates both with a Social Darwinian interpretation of industrial capitalism and with a Marxist critique of it. Andrew Carnegie, in an essay titled "Wealth" (1889), carries out a typical Social Darwinian conflation of the dynamics of competition in the capitalist market with inexorable natural processes:

We assemble thousands of operatives in the factory, in the mine . . . to whom the employer is little better than a myth. All intercourse between them is at an end. . . . Under the law of competition, the employer of thousands is forced into the strictest economies, among which the rates paid to labor figure prominently, and often there is friction between the employer and the employed, between capital and labor, between rich and poor. . . . But, whether the law [of competition] be benign or not, we must say of it, as we say of the change in the conditions of men to which we have referred: It is here; we cannot evade it; no substitutes for it have been found; and while the law may sometimes be hard for the individual, it is best for the race, because it insures the survival of the fittest in every department. (98)

If Carnegie apologizes for the strict economies of a dominant social class here, he also would seem to anticipate an imaginary set of practices in the way his arrangement of alienated factory workers, distant and impersonal employers, rational economic calculation, and the law of natural selection resembles the science fiction figure of the emotionless brain, ruling over its atavistic organic servants, enacting the natural and inevitable result of evolutionary "progress." But the stunting of emotional affect in the figure of the cyborg might be connected just as plausibly to the phenomenon Marx calls the fetishism of commodities, the tendency for a capitalist economy's elaborate social division of labor and far-flung web of commodity exchange to make relationships between people take on the fantastic form of relationships between things (163–65). Georg Lukács called the resulting appearance—that socially constructed arrangements were natural, inevitable ones—"reification," and considered it an endemic feature of bourgeois ideology (*History and Class Consciousness* 83–110).

The separation between the brains and their subjects is never simply that of class position, however. Science fiction stories about these hypercerebral future beings never lack the anachronism of their immediate interaction with some more or less contemporary version of homo sapiens, so that the brains' subjects are not merely the past but *their own* past. Thus, the figure inevitably refers to colonial situations, racial ideology, and the discourse of racial division. What marks the great brains as racialized figures? It is not merely the domination they exercise over their human subjects or the appeal to a hierarchical and progressive version of evolution they invariably use to justify it. The entanglement of the fictional motif with the discourse of racism comes into focus when we describe the contradictions attendant upon the combination of their anatomies with a social script. That script first identifies, or confuses, the cyborgs' anatomical distortion with the technological achievements of an advanced industrial society, but then, when putting this "acquired factor" into action to enslave a supposedly barbarian, anatomically inferior "race," explains the same set of differences as the very work of nature. What especially enters this contradiction into the register of the myth of race is the rendering of the brains' mercilessness as the actual bodily absence of "the bowels of mercy." That they cannot feel their own mutilation as anything except another sign of their superiority dramatizes the way the deterministic discourse of race serves as a kind of self-justifying, anesthetizing hallucination. But at the same time, their physically determined inability to feel mercy—a spectacular display of anatomy as destiny—seems to exonerate them from moral responsibility for participating in that rationalization of cruelty, enslavement, eugenic purification, and even genocide. In a peculiar reversal, racism itself becomes an expression of anatomy.

The Onlookers

The anonymous, mythic quality of the figure of the hypertrophied brain is finally most evident, perhaps, in the way the contradiction between its critical and spectacular effects adheres to manifestations of racial ideology throughout early science fiction. For, although the figure of the cyborg is undoubtedly an estrangement of the imaginary, ideological superiority of white, imperial masters over non-whites, its critical, decentering potential in relation to the construction of race nonetheless cohabits, time and again, with explicitly brutalizing, crudely stereotypical depictions of non-white characters. The intimacy shared in early science fiction by critical metaphor and uncritical spectacle may well reflect a dichotomy that is endemic to modern mass culture in general, as Fredric Jameson argues in "Reification and Utopia in Mass Culture," or it may register the unevenness of science fiction's production and reception across a social field characterized at one pole by the interests of commercial profit and at the other by those of cultural prestige, as Pierre Bourdieu's analyses of cultural production would suggest. If this book has been at all accurate in its analysis, such a pattern also has to do with the ambivalence of colonial ideology insinuating itself into the fabric of science fiction's fascination with the new and the strange. Let me conclude this discussion of the motif of the artificial human by looking at an aspect of it that self-reflexively portrays this ambivalence.

The coming to life of artificial beings or the catastrophic transformation of familiar beings into new hybrid or cyborg forms often takes place in a laboratory equipped not only with scientific apparatus but also with one or more spectators. Sometimes a dialogue between the scientist and the spectators articulates opposite reactions to the experiment, as in *The Island of Dr. Moreau* or "The Man Who Evolved." Sometimes the reactions of the spectators display an array of perspectives. One of the best examples of this strategy is the well-known, often imitated, and often parodied creation sequence in the Universal Studios *Frankenstein* of 1931 that ends with Henry Von Frankenstein gibbering, "It's alive! Alive!" What easily can be forgotten about Colin Clive's scenery-chewing performance as Dr. Frankenstein is that he puts the whole show on for three spectators interior to the drama—his fiancée Elizabeth, his friend Victor Clerval, and his ex-colleague Dr. Waldmann, each of whom definitely has a very different take on the events; respectively, concerned sympathy, jealous mistrust, and scientific curiosity. Frankenstein's scientific success at bringing an artificial human to life is framed immediately not only by his own hysterical identification with it but also by Waldmann's diametrically opposed critical detachment, and the sexual dynamics of his achievement likewise are framed by the opposing viewpoints of his lover and his rival. Thus the unnamed monster comes into the world in a setting that almost schematically maps out the intellectual and emotional compass points of ambivalence, and the portrayal of racial ideology that emerges so explicitly in the film's conclusion, when the monster ends up being burned to death by a mob gathered around an enormous burning cross, has been prepared for and even subjected to a kind of critical dissection in the creation scene's display of attitudes toward Frankenstein's project.

The lab scene is also one of a rather small group of subjects that dominates Gernsback-era cover art (e.g., spaceships, future urban landscapes, extraterrestiral landscapes and beings, humanoid machines, etc.). Some of these lab scenes make the onlookers' ambivalence their main subject, for instance the cover of the August 1926 issue of *Amazing*, where the detached, corpse-like head's glassy gaze is met, on the one hand, by the sinister calculation of the onlooker whose color matches that of the cyborg, and, on the other, is blocked defensively by the upflung hand of the one who retains his fleshly hue (fig. 4). But let us finish with the charmingly odd illustration that graces the cover of *Science Wonder Stories*, October 1929 (fig. 5). This scene is dominated by a confrontation in the foreground between two helmeted figures. On the right, and clearly in charge, sits a scientist who manipulates a control board in front of him (presumably him, not her, given the figure's masterful position in this institutional context, though its gender is impossible to determine), meanwhile turning toward the other figure as though to observe the results of whatever he is trying to do. On the left sits the apparent subject of the experiment, one capable only of display, not of gazing back at the experimenter. The dinosaur that appears on the screen of this figure's helmet no doubt resides deep in the subject's psyche, since the story being illustrated is "Into the Subconscious" by Ray Avery Meyer.[7] Altogether the two figures display a fairly muted but unmistakable cyborg-hybrid relationship, the experimenter tending towards identification with the machinery in which they are enveloped, the subject marked as part animal in a particularly striking display of evolutionary regression. Not surprisingly, then, the two figures are racialized as well, one wearing a white suit beneath the brass helmet and displaying white hands on the control panel, the other rather underdressed and looking a bit greenish. But who do we find in the background, witnessing from a distance this bizarre acting out of the colonial gaze? On the right, looking knowingly on, seems to be Sigmund Freud, or at least a close relative of his. On the left, looking quite startled, is his naïve counterpart, who apparently did not at all expect an extinct predator to be lurking inside the subject's head. Thus the onlookers grasp the exotic human being put on display in the foreground according to the ambivalent alternatives dictated by colonial ideology, as scientific data and as sensational anachronism.

The entire illustration is too whimsical and funny for it to sustain any belaboring of the colonial history and racial ideology that nonetheless loom through it, but it is precisely that whimsical containment of its thematic potential that we might take as its emblematic value for the genre of science fiction. One cannot really read the genre well by identifying exclusively with the knowing, serious gaze of the Freud figure any more

FIGURE 4. Frank R. Paul, front cover illustration, *Amazing Stories*, August 1926. Courtesy of Cushing Memorial Library and Archives, Texas A&M University. Used with permission of The Frank R. Paul Estate.

FIGURE 5. Frank R. Paul, front cover illustration, *Science Wonder Stories*, October 1929. *Courtesy of Cushing Memorial Library and Archives, Texas A&M University. Used with permission of The Frank R. Paul Estate.*

than with the wide-eyed wonder of his counterpart, nor can the genre be limited to the conventions of interpretation being used by one or the other. Instead, one needs to attempt to understand the social architecture that dictates the various positions distributed across this imaginary laboratory. If the foreground articulates a scientific but systematically uneven production and distribution of knowledge and power, while the background articulates an ideologically polarized reception of those products, yet the difference between the two perspectives pictured in the background does not reproduce the power differential enacted in the foreground, for the spectators both resemble the gazing scientist rather than the exotic. In fact, the two spectators look like colleagues, so that the lesson the one seems to be absorbing remains potentially available to the other as well. Their reactions are perhaps not so much contradictory as sequential. For if all of this maps out the reception of colonial and imperial practices by the homeland audience—not as deliberate allegory, but in the ideological and epistemological framework the artist brings to visibility—it nonetheless remains a scene of spectacular pleasures, without which its critical potential would remain forever mute.

chapter five

Visions of Catastrophe

Representations of disaster establish themselves early on as one of science fiction's most recurrent features. One can derive the collective, anonymous repetitiousness of early science fiction's vocabulary of disaster from its deep roots in the Christian apocalyptic tradition, and the persistence of last-man fantasies, fantasies of inundation, and the like also suggests a need for psychoanalytic interpretation.[1] While such explanations respond well to the recurrence and repetitiousness of stories of disaster, however, they also can tend to cast the fiction's specific allusions to the political and economic realities of the day as merely the passing occasions for such repetition. But these allusions are not merely superficial trappings attached to an archetypal theme. For, although science fiction disasters are often about the end of the world, whether it be the coming of a disaster that recalls the fire and brimstone visitations of the wrath of Jehovah, or the dawning of Armageddon, a war to the death of a race or a civilization, what is most persistently at stake in them is not the world's end but its transformation by modernity.

Science fiction sometimes is seen as a genre that embraces modernity wholeheartedly, but its visions of catastrophe display a more divided and complex set of attitudes. This is especially true when the fiction deals with the anxieties that colonial and imperial projects generated in the homelands. Here one finds, in fact, that visions of catastrophe appear in large part to be the symmetrical opposites of colonial ideology's fantasies of appropriation, so much so that the lexicon of science-fictional catastrophes might be considered profitably as the obverse of the celebratory narratives of exploration and discovery, the progress of civilization, the advance of science, and the unfolding of racial destiny that formed the Official Story of colonialism. Moreover, such logical or emotional inversion of the fantasies of appropriation is not just an imaginary effect. Environmental devastation, species extinction, enslavement, plague, and genocide following in the wake of invasion by an alien civilization with vastly superior technology—all of these are not merely nightmares morbidly fixed upon by science fiction writers and readers, but are rather the bare historical record of what happened to non-European people and lands after being "discovered" by Europeans and integrated into Europe's economic and political arrangements from the fifteenth century to the present. The way that history haunts science fiction's visions of catastrophe is the point of departure for this book's final chapter.

The antithetical relation of colonial or imperial triumphalism to science-fictional catastrophes is in some instances a straightforward matter of the fiction's reversing the positions of colonizer and colonized, master and slave, core and periphery. This relatively simple procedure yields complex results in the three influential and momentous texts with which we will begin: George Chesney's *The Battle of Dorking* (1871), Richard Jefferies's *After London; or, Wild England* (1885), and H. G. Wells's *The War of the Worlds* (1898). Written against the backdrop provided by the climax of Britain's imperial expansion, each of these bases its main fictional strategy, the exhibition of the mighty humbled, on the premise of England's imperial supremacy and its centrality to the world economy. Next, in a wider and more diverse group of texts written from the 1890s to the 1930s, we observe the way that fantasies of appropriation and conquest sometimes project a set of internal contradictions onto an exterior where they, or their surrogates, can be violently eliminated. The association of such exiling or violent purgation of internal contradictions with the consolidation of a utopian enclave—as in J. M. Brown's *Riallaro* and *Limanora*, for example—is a well-known structural feature of many utopian fictions. In the texts considered here, however, the emphasis lies more heavily on defensive reactions to an outside threat than on social planning, suggesting, I will argue, that the pattern of purification and violence alludes to the mounting imperial competition of the pre–World War I and interwar decades. Finally, I will ask how tales of invasion can help us speak to the transition from colonial to postcolonial visions of modernity and its attendant catastrophes. Here we will concentrate on a nonmilitary form of invasion—contagion—a certain form of which achieves striking, symptomatic popularity in post–World War II American science fiction.

The Mighty Humbled, 1871–1898

England's ascendancy as an imperial power was never greater than in the three decades that ended the nineteenth century, although imperial competition was also steadily becoming stronger and more diverse. The same three decades also show a steadily increasing publication of work that retrospectively can be identified as science fiction, a trend in which there is perhaps no episode more significant than the phenomenal impact of George Chesney's *The Battle of Dorking*. After its initial publication in *Blackwood's* in 1871, Chesney's vision of England's ineffectual response to a surprise German invasion sparked an extensive public debate over England's military preparedness that even drew the prime minister onto the defensive, and subsequently the story became the model for an entire subgenre, the future war narrative.[2]

The Battle of Dorking's initial shock value for its English readers depended upon an illusion of England's invincibility that was Chesney's main polemical target. The closing scenario, which finds German soldiers occupying a South England parlor—putting their boots on the furniture, smoking cigars, drinking brandy—no doubt recalls the Germans' occupation of Paris a year before, but also is a significant instance of that reversal of the strategies of the historical novel that Fredric Jameson describes as "transforming our own present into the determinate past of something yet to come" ("Progress versus Utopia" 152). If England's present military posture is the determinate past of this scene of humiliation, the horrific near future imagined in the closing scenario is itself the determinate past of Chesney's opening: "You ask me to tell you, my grandchildren, something about my own share in the great events that happened fifty years ago." Thus Chesney's narrative opens with an almost explicit inversion of the temporal scheme of Walter Scott's *Waverley, or 'Tis Sixty years Since* (1814). It is not an ideology of progress that joins Chesney's fifty years hence to the British present, however, as it would be in that similarly phenomenal publication of the following decade, Edward Bellamy's *Looking Backward* (1888). What changes in Chesney's vision of the English future is England's place in the global economy.

Listen to how Chesney's narrator laments British short-sightedness from a perspective situated two generations in the future after England's ignominious defeat by German invaders:

Fools that we were! We thought that all this wealth and prosperity were sent us by Providence, and could not stop coming. In our blindness we could not see that we were merely a big workshop, making up the things which came from all parts of the world; and that if other nations stopped sending us raw goods to work up, we could not produce them ourselves. . . . We were so rich simply because other nations from all parts of the world were in the habit of sending their goods to us to be sold or manufactured; and we thought that this would last for ever. And so, perhaps, it might have lasted, if we had only taken proper means to keep it; but, in our folly, we were too careless even to insure our prosperity, and after the course of trade was turned away it would not come back again. (8)

Chesney, who had just returned to England from a successful administrative career in India in order to become the organizer and first president of the Royal Indian Engineering College, is mainly concerned with reminding his readers that the rest of the world's "habit" of supplying England with the raw materials that enable it to be the workshop of the world actually depends on the military coercion that keeps things in that propitious course: "we [that is, we English] ought to insure against the loss of our artificial position as the great centre of trade, by making ourselves secure and strong and respected" (39). The power of the word "artificial" in this sentence depends, of course, on the ease with which England's imperial position seemed "natural" to Chesney's contemporaries. Chesney's fantasy of England being invaded successfully by an imperial competitor is thus a calculated reversal and unmasking of the kind of fantasy of appropriation that erases violence and agency from the reality of colonial expropriation. His version of that expropriation remains mystified by his representing it as dependence, but he does at the same time expose its contingency, that is, its reliance on military force. His explicit polemical intentions are remarkably clear and effective, then. Perhaps of more lasting importance, however, are the emotional and ideological values he calls upon, which are the same strongly ambivalent ones that would characterize the host of invasion fantasies that followed in *The Battle of Dorking*'s wake: complacency versus panic, repletion versus deprivation, and the sense of providentially granted security versus a contingent, threatened, "artificial position."

Chesney's basic strategy, the reversal of the homeland's position as imperial center, conqueror, and colonizer into an imaginary one that is on the margin, conquered, or colonized, is one that characterizes not only many other invasion fantasies but a wide variety of science fiction visions of personal, national, and global catastrophe. An important and influential example is Richard Jefferies's 1885 *After London; or, Wild England*, which stands at the head of another subgenre of stories in which the imperial homeland finds itself fallen into ruins or reduced to savagery. Where Chesney plays with England's position in economic geography, Jefferies transforms the physical geography of England itself, turning mighty London into a half-submerged swamp on the edge of an inland sea that covers much of southern England. This sea then becomes the quasi-Mediterranean site of the hero's circumnavigation of Jefferies's future wild England. *After London* did not inspire the immediate onslaught of imitations that *The Battle of Dorking* or *King Solomon's Mines* did, but the lasting influence of its post-apocalyptic scenario can be traced in works as diverse as Hudson's *A Crystal Age* and John Collier's *Tom's A-Cold* (1933). More importantly, Jefferies's fictional canvas is broader and more complex than Chesney's, and no fictional work before Jefferies creates a future society and landscape with the same detailed realism. Yet, like *The Battle of Dorking*, *After London* is based firmly on the premise of England's contemporary world supremacy. Although Jefferies is far more critical of that premise than is Chesney, his fiction is nonetheless just as much involved in the ambivalent and contradictory values of colonial ideology.

After London is a crucial instance of the way that the confluence of realism, the romance revival, and scientific discourse in the 1880s opened up a generic possibility that would develop into science fiction. The novel is at once exceptional, typical, and symptomatic. Its exceptional quality can be gauged by the opinion of informed contemporaries. The Darwinian scholar Grant Allen's review of *After London* praised Jefferies for his acute use of evolutionary and ecological science in constructing his future setting. William Morris, too, was a great admirer of *After London* because it "put into definite shape, with a mingling of elusive romance and minute detail that was entirely after his heart, much that he had half imagined" (Miller and Matthews 441, quoting J. R. Ebbatson). In a summary of the work in an 1884 letter to C. J. Longman, Jefferies himself stressed its conventional realism: "All these matters are purposely dealt with in minute detail so that they may appear actual realities, and the incidents stand out as if they had just happened." In the same letter, Jefferies describes the book as a three-volume piece, but when Cassell and Co. published it the following year it appeared in a single volume, the same format in which Cassell published romances by Stevenson, Haggard, and Julian Hawthorne. This typical publishing format is also symptomatic. If we are to judge by comparing the description of *After London* in the Longman letter with the volume as it actually appeared, we can guess that a substantial fictional ethnography concerning "the manner of life, the hunting journeys through the forests, the feasts and festivals, and, in short, the entire life of the time" has been cut under the pressure of the publishing milieu, and the novel's puzzlingly abrupt ending may be a result of the same curtailing of Jefferies's intentions (Miller and Matthews 434–41; the letter to Longman is quoted at length on 434–35).

After London is a landmark in the emergence of science fiction primarily because of its construction of an imaginary future with a meticulously realist texture. Jefferies gives setting priority over character throughout the novel, as he says in the letter to Longman: "First, you see, I have to picture the condition of the country 'After London', and then to set my heroes to work, and fight, and travel in it" (435). Jefferies's acclaimed skills as a naturalist are everywhere evident in the novel, and its most exciting sequence, the protagonist's journey into the poisonous ruins of London, consists almost entirely of carefully rendered descriptions of the hellish landscape. Nonetheless, when Grant Allen praises Jefferies's handling of evolutionary and ecological discourse he is referring primarily to Part One, "The Relapse into Barbarism," which delivers us a fifth of the way through the novel without our having met any of the characters.

Standing quite independent of the narrative section that follows it, "The Relapse into Barbarism" describes the flora, fauna, and social order of a post-catastrophic England in which the former Thames valley has become a great inland lake. Its narrator attempts to retrace the processes by which the great forest reclaimed the former meadows, the running streams of the cultivated landscape grew errant and boggy, and domestic cats, dogs, and cows turned wild and split into new species. Although the narrator bewails the loss of the ancients' secrets, his own procedures are distinctly scientific. He relies on first-hand observation for his description of the present, and empirical testimony for his reconstruction of the past: "The old men say their fathers told them that soon after the fields were left to themselves a change began to be visible" (1). He disclaims any ability to explain the catastrophe that caused the great landscape changes and the depopulation of England. Instead, he retains his scepticism in the face of his rivals' fancies:

> It has, too, been said that the earth, from some attractive power exercised by the passage of an enormous dark body through space, became tilted or inclined to its orbit more than before, and that this, while it lasted, altered the flow of the magnetic currents, which, in an imperceptible manner, influence the minds of men. Hitherto the stream of human life had directed itself to the westward, but when this reversal of magnetism occurred, a general desire arose to return to the east. And those whose business is theology have pointed out that the wickedness of those times surpassed understanding, and

that a change and sweeping away of the human evil that had accumulated was necessary, and was effected by supernatural means. The relation of this must be left to them, since it is not the province of the philosopher to meddle with such matters. (20–21)

Parodying and reducing to absurdity the imperialist ideology of the westward progress of civilization, and outright rejecting any hint of supernatural agency, Jefferies's narrator thus sets up his turn to a description of the present social order in the deterministic context of ecological transformation and evolutionary change.

In a development that is pointedly parallel to the speciation of the domestic animals, human communities in England "after London" have split into three distinct kinds: primitive "Bushmen," who live in small kinship groups in the forests and rely on day-to-day hunting and gathering; gipsies, who have retained their nomadic and patriarchal ways; and the brutal, quasi-feudal, slave-owning society of the narrator himself. The moment that most clearly links *After London* to *The Battle of Dorking* before it and *The War of the Worlds* after it comes when the narrator reveals that the scattered descendants of the English have become the prey of invaders from Wales and Ireland. The Welsh claim "that the whole island was once theirs, and is theirs still by right of inheritance" (35), and the Irish, too, "say that in conquering and despoiling my countrymen they are fulfilling a divine vengeance. . . . [for] now the hateful Saxons (for thus both they and the Welsh designate us) are broken, and delivered over to them for their spoil" (36–37). The Welsh and Irish rationalizations of their opportunism carry no more weight than the theological interpretation of the great change, but the point borne home by the permutations of predation is that the self-image of the British Empire is itself just such a self-serving construction. Yet if Jefferies's reversal of British colonial relations to Wales and Ireland links the book most tightly with Chesney and Wells, it is instead the description of London turned poisonous that best unites "The Relapse into Barbarism" with the narrative section, "Wild England." The finely wrought blending of biological and anthropological imagery on Jefferies's evolutionary canvas implies that colonialism and imperialism are more or less inevitable expressions of predatory competition, but it indicts modern urban civilization itself as an entirely untenable species—so to speak—of human community.

The two parts of the novel do not fit together entirely happily, however, and the novel's incoherence epitomizes the contradictions of colonial ideology. "Wild England" has the form of a quest romance in which the central character, Felix Aquila, sets out to circumnavigate England's central lake in an attempt to win the riches or power that will allow him to claim the hand of his lady love. It works best in conjunction with the steadfastly impersonal, deterministic perspective of the "Relapse" when it attains the same impersonality, as in the marvelous hallucinatory phantasmagoria of Aquila's journey through the ruins of London, and in the way that not only his survival but his success in coming away with a treasure in jewels depend not on heroism but on utter chance. "Wild England" also explores the cultural relativism that defines virtue in one society as ignobility in another, particularly in the portrait of the Baron Aquila, Felix's father, who is the very definition of rural virtue in the Horatian tradition that dominated English poetry and fiction in the eighteenth century—a nobleman who, disgusted by the corruption and deceit of courtly politics, retires to his farm and turns it into a land of "milk and honey" (96). But all this earns him in the postcatastrophic England of *After London* is the covetousness of his enemies and the contempt of his sons. Jefferies then extends the narrator's bitter complaints in "The Relapse" about the ruling class's greed and brutality by having Aquila thrown, briefly, into the lower class, where he experiences the rulers' injustice and witnesses their pointless atrocities firsthand.

Nonetheless, the intensely personal focus of the second part tends to undermine the detached perspective of the first part, a problem that is exacerbated by the fact that Felix Aquila is, all commentators agree, a thinly disguised portrait of Jefferies himself as a young man (Keith 119; Miller and Matthews 431; Taylor 122). Is it coincidence that, where the quest romance seems to turn decisively into gratifying daydream, naïve colonialist ideology suddenly rules the plot? An explicit colonialist motive runs throughout Aquila's journey in his desire to identify locations of strategic importance where he might build a powerful fortress: "Who held this strait would possess the key of the Lake. . . . [T]he opportunity of empire [lay] open here to any who could seize it" (180). But this realistic motive turns into an all-too-familiar fantasy in the novel's last episode, when Aquila arrives in a society of shepherds who, when they find that he has survived a trip through the ruins of London, regard him with superstitious awe. Then, when he displays his skill with the bow and arrow, they declare him their king and nearly worship him. Jefferies's sense of irony does not fail entirely here, since the skill at archery that earns Aquila his promotion to quasi-divine status among the shepherds is one that is considered unmanly and contemptible in his own society. But the young man venturing into the wilderness, seizing opportunity, succeeding on his own merits, and ruling, by virtue of an unevenly distributed technology, over the simple natives, thereby taking control of their land and government and acquiring fantastic wealth and power—all of this is as if the story of catastrophe, of imperial splendor falling into ruins and savagery, is at a stroke transformed into its celebratory counterpart, the litany of exploration, discovery, improvement, and affluence. To put it another way, the satirical power of Jefferies's vision of poisoned London co-exists in the text with an antimodernism that more closely resembles the nostalgic position of the romance revival.

Just as the neo-Mediterranean lake in *After London* shrinks the world to the size of southern England, London and its environs are clearly the center of the world in the view of Wells's Martian invaders, whose invasion of the planet is curiously circumscribed by its focus upon the great city. Wells's scenario shares a certain ethnocentrism (or paranoid narcissism) with the entire future war genre it springs from and crucially transforms. By the late 1890s, the device of portraying the imperial homeland as the victim of a surprise attack by one of its imperial competitors was already well worn.[3] The frequency with which contemporary writers imagined their countries attacking and being attacked by others in the bellicose milieu of late-nineteenth- and early-twentieth-century Anglo-American popular culture is quite impressive. According to Bleiler's subject index in *Early Years*, British writers of the period imagined their country coming to blows with Afghanistan, Andorra, Austria, Brazil, China, France, Germany, Italy, Japan, the Netherlands, Peru, Russia, Spain, Switzerland, Turkey, and the United States (884–85).[4]

I. F. Clarke's *Voices Prophesying War*, the definitive work on the future-war genre, shows how, during the period of the first great industrial arms race from 1870 to 1914, the genre's imagined strategies for the preparation and conduct of the war to come became an important means of intervention in the political discourse of England, the United States, France, and Germany. However, by the 1890s, stories of future war focused less often on public policy and more and more on extravagant military adventure, a development that could be taken to indicate that its basic strength always lay at least as much in its fantastic appeal as in its polemical vigor. Wells's accomplishment stems from his deep understanding of that fantastic appeal. First, for the myriad imperial competitors who, in the polemical logic of the future-war genre, are always doing to us what we have been or ought to be doing to them, Wells substitutes his distorted mirror-image of invasive colonialists, the Martians. Second, while retaining the genre's fundamental narcissistic paranoia in the odd concentration on southern England that he gives the Martians' campaign of planetary conquest,

Wells also explodes the genre's parochialism by expanding the terms that define empire, so that nationalist competition disappears into or beneath the grander canvas of racial migration and species survival.

This double movement of criticism and exploitation of imperialist ideology reverberates throughout *The War of the Worlds*. In the opening, for example, when Wells's narrator proposes the analogy between the Martian invasion and the genocidal colonial settlement of Tasmania, he leads up to it by suggesting a parallel comparison between the Martians' indifference about the effects of their actions on humans and humans' recklessness with regard to animals. This play between a political analogy and a biological one is something Wells had employed with great success in *The Time Machine*. However, the tendency to see colonial warfare as part of a natural, evolutionary process is also a standard feature of Social Darwinian ideology. Before Wells announces the critical, political analogy between the Martian invasion and the genocidal "war of extermination waged by European immigrants" against the Tasmanians, in the sixth paragraph of *The War of the Worlds*, he already has introduced a naturalizing, biological analogy by modeling the relationship of Mars to Earth on the imaginary relationship of Europe to the tropics. The Martians cast "envious eyes" on Earth because their own world is cold and its resources exhausted. However, the pressure of this inimical environment on Martian civilization has "brightened their intellects, enlarged their powers, and hardened their hearts." In the gaze of this ancient civilization, the younger, warmer world of Earth appears "a morning star of hope, ... green with vegetation and grey with water, with a cloudy atmosphere eloquent of fertility." Earth is "crowded with life, but crowded only with what they regard as inferior animals." All of this conforms to contemporary racist ideology's belief in the natural superiority of Europe's temperate climate over the unchallenging tropics as a spur to civilization.

According to no less an authority that Alfred Russel Wallace, in his groundbreaking 1864 lecture to the Anthropological Society of London, "The Origin of Human Races and the Antiquity of Man Deduced from the Theory of 'Natural Selection,'" under the influence of

> the harsh discipline of a sterile soil and inclement seasons . . . a hardier, a more provident, and a more social race would be developed, than in those regions where the earth produces a perennial supply of vegetable food, and where neither foresight nor ingenuity are required to prepare for the rigours of winter. And is it not the fact that in all ages, and in every quarter of the globe, the inhabitants of temperate have been superior to those of tropical climates? All the great invasions and displacements of races

have been from North to South, rather than the reverse; and we have no record of there ever having existed, any more than there exists today, a solitary instance of an indigenous inter-tropical civilization. (21)

Echoing Wallace, Wells's narrator also reiterates the position, shared by Martians and Social Darwinians, that colonial expropriation is an inevitable expression of the "incessant struggle for existence." Even Wells's move to the topic of genocide is anticipated by Wallace's lecture, in which Wallace shortly goes on to propose that "It is the same great law of *'the preservation of favoured races in the struggle for life,'* which leads to the inevitable extinction of all those low and mentally undeveloped populations with which Europeans come into contact" (21; the emphasis of the subtitle of Darwin's *The Origin of Species* in the quotation is Wallace's). Thus, Wells's Martian invasion models European colonialism within a frame of reference where Tasmanian genocide and the extinction of the dodo seem very similar—that is, where animals and aborigines seem almost equally inferior and helpless in the eyes of the European.

The dominant strain of Wells's critique of colonialist ideology in *The War of the Worlds* is indignation against colonial arrogance, an emotion rooted in the political and historical moment from which it arises, that of the climax of British world dominion. The motive of humiliating imperial pride emerges most strongly at the rhetorical climax of the novel, when the narrator, having finally escaped from the ruined house where he was trapped for fifteen days only to find himself in "the landscape, weird and lurid, of another planet," feels "a sense of dethronement, a persuasion that I was no longer a master, but an animal among the animals, under the Martian heel. With us it would be as with them, to lurk and watch, to run and hide; the fear and empire of man had passed away" (165). Here, once again, the double movement of colonial ideology in the text makes itself felt. If, on the one hand, Wells proposes an ethical critique of European colonialism (you are to see in these horrible aliens an image of your own horrible selves), on the other hand, the reduction of humankind to "an animal among the animals" simultaneously undermines ethical judgment *per se* by casting doubt on the notions of choice and self-determination that usually provide its basis. Are we to understand the Martians fleeing their desiccated planet as rational agents seizing control of their destiny, or as victims of circumstance driven to desperate measures by the pressure of climatic change? The narrator himself, especially at the moment when he emerges from his captivity, presents the same kind of dilemma in the question of his responsibility for the death of the curate, whom he has killed—

or been forced to kill—in order to keep him from giving away the narrator's hiding place to the Martians.

The connection between this ethical dilemma and Wells's critical handling of the contradictions of colonial ideology becomes clearer in the light of the Martians' status as a kind of ultimate figure of progress. For the Martians do not so much represent the result of an extraterrestrial evolutionary development as they body forth the future of mankind itself as projected more playfully by Wells in his 1893 essay "The Man of the Year Million" (later titled "Of a Book Unwritten"). The remarkable ethnographic passages describing the Martians and their machinery, their anatomy, the well-preserved specimen in the Natural History Museum, and so on, are all modeled, as Wells says in the essay, on the study of "primitive man in the works of the descriptive anthropologist" (*Certain Personal Matters* 161). But the Martians are men for whom the second nature of technology has so shaped their relationship to the world that their machines seem more alive, less "artificial," than they themselves do. Is this confusion a sign of their sophistication or of their decadence? The identity of mechanical progress and organic atrophy in the Martians' prosthetic technology suspends the opposition between nature and culture and undermines an understanding of evolution tied to ideologies of progress by engaging both evolutionary discourse and anthropology in the crux between biological determinism and cultural or technological rationality. The Martians' diet baffles the notion of progress in the same way. On the one hand an ultra-civilized technical procedure that is part and parcel of their prosthetic technology, on the other hand it clearly evokes vampirism, and, insofar as the Martians embody a possible future for humanity, it also conjures up anxieties about cannibalism. The Martians' diet therefore marks them as simultaneously the apex of technological sophistication and exemplars of the most repulsive savagery. It is as impossible to tell progress from degeneration, civilization from savagery, culture from nature, or reason from instinct as it is to draw the line between human and animal.

As long he holds these oppositions in suspension, Wells effectively subverts any self-congratulatory interpretation of the "survival of the fittest." Far from concluding that colonial nations' superior efficiency in the art of slaughter proves they are "fittest" to rule the lands and people they colonize, Wells empties this brutal superiority of any sense of privilege or deserving ("What ugly *brutes!*" is one of the initial refrains of human reaction to the Martians [65, Wells's emphasis]). Yet when Wells's displacement of colonial invasion (or imperial warfare) into inter-species struggle transforms the Martians and humanity alike into animals among animals, this very leveling of motives threatens to revalidate a naturalizing, quasi-Darwinian apology for the colonial violence the novel estranges and critiques.

The novel's conclusion very aptly reprises this pervasive double movement. The amoral, merely biological activity of the microbes that infect the Martians appropriately humbles their imperial ambitions. At the same time, it is difficult to square this amoral process with the interpretation forced upon it by the narrator, who takes it as a form of providential intervention. It seems that in seeking closure to his story the narrator momentarily gives way to the simple logic of good and evil, heroes and villains, that he warns us against in the opening and successfully suspends for most of the narrative. Of course, it is possible to separate the narrator's opinion from the author's. The narrator's thanksgiving to a provident divinity could be taken as an ironically anthropocentric, yet dramatically convincing, reversion to the comforts of colonial ideology that shows how easy it is to forget the lessons of catastrophe when the disaster recedes. But it is difficult to find any good evidence for authorial detachment from the narrator's thanksgiving. Rather, it seems that the contradictory values we already have noted in Chesney and Jefferies find their way even into this great work of early science fiction.

Purification and Hyperbolic Violence, 1893–1934

The motif of the mighty humbled always depends on the anxieties of imperial competition, as Chesney's, Jefferies's, and Wells's fables can testify. In passing from the motif of mighty London humbled, in the previous section, to the patterns of purification and hyperbolic violence explored in this one, I do not mean to present a periodization of early science fiction. For one thing, the figure of the urban center of the world brought to its knees or reduced to savagery could be traced right into the twenty-first century. Also, although the broad contours of political and economic history inevitably impress themselves on the history of cultural production, the lives and careers of individual writers can intertwine themselves with that broad background in many different and quite inconsistent ways. Nonetheless, in selecting visions of catastrophe that seem more attuned to exploiting anxieties about conflict and competition than to unsettling vain feelings of security, I do mean to emphasize developments in science fiction that responded to an escalation of imperial competition that not only threatened Britain's world supremacy, but also erupted into the most widespread and devastating military conflicts in history.

I will begin with Garrett Putnam Serviss's *Edison's Conquest of Mars*, which appeared in January 1898, hot on the heels of *The War of the Worlds*.[5] Serviss's plot demonstrates the proximity between visions of catastrophe and fantasies of appropriation, as it neatly flips Wells's nightmare of invasion over into its reverse, a fantasy of conquest where the world-threatening disaster is revisited upon the Martian enemy. It is an interestingly typical example of the reception and transformation of Wells in the American popular publishing milieu that we associate most strongly with Hugo Gernsback.[6] Serviss, like Gernsback, wraps popular science in the attractive shell of adventure romance. But what is most interesting in relation to colonialism is Serviss's nationalism, which is that of a new imperial competitor bristling with eagerness to reshape the international order of things. Serviss fantasizes that reshaping taking place in two stages: first, a purification of the mundane world by eliminating international strife; second, a visitation of hyperbolic violence upon the exterior threat that galvanized Earth's new world order.

Serviss's reversals of Wells's narrative strategies begin when Serviss turns the imperial geography of the North versus the South to a rather different purpose than Wells. Serviss echoes Wells's opening when he describes the motives behind the Martian invasion:

Mars was desperate because nature was gradually depriving it of the means of supporting life, and its teeming population was compelled to swarm like the inmates of an overcrowded hive of bees, and find new homes elsewhere. In this respect the situation on Mars, as we were all aware, resembled what had already been known upon the earth, where the older nations overflowing with population had sought new lands in which to settle, and for that purpose had driven out the native inhabitants, whenever those natives had proven unable to resist the invasion. (35)

Logically, Serviss's analogy would seem to put the Earth in the position occupied by the American Indians in relation to European settlers. But the upshot is not, as it is for Wells, to criticize colonial violence or to undercut ethnocentrism (or anthropocentrism). Instead, Serviss simply deploys this Social Darwinian logic to justify Earth's invasion of Mars: "It was the evolution of earth against the evolution of Mars" (35). For Serviss, it is a matter of the young, pseudo-Southern, American-led Earth replying in kind to an episode of "the struggle for existence." This alliance of Social Darwinism to Serviss's nationalism is the ideological point of departure for the pattern of purification in *Edison's Conquest of Mars*.

The key organizing element in the pattern is the galvanization of a new global unity. Serviss's novel opens by describing the noble response of the survivors of the devastation the Martians left behind, where "differences of race and religion were swallowed up in the universal sympathy" (4). Although despair and panic threaten as astronomers discern the signs of preparation for a second invasion from Mars, the glad news of Edison's discovery of the secret of the Martian weapons and a means of overcoming them quickly dispels the gloom. The narrator describes "the pride that stirred me at the thought that, after all, the inhabitants of the earth were a match for those terrible men from Mars, despite all the advantage which they had gained from their millions of years of prior civilization and science" (6). The second and third chapters show the world banding together, putting aside national differences, in order to form a super-fund to finance the invasion of Mars. But all of this is a thinly veiled fantasy of American global hegemony, as Washington becomes "the new focus and center of the whole world. . . . [M]y heart was stirred at this impressive exhibition of the boundless influence which my country had come to exercise over all the people of the world" (17–19). Given the sense of destiny that underwrites such sentiment, it is no exaggeration to say that Edison, as the mechanism of humankind's providential salvation from the Martian invaders, takes over where Wells's microbes left off, except that Serviss restores the national chauvinism left implicit in Wells to its pride of place.[7]

This galvanization of global unity is already a response to an outside threat, of course, so that the homogenization of a previously fragmented and disorganized interior depends all along on the project of responding to a hostile exterior. What is crucial is that this newly strengthened, American-dominated world produces not only the capacity to respond to the Martian threat but also an apparently unlimited license to violence in carrying out its project. *Edison's Conquest of Mars* ends happily when the fleet from Earth, having preempted the second Martian invasion by launching one of their own, succeeds in destroying a dam and causing a flood that wipes out, at a minimum, the entire population of Mars's largest city. The narrator's reflection on this tactic is brief:

Now that we had let the awful destroyer loose we almost shrank from the thought of the consequences which we had produced. How many millions would perish as the result of our deed we could not even guess. Many of the victims, so far as we knew, might be entirely innocent of enmity toward us, or of the evil which had been done to our native planet. But this was a case in which the good—if they existed—must suffer with the bad on account of the wicked deeds of the latter. (162–63)

Thus Serviss ends up bringing Wells's plot full circle, as the human invaders reassume their blithe complacency about the possibly genocidal consequences of their actions.

Another contemporaneous American invasion fantasy, J. H. Palmer's *The Invasion of New York; or, How Hawaii Was Annexed*, illustrates, perhaps more clearly than *Edison's Conquest of Mars*, the linkage in nationalist and imperialist ideology that makes consolidating a purified interior depend on exporting its social contradictions. Dated 4 July 1897, Palmer's book is primarily an intervention in the Congressional debate, then in progress, over the annexation of Hawai'i. Palmer backs a policy of aggressive imperial expansion, seeing possession of Hawai'i as a key element in an incipient struggle with Japan for control of the Pacific.[8] His distinction is to be among the first to identify the Japanese as a major imperial competitor (Franklin, *War Stars* 39), as his novel narrates a surprise takeover of Hawai'i by the Japanese, followed by their invasion of San Francisco. This comes hard on the heels of the novel's title invasion of New York by Spain, America's competitor for its expansionist ambitions in Puerto Rico. The two occasions finally serve as reasons for America to display its military prowess, especially in a prolonged invasion of Japan. Like *Edison's Conquest of Mars*, *The Invasion of New York* is dominated by the plot of answering foreign invasion with massive retaliation. What is of most interest for our present purposes is the internal reaction that the Japanese invasion provokes in the United States, a consolidation of national unity that overcomes economic and class differences.

In the wake of the Japanese invasion, as Palmer imagines it, America is forced to confront its economic stagnation and high unemployment:

> At last the truth was borne in upon them that no legislative measures, no arrangement of labor against its natural ally, capital, could bring an overproductive population work.
>
> Gradually it came to be seen that the natural laws that had operated in all lands in all ages were in force here; that the inevitable rule of supply and demand had reached its equipoise, and that if any change were possible it must come from the disposal abroad of the great surplus now always in excess of home consumption. (115)

Thus Palmer looks to imperialism to solve the domestic economy's crisis of overproduction, issuing in the curious result that Palmer's militaristic nationalism predicates socialism at home in the interest of American capitalism abroad. What we might call the fortress response to invasion, the push to internal cooperation in reaction to external hostility that produces the world united in *Edison's Conquest of Mars*, no doubt can be discerned in the organized aggression of any group, from a street gang to an army. But Palmer fixes upon a specific form of fortification, based on the contrast in a capitalist economy between the internal organization of the factory or corporation and the anarchic "natural" competition of the market. In this situation, as Marx observed, there is a tendency for the value of freedom to run into the ideological contradiction of being strenuously insisted upon in one area and equally resisted in another: "It is very characteristic that the enthusiastic apologists of the factory system have nothing more damning to urge against a general organization of labour in society than that it would turn the whole of society into a factory" (477). In Palmer's aggressive imperialism, the nation is to the world as a factory is to the market. The natural alliance, as Palmer calls it, of labor and capital is really an erasure of capital's expropriation of surplus value from labor, a purification of the capitalist economy that expunges the class antagonism inherent to it. But that antagonism then gets exported along with America's surplus commodities, where they presumably disturb the "equipoise" of production and consumption to the detriment of rival national economies. Imperialist military competition would seem to follow inevitably, as each nation seeks to impose its surplus production on the others. Internal purification and external violence go hand in hand.

One of the most important ramifications of the opposition between the factory and the free market is its extrapolation into the opposition between a minutely, oppressively administered interior and an anarchic exterior in dystopian fiction. In E. M. Forster's "The Machine Stops" (1909), often said to be the first example of this generic development, the ethos of administration and the technology of the factory come together in the Machine of the story's title. Forster constructs the Machine's rationalized, sterilized domain, a conscious parody of Wells's socialist utopias, as the actual interior of the planet, and places that unified, conflict-free world in opposition to the natural light and unconfined space of the forbidden exterior, the planet's surface. Yevgeny Zamyatin's *We* may owe its preeminence in many critics' estimation of early-twentieth-century dystopias to the clarity with which Zamyatin exposes the same opposition between a panoptically supervised, factory-like interior space and the wild, primitive, sexualized, exoticized exterior it posits as "nature." The impact of Fordism on Aldous Huxley's *Brave New World* is well known, and equally obvious is the crucial thematic role of the Savage as the society's exterior alternative. Finally, although the combination of the police state of George Orwell's *1984* (1949) with never-ending imperialist war, and its mobilization of xenophobia and invasion anxiety to buttress the fortress-like rigidity of its totalized administration, are modeled on the historical examples of European Fascism and Stalinist dictatorship, the resemblance of Orwell's nightmare to Palmer's program for America is anything but coincidental. All of these dystopias, in short, involve the project of domestic order and unity going disastrously awry, so that the stories all center on protagonists who struggle to escape its effects, in the case of Forster's and Zamyatin's stories by literally trying to escape the interior space that the civilizing project has constructed.

The combination of socialism at home and capitalist-imperialist expansion abroad in *The Invasion of New York* nicely recapitulates the ambiguous class position of the imperial homelands' working classes as theorized by Lenin (see above, chapter one) and as reflected, I have argued, in *The Time Machine*. The strategy of ameliorating interior class division by means of imperialist aggression escalates into outright racial warfare in another, more disturbing version of the pattern of purification. George Griffith's *The Angel of the Revolution* (1893) is a good example. Griffith's point of departure, a technological innovation—a flying machine—that promises to make a decisive military difference, firmly places the novel within the conventions of the future-war genre and its political-ideological domain, the contemporary arms race.[9] Griffith imagines the lone inventor who possesses the secret of the flying machine being recruited into a hypersecretive terrorist conspiracy. The members of the conspiracy hide their activities within the organization under the cover of normal lives, in the most extreme instances having been induced hypnotically into being entirely unaware of this double life. This hyperbolic compartmentalization speaks, on the one hand, to the numbing of moral reflection in the conduct of military affairs, as Griffith notes in describing the transformation of his protagonist into a dedicated terrorist conspirator: "The man who a year before had been an inoffensive student of mechanics and an enthusiast dreaming of an unsolved problem, spoke of the frightful destruction of life and the havoc he had caused by just pressing a button with his finger, as coolly and quietly as a veteran officer of artillery might have spoken of shelling a fort" (83–84). On the other hand, it turns out also to register a split between the national and international position of the imperial public.

This, at least, is one way to understand the fact that, although the terrorist organization masks itself in America as the labor movement, where it boasts twelve million members, and "in its cosmopolitan aspect . . . was known to the rank and file as the Red International" (270), the revolution, when it comes, does not live up to this guise of international solidarity at all. Instead the workers' conspiracy metamorphoses into a racist fantasy where

> the Federation of the English-speaking races of the world, in virtue of their bonds of kindred blood and speech and common interests[,] . . . amidst a scene of the wildest enthusiasm called upon all who owned those bonds to forget the artificial divisions that had separated them into hostile nations and communities, and to follow the leadership of the Brotherhood to the conquest of the earth. (281)

This call to the "English-speaking races" moves the Brotherhood's project beyond the national dimension, in which its enemies were the behind-the-scenes capitalists who really directed the corrupt governments of Europe and America, and onto a truly global plane, where the threat becomes an Asiatic invasion that threatens to "sweep, innumerable as the locusts, resistless as the pestilence" (146) over Europe. The head of the Terror suggests to the protagonists, "Would it not be a glorious task for you, who are the flower of this splendid race, so to unite it that it should stand as a solid barrier of invincible manhood before which this impending flood of yellow barbarism should dash itself to pieces?" (146). Thus the task of purification changes from reformed administration within—"All the affairs of government were conducted upon purely business principles, just as though the country had been a huge commercial concern, save for the fact that the chief object was efficiency and not profit-making" (287)—to genocide without: "the conquering race of earth, armed with the most terrific powers of destruction that human wit had ever devised, was rising in its wrath, millions strong, to wipe out the stain of invasion from the sacred soil of the motherhood of the Anglo-Saxon nations. . . . The Federation was waging a war, not merely of conquest and revenge, but of extermination" (322, 318).

The flood of Yellow Peril stories that follow upon this one is nothing if not consistent in its genocidal fervor. M. P. Shiel's elaborately wrought *The Yellow Danger* (1898) and Jack London's short but intensely disgusting "The Unparalleled Invasion" (1916) are excellent examples. But the application of genocidal purification was hardly limited to the yellow hordes. King Wallace solves a host of social problems in *The Next War* (1892) by killing off all of America's blacks (Bleiler, *Early Years* 785). William DeLisle Hay's *Three Hundred Years Hence* (1880) imagines a unified, harmonious world being achieved by the extermination of all non-whites, period (Bleiler, *Early Years* 356). What is most impressive, however, is the frequency with which total extermination of the enemy is enacted as a resolution of conflict in the pulp science fiction milieu of 1926 onwards. The writers published in *Amazing Stories, Weird Tales, Science Wonder Stories, Wonder Stories,* and *Astounding Stories* imagine extraterrestrial invaders who try to wipe out humanity, human colonizers of other worlds who try to eliminate resistant natives, underground civilizations who want to take over the surface and exterminate the present inhabitants in the process, feminists from the fourth dimension who want to destroy all males, genocidal race wars and class wars, and even a war to extermination between Pedestrians and Automobilists.[10] It is as if competition for resources admits no half-way solutions, and the "struggle for life" has to be enacted with absolute finality in every situation. Genocidal violence is reduced to such a reflex mechanism that, for example, John W. Campbell's "The Last Evolution" (*Amazing Stories,* August 1932; reprinted in Campbell 1–21) portrays a war between the Earth and invaders from outside the solar system, in which the invaders' methods involve wiping out all life on the planet they intend to colonize—begging one to ask what value this humanoid species places in lifeless planets, not to mention why they do not go the simpler route of simply appropriating lifeless planets in the first place, instead of taking the trouble of trying to kill all the abundant, annoying life on a planet like Earth.

Such commonplace extravagance is no doubt partly explicable as a reaction to the horrors of modern, industrialized warfare that were exposed by World War I. But the genocidal or near-genocidal consequences of colonial expansion also ought to be taken into account, particularly in America where the settlement of the West continued to play such a vivid role in the popular imagination. The impact of American settlement on the American Indians—the consolidation of a unified continental geographical entity by a violent "purification" of the territory—certainly serves as the historical reference for Edmond Hamilton's "The Conquest of Two Worlds" (*Wonder Stories,* February 1932; reprinted in Hamilton 36–69), a story about genocidal campaigns against the indigenous inhabitants of Mars and Jupiter clearly meant as an allegory of the American Indian wars. In the crude mining towns that spring up on Mars in the wake of the near-extermination of the indigenous population, for example, "There could be seen among them occasional stilt-limbed, huge-chested Martians moving about as though bewildered by the activity about them, but most of the remaining Martians were on certain oases set aside for them as reservations" (49–50). The story's hero eventually turns traitor and leads the Jovians in a doomed campaign against the human invaders, finally assisting them in what amounts to racial suicide rather than submit to the fate of the Martians. Nonetheless, this rare example, for its decade, of American bad conscience regarding the Indian wars seems as resigned to the inevitability of the Martians' and Jovians' fate as it is critical of the arrogant self-righteousness of the conquerors.

In post–World War I British science fiction, one tends to find more anxious, less epic, darker visions of catastrophe. The hyperbolic violence associated with purification often overlaps with another hyperbole, where the decline of imperial power debouches into the decline of civilization or of the human species itself. Stories of the collapse of civilization into savagery and of the contemporary imperial center into ruins definitely rose in popularity after World War I.[11] British writers employed the postapocalyptic scenario of *After London* repeatedly in this context, often giving it an emphatically more bitter resolution. Edward Shanks's *The People of the Ruins* (1920), for instance, ends with the protagonist united with his Lady Eva—but united in suicide, as the forces of barbarism overrun the ruins of London. John Collier's *Tom's A-Cold* (1933), which Brian Stableford thinks "is so obviously influenced by *After London* that it almost qualifies as a sequel to it" (Wright, *Deluge* lvi), amply and admirably fulfills the tragic expectations invoked by its title allusion to *King Lear*, treating the postapocalyptic setting as a way of stripping bare the violent realities that underlie the acquisition and exercise of political power. The postapocalyptic novel that best combines the political thematics of the British interwar years with the evolutionary perspective so crucial to both Jefferies and Wells, however, is Alun Llewellyn's *The Strange Invaders* (1934).

Llewellyn's far-future setting is a fortress town built around the ruins of a Russian factory that now serves as a religious site, where a dimly remembered Stalinism has devolved into a parody of medieval Christianity. Thus Llewellyn expands the Russian revolutionary movement's degeneration into Stalinist dogmatism into a general collapse of modernity into a "dark age" version of pre-industrial society. Llewellyn's theme is not the dystopian malfunctioning of the project of purification, but rather the ossification of a utopian project into a kind of senility. Thus the protagonist's struggles within this enclave most pointedly satirize the blind orthodoxy of the priesthood. His small world is also torn apart by sexual jealousy, class violence, and political subterfuge, all in quite the same register as *The People of the Ruins* and *Tom's A-Cold*. What sets *The Strange Invaders* apart from such similar fictions of civilization's dissolution is its global context, in which the hyperbolic violence elsewhere consistently associated with purification takes a quite original and powerful turn.

The world of *The Strange Invaders* is in the grip not just of a return to the Dark Ages but of a new Ice Age. The polar ice cap, we are told, has advanced south far enough to cover what used to be Moscow. Winters are increasingly long and bitter, and the summer's harvest is less and less adequate for surviving winter's rigors. But the real threat comes from the South. Nomadic Tartars who are fleeing *en masse* northward tell unbelievable stories of a new species of giant lizards that eat human beings. The clashes between the nomads, who seek shelter in the fortress, but are far too numerous for the town's meagre food supply, and the townspeople, who end up massacring a large number of the Tartars in their sleep, comprise several magnificent scenes in the novel. What Llewellyn manages here is a version of the deterministic geography that underlies the Martian invasion in *The War of the Worlds*, rendered on a scale and with an intensity comparable to the great scene of the evacuation of London in Wells. It is also, of course, a reversal of the Wellsian scenario, since here the tropical South is invading a freezing, starving North, and an emergent species is attacking a worn-out, ancient civilization. Thus the climatic necessities and migratory quest for resources in *The Strange Invaders* turn the older imperial geography and its apology for colonialist expropriation on its head, in what is definitely a logical extension of the fundamental scheme of transposing the positions of the imperial center and the colonized margin that underlies so many invasion plots and postapocalyptic scenarios alike.[12]

But the distance between the imperialist context of Wells's or Chesney's attacks on British complacency or pride and the sense of a world system in crisis that pervaded the inter-war period is nowhere clearer than in the double bind in which Llewellyn places his characters. Neither Llewellyn's nomads nor the townsmen have any choice but to undertake a desperate defense of an already-doomed position, for the giant lizards arrive just behind the fleeing Tartars, and the massacre of the nomads takes place in the shadow of the lizards' inexorable advance. The lizards overrun the fortress in short order, but then (not being settlers, but only predators) they retreat to the south, apparently because winter is coming on. Just as the nomads were caught between the lizards behind them and the fortress in front, the townspeople now find themselves crushed into the margin between the ice advancing from the north and the lizards' inevitable return from the south. Thus, in the novel's final moments, the stern resolve of the few survivors standing "shoulder to shoulder . . . in comradeship . . . despite their dread" is a fatalistic acceptance of their destiny, a stoic adjustment to an inescapable position rather than a determination to shape it according to their desires.

The irresistible onslaught of the lizards, no less than Wells's Martian invasion, is a vision of modernity-as-catastrophe written on the evolutionary canvas of adaptation and extinction. And, like Jefferies's poisoned London, Llewellyn's lizards attain a sublime intensity that ultimately overpowers the novel's human drama. Here, at some length, is Llewellyn's description of the strange invaders as they approach the town:

> The plain, where it came down from the river, was alive with inter-weaving movement. They played together in the sun as though its brightness made them glad, running over and under one another, swiftly and in silence, but with an almost fierce alacrity, eager and unhesitating, unceasing. The eye was not quick enough to catch the motion of their rapid, supple bodies that seemed not to move with the effort of muscles but to quiver and leap with an alert life instinct in every part of them. They were brilliant. As he looked, Karasoin saw the play of colour that ran over those great darting bodies, a changing, flashing iridescence like a jewelled mist. Their bodies were green, enamelled in scales like studs of polished jade. But as they writhed and sprang in their playing, points of bronze and gilt winked along their flanks, and their throats and bellies as they leaped showed golden and orange, splashed with scarlet. Now and then one would suddenly pause and stand as if turned to a shape of gleaming metal, and then they could see plainly its long, narrow head and slender tail and the smoothly shining body borne on crouching legs that ended in hands like a man's with long, clawed fingers; five. (134–35)

The lizards, like the Martians in their machines, hover on the uncanny border between the organic and the mechanical. Llewellyn's description plays their solidity, their metallicism, against the "fierce alacrity" that turns their motions into a "jewelled mist," giving this herd of gigantic reptiles a delicacy and brilliance more like that of a flock of hummingbirds. There is no sense of individuality in the play of their "inter-weaving movement" across the plain. They are a totality, a herd, their advance more like the flowing of the river than a human march toward a goal. Yet there is the startling human likeness of their five-fingered hands. Where the Martians' prosthetic technology subverts the oppositions that stabilize ideologies of progress and legitimate colonial expropriation, the strange invaders seem even more adamantly to resist human comprehension altogether. Their brute reality is so foreign, such a violation of prior experience, that they can be apprehended only as paradox. Thus, in the continuation of the passage, the spectator reflects that,

> They were so much apart from all experience, the day so still, their motion so swift yet silent in the distance; they were surely a dream. They were playing. They ignored everything but themselves. Suddenly their indifference, their beauty, became terrible. (135)

In the context of Llewellyn's parody of Stalinism, the echo of William Butler Yeats's "A terrible beauty is born"—the refrain of his poem about the failed Irish uprising of 1916, "Easter, 1916"—cannot be accidental. Llewelyn confronts a failed revolution's fossilized orthodoxy about its historical destiny with the face of an inexorable but utterly indifferent and absurd progress. Given the echo of Yeats, it is hard to resist the suggestion that Llewellyn is supplying an image to flesh out the portentous question with which Yeats ends "The Second Coming:" "What rough beast, its hour come round at last, slouches toward Bethlehem to be born?"

Yet what makes the lizards so terrifyingly beautiful is that, in a decade when science fiction was obsessed by wars of extermination, Llewellyn's strange invaders stand out as one of its most compelling exemplars of the totalizing, genocidal single-mindedness of the drive to purification. The novel sketches the consolidation of a new global system that Llewellyn elaborates in terms of climate change and species adaptation. The lizards embody the indifference to humanity's welfare of the natural forces ushering in the new system, where the human survivors find themselves changed not so much into a food source as into an anachronism clinging to existence on the margins of the emergent world order. The lizards thus could be read as a metaphor for modernity itself in any of its more grimly transformational aspects, and it is of course tempting to associate their ruthless efficiency with the infamous political and racial purges of the 1930s. But such an interpretation would itself be anachronistic, perhaps. Finally, the lizards' metaphorical potential seems relatively weak compared to Llewellyn's brutal literalization of Wells's rhetorical climax in *The War of the Worlds*: "the fear and empire of man had passed away" (165). Llewellyn manages, in short, one of science fiction's most terrifying and compelling realizations of the mise-en-scène of Social Darwinian ideology: the inexorable advance of the newer and better-adapted "race" and the inevitable extinction of its less-well-adapted predecessor. The nonhumanity of the triumphant party estranges and at the same time recalls the inhumanity of the racial, political, or economic arrangements that such ideology was able to naturalize or apologize for. At the same time, like any really first-rate piece of science fiction, the realistic impact of its coherently imagined world adds impressive depth and power to its allegorical suggestiveness.

Contagion, 1938–1946

Colonial geography continues to provide an imaginary framework for much science fiction throughout the twentieth century, especially in the genre of space opera, where the most common of strategies is that of treating outer space, in effect, as an infinitely extended ocean that separates exotically diverse continents, not radically different worlds. The commercial success of the ongoing installments of *Star Wars* and *Star Trek* over the last three decades of the twentieth century attests to the enduring appeal of such quasi-colonial adventure. But the persistence of colonial geography is by no means restricted to such examples. Jefferies's inversion of core and periphery also continues to structure such distinguished postapocalyptic science fiction novels as J. G. Ballard's *The Drowned World* (1962) and Kim Stanley Robinson's *The Wild Shore* (1984), and Chesney's and Wells's inversion of victors and vanquished persists in one of the great treatments of colonialism and racism in post–World War II science fiction, Philip K. Dick's *The Man in the High Castle* (1962). But the late 1930s and early 1940s also produced at least one important and influential innovation on the plots of invasion and catastrophe that points toward a postcolonial framework of imagining imperial hegemony and cultural difference.

The innovation I have in mind is the one invented on the plot of invasion by John W. Campbell in "Who Goes There?" (*Astounding Science Fiction*, August 1938; in Campbell 290–353). As in Campbell's "The Last Evolution," the extraterrestrial invader in "Who Goes There?" threatens to wipe out all preexisting life on the planet, but the invaders' purification of the territory they mean to inhabit now takes the form of assimilation rather than slaughter. These aliens, as one character puts it, want to "*rule—be—all Earth's inhabitants*" (316, Campbell's emphasis), and the equivocation between ruling and being points to their strange form of takeover that, although prevented from happening in Campbell's story, would leave the world indistinguishable from its former self externally but also entirely alienated (so to speak) internally. Campbell's invaders threaten to achieve a perfect identity with their victims that makes an absolute difference because the process annihilates the host's desire and replaces it with an alien agenda.

In the 1950s, the plot of invasion by aliens who imitate and replace humans would become a staple of science fiction, for instance in Robert A. Heinlein's *The Puppet Masters* (1951), Jack Finney's *Invasion of the Body Snatchers* (1955), and Don Siegel's great film adaptation of Finney's novel (1956).[13] The plot of conspiratorial infiltration in such stories usually is associated with Cold War tensions that pit contemporary communism's totalitarian regimes, internationalist revolutionary ambitions, and propaganda machines against America's open society, domestic security, and free speech—a set of anxieties that is made quite explicit in an example like *The Manchurian Candidate* (1962). But I would suggest that here, as in earlier invasion fantasies, a disavowed self-recognition makes its uncanny reappearance in the figure of the imaginary enemy, and that one of the major reasons for the success of this scenario in the 1950s is that, in addition to playing upon the cloying conformism of postwar America and the witch-hunting excesses of McCarthyism, it also resembles the form of global hegemony being established by the United States in the wake of World War II and the subsequent, ongoing collapse of the older colonial system.

That new, postcolonial form of hegemony involved a recession of direct governmental control in favor of more pervasive economic penetration by a more stable and enveloping world system of trade and finance, and, concomitantly, by American cultural values. Might not the sense of America's overwhelming cultural and economic ubiquity, taking the place of an older global economy's reliance on colonial expropriation and imperial control, have lent considerable power to a type of science fiction story that we find repeated during the same years, in which, instead of natives being massacred by super-weapons, a surreptitious or invisible foreign presence transforms signs and values, empties out older cultural artifacts and rituals, and refills them with fundamentally different motives and assumptions?[14] I can do no more here than suggest that this figure of invasion by assimilation speaks to and about anxieties concerning America's economic and cultural inundation of the postcolonial world, about the invisible but ever more pervasive power of new forms of multinational capitalism, or about the hybridization of the postimperial homelands.[15] However, in "Who Goes There?" there is certainly a turn away from the older military plot to imagining an invasion that disguises itself as a natural process, in which the figure of contagion plays a central part in representing the surreptitious, parasitic incursion of the invaders into the protagonists' community.

The invasion imagined in "Who Goes There?" appears to be a studied revision of *The War of the Worlds*. Campbell retains Wells's fundamental allusion to colonial history by turning humanity into the target of aliens who possess a dauntingly superior technology, and the setting of the Antarctic research station alludes to a long tradition of polar expeditions in scientific exploration stories (in acknowledgement of which, Campbell has our heroes very nearly shoot an albatross near the end of the tale). However, Campbell pushes the aliens' technological advancement to the edges of his story. The marvelous spaceship found buried in the ice at the beginning of the tale quickly (and spectacularly) disappears almost literally in a puff of smoke, and the antigravity device the humans discover the alien building at the end never gets put to use. Instead of Wells's master trope of technological unevenness—the Martians' devastating heat ray or their glittering, uncannily lifelike machines—Campbell seizes upon the logic of infection and contagion that already is present in *War of the Worlds*, as in the passage where Wells describes the Martian cylinder "sticking into the skin of our old planet Earth like a poisoned dart" from which the "fringe of inflammation" gradually spreads (75), or in the extravagant growth of the Red Weed across the Earth's landscape later in the story, or, of course, in the microbial infections that finally destroy the Martians. Like a disease, Campbell's invaders arrive by accident. The isolated setting likewise emphasizes the plot of trying to contain an epidemic. The aliens' absorption and imitation of their hosts resembles infection not only in its spreading by contact, contagiously, but also in the method that the humans adopt in trying to combat it, the blood serum tests by which they attempt to identify the inhabitants of the station who have been absorbed and are being mimicked by the aliens.

The fact that the blood serum tests prove ineffectual coheres with the way the whole story's biological premise ultimately gives way to an ideological ground. When, early in the story, Campbell rehearses the scientists' debate over whether or not it is safe to thaw out the frozen alien they have discovered outside the spaceship, the discussion is laden with foreshadowing of the quite unexpected form of infection they will release, as when the biologist urges that any risk of contamination is outweighed by the unique importance of the specimen: "*never in all time to come can there be a duplicate*" (301, Campbell's emphasis). The key moment connecting biology and ideology comes a little later, however, when the biologist argues, "You can't thaw higher forms of life and have them come to. . . . Though the individual cells revive, they die because there must be organization and cooperative effort to live" (304). He turns out to be dead wrong about the alien, of course, for the crucial fact about it, the one that eventually enables the humans to unmask the imitations among them, is that "every piece [of the alien] is self-sufficient." Even a blood sample becomes "a new individual, with all the desire to protect its own life that the original—the main mass from which it was split—has" (344–45). As a consequence, the blood samples taken from the alien-infected humans selfishly betray their donors by trying to escape the test tube when threatened by a hot wire. Thus, in sharp contrast to the quasi-totalitarian group minds of Heinlein's puppet masters or Finney's and Siegel's body snatchers, Campbell's aliens are ruled by a principle of individual self-interest so radical that it overrides the "organization and cooperative effort to live" that the humans expect from a higher form of life.

The way the aliens' individual self-interest overrides all else is of a piece with the story's relentless reduction of all conflicts and motives to the instinctual struggle for survival. The isolated setting strips away any political or economic context, as if to suggest that the camp is a kind of laboratory environment where human nature can be examined independent of such historical and cultural variables. Yet what appears in the place of nature is not just an instinctual drive to survive but a naturalized version of every-man-for-himself free-market ideology. In keeping with that naturalized imperative, the most desperate expressions of anxiety seem to focus less on the threat of death than on the aggressive surveillance everyone feels subjected to by everyone else (the scientists' argument about the meaning of the alien's baleful expression early in the story leads to repeated exclamations about the mistrust and hostility with which the humans regard one another after the outbreak of the alien infection) and finally on the absence of any way to escape such surveillance, that is, on the absence of any privacy in the station. Hence the most revealing image of alien contagion is the alien's breach of the most intimate borders of privacy, its apparently unintentional telepathic broadcasting of its thoughts—as if the Wellsian motif of microbial subversion were translated into psychological terms, as a loss of individual autonomy at the level of one's interior discourse. The anxiety Campbell's characters end up registering, then, is just as much an expression of individualist ideology as the aliens' weird cellular organization. The intimacy of the threat envisioned in Campbell's invasion story, its penetration of individual privacy and interiority, points toward that ideological ground and emphatically marks Campbell's story as a turning point away from the military fantasies of the 1930s milieu.

If all particular political or economic reference in "Who Goes There?" disappears into the ideological universality of self-interest, that erasure itself might well be taken, even in 1938, as an apt metaphor for the increasingly hegemonic power of the exportation and broadcasting of American culture in its alliance with the financial flows of capital in the world market. But the erasure of social history by the logic of the story means that the suggestion of connecting it to such an incipiently postcolonial scenario can be no more than that, a suggestion. What one can do with more confidence is put the story into its literary-historical context. Campbell transforms Wells's colonial invasion scenario into a quasi-biological story of invisible takeover by alien parasites. Whatever the social or historical reasons for its later popularity, this form of invasion fantasy proves to be powerfully resonant, not just during the red scares of the 1950s, but throughout the latter half of the twentieth century. These later stories of contagious invasion typically do not imitate the isolated, laboratory-like setting, restricted cast of characters, and consequent disappearance of political and economic context found in Campbell's tale, but rather introduce the alien into the midst of a decidedly commonplace setting among average, unremarkable characters. One such example, which precedes the red scares but follows Word War II, is Henry Kuttner and Catherine L. Moore's "Vintage Season" (*Astounding*, September 1946). As a final exhibit, then, consider the social dynamics portrayed in Kuttner and Moore's tale of disguised invasion and catastrophic contagion.

The mysterious strangers in disguise who infiltrate the unnamed city in "Vintage Season" are anything but invaders bent on conquest. They are merely tourists, spectators, who have come to enjoy the beautiful weather and the quaint local culture. By making these tourists time travelers from the future visiting the present, Kuttner and Moore seize upon a basic ideological understanding of the relationship between the "developed" economic core and the "developing" periphery and combine it with the fundamental strategy of the Wellsian invasion plot, putting the common man Oliver Wilson, his fiancée Sue, and their contemporary American city in the place of simple natives and their exotic locale. But like the pod people of *Invasion of the Body Snatchers*, the tourists of "Vintage Season" cannot entirely disguise their internal difference from the natives. Despite the fact that these tourists don the local costume and speak the local language, they carry themselves with a sense of superiority, an "assurance that the earth turning beneath their well-shod feet turned only to their whim" (233), that sets them apart. Oliver, who deals closely with them, senses "a gulf . . . so deep no human contact could bridge it" (235). That sense becomes most drastic in retrospect, when Oliver realizes that Kleph, the visitor who apparently crosses the gulf to form a sexual liaison with him, had never seen him "as a living, breathing man" (273), but only as a passing entertainment. However, unlike the invaders in the red scare fables of the 1950s, these tourists are not dehumanized subjects of a totalitarian regime. They are clearly people just like Oliver and Sue, whose internal, unapproachable distance is entirely a function of their economic and cultural privilege.

Kuttner and Moore use the figure of taste to dramatize the gap between the cultural values of the visitors and the locals, as when Oliver embarrasses his visitors by serving them fish, or when Kleph feeds Oliver candy that he finds nauseating. The stakes rise a bit later, when Kleph shows

Oliver a piece of a symphony composed by the "advanced" artist, Cenbe, which leaves Oliver "sickened to the depths of his mind." Yet "only appreciation showed upon [Kleph's] face. To her it had been magnificence, and magnificence only" (255). The development of the figure climaxes in the final conversation between Cenbe and Oliver, where Cenbe draws an invidious distinction between his own artistic interest in the past and the voyeuristic dilettantism of the other tourists, but undercuts the opposition by calling himself a "connoisseur." The structure of this clash of cultural values becomes most obvious in a confrontation between Kleph and Sue that strikingly recalls the dynamics of the colonial gaze, that is, of looking and being looked at across the social divide formed by colonial political economy. It comes about when Sue has begun to suspect something about Kleph's designs on Oliver. Sue, who has a "fashionable figure," tries to stand up to the smaller, more rounded Kleph, but

> in the silence there was an abrupt reversal of values, based on no more than the measureless quality of Kleph's confidence in herself. . . . Kleph's curious, out-of-mode curves without warning became the norm, and Sue was a queer, angular creature beside her.
> . . . Kleph was a beauty, suddenly and very convincingly, beautiful in the accepted mode, and Sue was amusingly old-fashioned, an anachronism. (251)

When not only Sue but her entire world are redefined as an "anachronism" in this remarkable moment, Kuttner and Moore capture the transforming power of colonial ideology upon the colonized. This imposition of Kleph's codes of normalcy and beauty subdues and diminishes Sue and Sue's culture in the most intimate fashion by seizing upon the mechanisms of desire itself. This cultural mechanism is what comes into the foreground of the postcolonial invasion plot, which consistently centers on the invaders' redefinition of the norm and their consequent preemption or usurpation of their victims' desire.

The effects of the tourists' economy on the local one also play into the dynamics of power and desire in "Vintage Season," affording a striking example of the inversion of a fantasy of appropriation into a vision of catastrophe. The harbinger of the tourist invasion is a sudden, inexplicable rise in the value of Oliver's house. The fact that Oliver cannot sell his house and realize the tripling of his real estate's value because Kleph's party holds him to his first, far less lucrative agreement to rent it to them renders them literally parasites, unwanted guests whom he cannot force off his property. But the real source of the disruption of real estate values, the real reason the tourists find Oliver's house so attractive a lodging, is its proximity to the story's science fiction catastrophe. Because the tourists come from the future, they know that his house affords the best and safest spot from which to view the collision of a meteor that devastates much of the city and instigates a deadly plague that soon will kill all of its inhabitants. Thus the promise of riches their visit seems to offer to Oliver is entirely illusory. What the tourists' visit really means to Oliver, Sue, and the city is that their entire way of life is about to end. The tantalizing infection of real estate values by the visitors' economy turns out only to foreshadow the deadly plague.

The meteor collision and plague give the tourists' motives a decidedly more sinister cast that Kuttner and Moore use to explore the problems of agency and destiny central to so much colonial ideology. The visitors' apparently innocent interest in sites and artifacts that hold profound historical interest for them, but are marginal to the natives, turns into a grisly voyeurism as they gather to drink their euphoria-inducing drug while they watch the city being destroyed. The distance Oliver initially senses in their attitude toward him now becomes fully exposed. In their eyes, he was always already dead. The gap between them is as immutable as nature itself. But the visible sign of this unbridgeable distance is not natural at all. The scar of inoculation each visitor carries as protection against the plague that they know the meteor collision will release is clearly the product of a medical procedure that they knowingly and deliberately are withholding from Oliver and his contemporaries. Thus the gap between the privileged visitors and the doomed natives is actually a matter of social consensus articulated by "the rules" the visitors need to agree to before embarking on their tour. The inevitability of history becomes rather difficult to tell apart from a naturalizing ideology that protects and disavows responsibility for the hierarchical difference between the tourists and the natives.

The best spokesman for "the rules" is the artist, Cenbe, who arrives just in time for the catastrophic meteor collision, but is really interested in its aftermath, the plague, which he is using as material to construct his "symphony"—a work of art actually closer to a documentary film with a symphonic soundtrack. Cenbe tells Oliver—who is already stricken with the plague, and whose face will become one of the most haunting and intimate images on Cenbe's canvas—that it would indeed be possible for the visitors from the future to intervene in the past, save the lives of Oliver and his contemporaries, and change history. But if one changes the past, it changes the future, too, necessarily. The lines of probability are switched into new patterns—but it is extremely difficult, and it has never been allowed. The physio-temporal course tends to slide back to its norm, always. . . . And our time-world is entirely to our liking. There may be a few malcontents there [in the future], but they are not allowed the privilege of temporal travel. (272)

Kuttner and Moore make it quite obvious that Cenbe's appeal to the natural laws of temporal inertia protects the status quo in his own society. It is not science but "the rules" that construct his own privilege as destiny and restrict his own agency to tragic representation of the mass suffering he must accept as constitutive of the future world order and, most emphatically, of his position within it. What the story exposes here is not merely the question of tragedy itself, then. It is also the ideological strategy that allows for the construction of a world order where the hierarchy of "developed" and "developing" areas makes its allocation of resources and distribution of agency seem the result of nature itself. The disappearance of ideological construction into natural embodiment is one of the strongest threads of continuity linking "Vintage Season" to "Who Goes There?" In sharp contrast to Campbell, however, Kuttner and Moore make that disappearance into the visible crux of their nonmilitary, postcolonial invasion story.

What connects "Vintage Season" to *The Puppet Masters* or *Invasion of the Body Snatchers* is not literary influence. Those later invasion narratives may well be more directly indebted to Campbell's "Who Goes There?" but what all of them share with "Vintage Season" is the common historical and ideological material they are working on. I suggest that this material concerns the growth of American political, economic, and cultural power in the lead-up to and, especially, the aftermath of the Second World War. Their lack of emphasis on military themes in comparison to the plots of purification and violence surveyed earlier corresponds to the transition from early-twentieth-century imperialism in crisis to an emerging postcolonial world system. Weaponry becomes less important because, in the struggles these plots unfold, the technology most at stake is not military but rather has to do with communications, and the exercise of hegemony has less to do with coercion and more to do with defining choices and co-opting desires. The anxiety this group of stories most insistently registers concerns the impact of publicity on private lives—the power of broadcasting and of organized public spectacle to penetrate and even usurp individual free will and identity. "Vintage Season" has the distinction of being more explicitly, self-consciously critical about these themes than the others. If it seems as if nature itself is the antagonist that dooms Oliver, Sue, and their city in "Vintage Season," Kuttner and Moore are careful to show us "the rules" that hold this version of nature in place. Yet some things change remarkably little in the half century that separates Wells from Kuttner and Moore. How does their time travelers' disavowal of responsibility differ from the arrogant disregard exercised by Wells's Martians or Dr. Moreau? The time tourists seem more passive, like mere spectators and not active manipulators of the situation. But in their maintenance of the separation between themselves and their hosts, in the way that separation denies their hosts full, contemporaneous humanity, there is all too little difference.

Notes

Chapter One: Introduction (pages 1–33)

1. For a general introduction to the cultural reception of evolutionary theory in Victorian England, see Fichman; on the impact of evolutionary theory on Victorian anthropology, see Stocking, 145–85; on Social Darwinism, see Hawkins.
2. See Anne McClintock's analysis in *Imperial Leather* of the relation between "panoptical time" and "anachronistic space" in imperialist science and popular culture, 36–42.
3. Mulvey constructs her analysis of the cinematic gaze in terms of gender ideology and its uneven distribution of power between the male gaze and the female object of that gaze. However, the application of Mulvey's term to representations of colonial and postcolonial subjects is not being suggested here for the first time. See E. Ann Kaplan's *Looking for the Other: Feminism, Film, and the Imperial Gaze*.
4. On Gartley's photography, see Andrews; on the use of such photography in the promotion of the tourist industry, see Bacchilega and Davis.
5. I am indebted for the ideas in these two sentences to Carl Freedman's thesis in *Critical Theory and Science Fiction*.
6. One needs to be cautious about Kincaid's formulation, however. Reducing science fiction to "whatever we are looking for when we look for science fiction" means nothing unless "we" know something about who we are and, more to the point, "we" can be identified on the basis of those who recognize a certain set of conventions. The fact that generic identity always resides in a reading audience, far from reducing the generic conventions to individual whimsy, should operate as a reminder of their historical grounding.
7. The broad and loose approach to defining science fiction taken here corresponds to the practice of Thomas Clareson in *Science Fiction in America, 1870s–1930s: An Annotated Bibliography of Primary Sources* and Everett Bleiler in *Science-Fiction: The Early Years*. The ensuing discussion will show how my position differs from Bleiler's claim that science fiction is "only a commercial term" (*Early Years* xi). The more drastic difference, however, lies between my approach and that of Darko Suvin, who painstakingly excludes material that does not conform to his strict formal definition of science fiction in the bibliographical section of *Victorian Science Fiction in the UK*.

8. Samuel R. Delany's insistence that the history of science fiction goes back no further than about 1910 is directed against professional academic constructions of science fiction that have sought to lend it the prestige of "literature," in the sense implied by Suvin's use of the term "sub-literary," by connecting science fiction to the long traditions of satire, utopia, and marvelous journeys. Delany stresses, in contrast, the importance of the science fiction subculture of writers and fans for understanding the development of science fiction in the mid-twentieth century; see *Silent Interviews*, 152–57. Justine Larbalestier's *The Battle of the Sexes in Science Fiction* is an excellent example of what can be done along the line of research that Delany advocates. On the relation of Bourdieu's sociological analyses to the problem of understanding literary canon construction in general, see John Guillory's *Cultural Capital*.

9. The "miraculous birth" of science fiction in one or the other of these two texts is an idea that Fredric Jameson throws off, apparently rather off-handedly, twice in his *Archaeologies of the Future* (1, 57).

10. The most influential identifier of Shelley's *Frankenstein* as standing at the origin of science fiction in English is Brian Aldiss, who first elaborated the claim in *Billion Year Spree* (1974; revised as *Trillion Year Spree* in 1986); see Aldiss, 25–52; other thoughtful discussions of the importance of this early text to the history of science fiction include Alkon, *Science Fiction before 1900*, the first sentence of which is, "Science fiction begins with Mary Shelley's *Frankenstein*," and Freedman, *Critical Theory and Science Fiction*, 48–50. On the publication history and critical reception of *Frankenstein* in the nineteenth century, see St. Clair.

11. The best surveys of the lost-race motif are Thomas Clareson's chapter, "Journeys to Unknown Lands," in *Some Kind of Paradise*; Clareson's "Lost Lands, Lost Races;" and Nadia Khouri's "Lost Worlds and the Revenge of Realism." Neither Clareson nor Khouri attends consistently to the difference between the adventure-fantasy and satirical-utopian strains of the motif, nor do either of them give anything close to adequate attention to the colonialist and imperialist contexts of lost-race fiction. Khouri in particular reads the material almost entirely as a naïve expression of class ideology.

12. The classic analyses of this sense of "literature" are the chapter entitled "Literature" in Williams's *Marxism and Literature* and Macherey and Balibar's "Literature as an Ideological Form."

13. An excellent overview of the long-term interdependence of capitalist expansion, industrialization, and colonialism is Eric Hobsbawm's *Industry and Empire: The Birth of the Industrial Revolution*; as are also the chapters on the establishment of the world economy in Hobsbawm's *The Age of Capital: 1848–1875* (29–68) and imperialist economy and culture in *The Age of Empire: 1875–1914* (34–83). All of my remarks in what follows about the intertwining forces of colonialism and capitalism in European social history are greatly indebted to Hobsbawm.

14. For a more detailed analysis than Jameson's of the emergence and function of future settings, see Paul Alkon's *Origins of Future Fiction*. Alkon's book establishes a long history to the device, but he does not extend his analysis past the middle of the nineteenth century.

Chapter Two: Fantasies of Appropriation (pages 34–60)

1. This reassessment of Verne has emphasized, among other things, his incorporation of colonially important scientific discourses such as cartography into his fiction and the resulting generic innovation and hybridity of his *romans scientifique*. See Arthur B. Evans, *Jules Verne Rediscovered*; Timothy Unwin, *Jules Verne: Journeys in Writing*; Edmund J. Smyth, ed., *Jules Verne: Narratives of Modernity*; and the essays by Arthur B. Evans, Timothy Unwin, Terry Harpold, and Gregory Benford in the Jules Verne Centenary special issue of *Science Fiction Studies* 32 (March 2005).

2. For critical and scholarly work on the lost-race motif, see Clareson and Khouri (chapter 1, note 11). The sole book-length treatment of the subject, Allienne R. Becker's *The Lost Worlds Romance: From Dawn Till Dusk*, is unfortunately of little value. The best critical commentary on the lost-race motif beyond the work of Clareson and Khouri is contained in the incisive, intelligent, but of course scattered summaries in Bleiler.

3. On the convention of hollow-earth journeys, see Fitting. In the 1965 Scholar's Facsimiles reprint of *Symzonia*, J. O. Bailey argues in his introduction that Adam Seaborn is a pseudonym for John Cleves Symmes, and the novel is attributed to Symmes on the title page. As Bleiler argues, however, "this attribution is not tenable, since, among other reasons, the work obviously satirizes Symmes" (*Early Years* 662). "Adam Seaborn" is clearly a pseudonymous persona in the tradition of Lemuel Gulliver, but it is the only name that can be attributed to the author of *Symzonia*.

4. One can gauge the impact of Haggard's success from the fact that Bleiler lists fourteen examples of lost-race fiction from 1870 to 1885, twenty-three from 1886 to 1889, and ninety-two from 1890 to 1899. The increase takes place on both sides of the Atlantic and involves both single-volume novels and a large number of American dime novels. The genre fades a bit for the two decades after that, but enjoys some resurgence in the 1920s. From 1910 on, the majority of lost-race pieces appear in the pulp magazines, especially *All-Story*, *Argosy*, *Weird Tales*, and the Gernsback publications. See also the very helpful summaries and discussion of the information that can be gleaned from Bleiler's and Clareson's bibliographies in James, "Science Fiction by Gaslight," 31–38.

5. I have learned from and drawn upon Nicholas Daly's discussion of the romance revival, where Daly quotes the same passage from Lang (18).

6. On "virgin land," see McClintock, chapter 1, "The Lay of the Land," 21–74.

7. For an informative account of the contours of racist representation of "natives" in British imperialist adventure fiction, see Street, esp. chapter three.

8. Haggard's anticapitalism is very much of a piece with his anticolonialism. Quatermain's disdain for the world where "Money is the moving power, and Self-interest the guiding star" (630) partakes more of nostalgia for the gentlemanly order of the rural manor than of socialist critique. This has much to do with Haggard's class position, as Anne McClintock argues in *Imperial Leather*: "Haggard was . . . representative

of a specific moment in imperial culture, in which the nearly anachronistic authority of the vanishing feudal family . . . was displaced onto the colonies and reinvented within the new order of the colonial administration" (239).

9. Wallerstein calls this kind of trade between different economic systems "an exchange of preciosities. That is, each can export to the other what is in *its* system defined as worth little in return for the import of what is defined as worth much. . . . In an exchange of preciosities, the importer is 'reaping a windfall' and not obtaining a profit" (14, Wallerstein's emphasis).

Chapter Three: Dramas of Interpretation (pages 61–96)

1. See China Miéville's explanation of the difference between traditional science fiction and fantasy in terms of the "not-yet-possible" versus the "never-possible" (44–45).

2. In addition to invoking Lacan, Bould quotes Carl Freedman's "Towards a Theory of Paranoia: The Science Fiction of Philip K. Dick": "The paranoiac is the most rigorous of metaphysicians. The typical paranoid outlook is thoroughgoing, internally logical, never trivializing, and capable of explaining the multitude of observed phenomena as aspects of a symmetrical and expressive totality" (Bould 78).

3. "The Country of the Blind" is an excellent example of the problems that beset the definition of early science fiction. Bleiler does not include it in *Early Years* because he thinks it is not science fiction, but Warrick, Waugh, and Greenberg's SFRA anthology gives it canonical status.

4. Theoretical impossibilities are always subject to change, of course; for a treatment of time travel that rigorously respects contemporary physical theory, see Gregory Benford's 1980 *Timescape*.

5. For example, Robert A. Heinlein (writing as Anson MacDonald), "By His Bootstraps" (Healy and McComas 882–932; originally in *Astounding*, October 1941); or Henry Kuttner (writing as Lewis Padgett), "Time Locker" (Healy and McComas 286–307; originally in *Astounding*, January 1943); an early move toward the problem of the time loop is Stanley Weinbaum, "The Circle of Zero" (Ashley 2: 78–94; originally in *Thrilling Wonder Stories*, August 1936).

6. Like the explorers of adventure fiction, time travelers in early science fiction are almost always male. Female time travelers do occur in Harold Steele Mackaye's *The Panchronicon* (1904), Murray Leinster's "The Runaway Skyscraper" (*Argosy*, 22 February 1919), and Ray Cummings's "The Giant World" (*Weird Tales*, January–March 1928), but they are all secondary characters accompanying male protagonists (Bleiler, *Early Years*, 175, 434, 468–69).

7. This is apparently the way Olaf Stapledon understood Beresford's invention. In Stapledon's *Odd John* (1935), Stapledon's narrator calls Stott a parallel example of the "supernormals" or "wide-awakes" of which Odd John is a member (6–7).

8. *The Definitive Time Machine* contains a good selected and annotated bibliography of critical work on *The Time Machine* up to the mid-1980s (122–27). There is an

updated, selected bibliography in the 2001 Broadview edition, but it is not annotated (284–91).

9. All quotations of *The Time Machine* are from *The Definitive Time Machine* edited by Harry Geduld.

10. On the sphinx's allusion to colonialism, see Debelius; on its blending of animal and human in the context of evolutionary theory, see Huntington, *Logic of Fantasy*, 44–45.

11. Quotations of "The Red One" are from the text in London, *The Complete Short Stories*.

12. On Balatta's significance in the resolution see López, 399–402; or for a Jungian reading, Reesman, 168–70.

13. London's use of dramatic irony and his distance from the opinions attributed to Bassett are cruxes of critical argument over "The Red One." Berkove tends to use dramatic irony to exonerate London from any taint of Bassett's racism. Petersen accuses Berkove of virtually rewriting the story and argues instead for the importance of Bassett's "dialectical oscillation between scientific truth and utopian romance" (54).

Chapter Four: Artificial Humans and the Construction of Race (pages 97–122)

1. On the eugenics movement, see Graves, 86–104; Hawkins, 216–46; and Stepan, 111–39. On its relation to Nazism and the holocaust, see Graves, 128–39; and Hawkins, 272–91.

2. The Oxford World's Classics edition of *Frankenstein* cited here is unremarkable, but in the context of Shelley's late-nineteenth-century reception it is important to use Shelley's 1831 revised version of *Frankenstein*, which is the basis of the Oxford edition as it is of the similar Penguin and Bantam editions, rather than one of the several more careful and informative editions based on the 1818 text of the novel.

3. All quotations of *The Island of Dr. Moreau* are from the variorum edition edited by Robert Philmus.

4. The early manuscript also contains deleted references to *Frankenstein* and the "state of nature" in Prendick's first encounter with Moreau (105) that suggest that Wells, like Constable, interpreted the Lockean *tabula rasa* of Shelley's creature in the context of the romance revival's opposition of civilization to "nature."

5. Pushing the logical implications of Moreau's racism to their extreme, Gomel argues for the similarity between Moreau's project and the Nazi holocaust in "From Dr. Moreau to Dr. Mengele: The Biological Sublime." For a reading of *Moreau* that argues for Wells's own allegiance to a eugenicist program of "vivisection morality," see Leon Stover's introduction to his edition of *Moreau*. Stover's scholarship is impressive, but his reading of *Moreau* is seriously weakened by its relative disregard for the novel's satirical strategies.

6. For a fuller elaboration of this reading of *War with the Newts*, see Rieder, "Science Fiction, Colonialism, and the Plot of Invasion," 383–86.

7. I have not had an opportunity to read Meyer's story, which, so far as I know, has never been reprinted.

Chapter Five: Visions of Catastrophe (pages 123–55)

1. On the religious roots of science fiction apocalypses, see the essays by David Seed, I. F. Clarke, and Edward James in the collection *Imagining Apocalypse*, edited by Seed, and Patrick Parrinder's essay in the earlier volume *Anticipations*, also edited by Seed. On last-man stories, see the excellent introductory essay to Volume 8 of Clarke's *British Future Fiction*. A psychoanalytic interpretation might well be launched from Freud's discussion of Dr. Daniel Paul Schreber's apocalyptic delusions in "Psycho-Analytic Notes on an Autobiographical Account of a Case of Paranoia" (*Dementia Paranoides*); cf. the importance given to the mechanisms of paranoia in interpreting the generic construction of science fiction by Carl Freedman, "Towards a Theory of Paranoia: The Science Fiction of Philip K. Dick" and Mark Bould, "The Dreadful Credibility of Absurd Things."

2. For a complete account, see Clarke, *Voices Prophesying War*.

3. Perhaps the best exposition of the degree to which the invasion fantasy had become a cliché is P. G. Wodehouse's hilarious 1909 parody, *The Swoop!: or, How Clarence Saved England*.

4. U.S. writers took on a similar number and range of imaginary enemies. Bleiler's list includes Argentina, Austria, Brazil, Canada, China, Colombia, France, Germany, Great Britain, India, Italy, Japan, Mexico, the Netherlands, Persia, Russia, Spain, Turkey, and Venezuela (*Early Years* 921).

5. *The War of the Worlds* first appeared in *Pearson's Magazine* from April–December 1897. Its date of publication is almost always given as 1898 because Wells made some important additions to the novel when it appeared in book form.

6. For an argument for the importance of a broad distinction between British "scientific romance" and American "science fiction," see Stableford.

7. H. Bruce Franklin, in *War Stars*, documents the United States long-lasting fascination, from Robert Fulton's submersible to Ronald Reagan's Star Wars program, with the fantasy of a super-weapon that would bring an end to all wars by putting unquestionable military superiority in the hands of the United States. The fact that possession of the super-weapon usually is understood as an expression of merit or innate genius, not of an uneven distribution of the resources on which technological development and innovation are based, acts as guarantee of the justice and wisdom of the arrangement.

8. In order to get a good sense of Palmer's place in the debate over the annexation of Hawai'i, *The Invasion of New York* should be read alongside Queen Lili'iuokalani's own attempt to influence it, *Hawaii's Story by Hawaii's Queen* (1898); and consult Fuchs and Silva.

9. One of the odd delights of this publication is that Frederick Jane's illustrations

of the flying machines equip them with the masts of yachts—without the sails, of course.

10. The war between the Pedestrians and Automobilists is in David H. Keller's "The Revolt of the Pedestrians," *Amazing Stories*, February 1928; the feminists from the fourth dimension arrive in M. F. Rupert's "Via the Hewitt Ray," *Science Wonder Quarterly*, Spring 1930; the entire sentence summarizes information that can be gleaned from the seventy entries under "Genocide, planned or accomplished" in Bleiler's subject index in *The Gernsback Years*.

11. On the popularity of disaster stories after the Great War, see Brian Stableford's introduction to Sydney Fowler Wright's *Deluge*, xxi–xxv; and Clarke, *British Future Fiction*, 8:1–2.

12. Migratory colonization under the pressure of climate change is a commonplace of 1930s American magazine science fiction, but it almost always is mapped onto the solar system rather than the globe, on the model worked out by Olaf Stapledon's *Last and First Men*—for example, in the remote future, as the sun grows colder, humanity relocates on Venus. The vision of a planetary future beset by shrunken or exhausted resources is much more rare. The best example is Laurence Manning's remarkable "The Man Who Awoke" (*Wonder Stories*, March 1933; revised version in Manning 1–36), in which a time traveler from the present finds himself reviled by the citizens of a future that designates our era the Age of Waste.

13. For a good survey of this motif in 1950s science fiction cinema, see Sobchak, 120–29.

14. Super-weapons remain prominent in 1950s science fiction, of course, but in the post-atomic-bomb era they are more often associated with apocalyptic and postapocalyptic scenarios or with the spawning of monstrous mutations than with invasion plots.

15. On the invisibility of late capitalist social power, see Fredric Jameson's conclusion regarding postmodern architecture: "This latest mutation in space—postmodern hyperspace—has finally succeeded in transcending the capacities of the individual human body to locate itself, to organize its immediate surroundings perceptually, and cognitively to map its position in a mappable external world. . . . This alarming disjunction point between the body and its built environment . . . can itself stand as the symbol and analogue of that ever sharper dilemma which is the incapacity of our minds, at least at present, to map the great global multinational and decentered communications network in which we find ourselves caught as individual subjects" ("Postmodernism" 82–83). The figure of hybridization becomes especially prominent in late-twentieth-century versions of the invasion/assimilation plot such as Octavia Butler's *Lilith's Brood* (1989) and Gwyneth Jones's Aleutian trilogy (1991–1998); see Rieder, "Science Fiction, Colonialism, and the Plot of Invasion," 386–91.

Works Cited

Abbott, Edwin A. *Flatland: A Romance of Many Dimensions.* 1884; reprint, New York: Dover, 1951.
Aldiss, Brian, with David Wingrove. *Trillion Year Spree: The History of Science Fiction.* London: Gollancz, 1986.
Alkon, Paul. *Origins of Futuristic Fiction.* Athens: University of Georgia Press, 1987.
———. *Science Fiction before 1900: Imagination Discovers Technology.* New York: Twayne, 1994; reprint, New York: Routledge, 2002.
Allen, Grant. *The British Barbarians: A Hill-Top Novel.* New York: Putnam, 1895; reprint, New York: Arno, 1975.
Andrews, Lew. "'Fine Island Views': The Photography of Alonzo Gartley." *History of Photography* 25 (2001): 219–39.
Arocena, Felipe. *William Henry Hudson: Life, Literature, and Science.* Translated by Richard Manning. Jefferson, N.C.: McFarland and Co., 2003.
Ashley, Michael, ed. *The History of the Science Fiction Magazine. Vol. 1: 1926–1935.* Chicago: Henry Regnery Co., 1974.
———. *The History of the Science Fiction Magazine. Vol. 2: 1936–1945.* Chicago: Henry Regnery Co., 1975.
Asimov, Isaac. *Before the Golden Age: A Science Fiction Anthology of the 1930s.* Garden City, N.Y.: Doubleday, 1974.
Aubrey, Frank. *The Devil-Tree of El Dorado.* New York: New Amsterdam, 1897.
———. *A Queen of Atlantis: A Romance of the Caribbean Sea.* London: Hutchinson, 1899; reprint, New York: Arno, 1974.
Bacchilega, Cristina. "Hawai'i's Storied Places: Anne Kapulani Landgraf's Re-Vision of Landscape and Illustration." *History of Photography* 25 (2001): 240–51.
Baines, Paul. "'Able Mechanick': *The Life and Adventures of Peter Wilkins* and the Eighteenth-Century Fantastic Voyage." In *Anticipations: Essays on Early Science Fiction and its Precursors,* edited by David Seed, 1–25. Syracuse, N.Y.: Syracuse University Press, 1995.
Ballard, J. G. *The Drowned World.* Harmondsworth, England: Penguin, 1962.
Barthes, Roland. "Textual Analysis of Poe's 'Valdemar.'" In *Untying the Text: A Post-Structuralist Reader,* edited and introduced by Robert Young, 133–63. Boston: Routledge and Kegan Paul, 1981.

Becker, Allienne R. *The Lost Worlds Romance: From Dawn Till Dusk*. New York: Greenwood, 1992.
Bellamy, Edward. *Looking Backward 2000–1888*. Edited by John L. Thomas. Cambridge: Belknap Press of Harvard University Press, 1967.
Benford, Gregory. *Timescape*. New York: Simon & Schuster, 1980.
———. "Verne to Varley: Hard SF Evolves." *Science Fiction Studies* 32 (2005): 163–71.
Bennet, Robert Ames. *Thyra: A Romance of the Polar Pit*. New York: Henry Holt & Co., 1901.
Beresford, John Davys. *The Hampdenshire Wonder*. London: Sidgwick & Jackson, 1911; reprint, New York: Arno, 1975.
Berkove, Lawrence I. "Jack London's 'Second Thoughts': The Short Fiction of his Late Period." In *Jack London: One Hundred Years a Writer*, edited by Sara S. Hodson and Jeanne Campbell Reesman, 60–76. San Marino, Calif.: Huntington Library, 2002.
Bleiler, Everett F., with the assistance of Richard J. Bleiler. *Science-Fiction: The Early Years*. Kent, Ohio: Kent State University Press, 1990.
———, with the assistance of Richard J. Bleiler. *Science-Fiction: The Gernsback Years*. Kent, Ohio: Kent State University Press, 1998.
Bould, Mark. "The Dreadful Credibility of Absurd Things." *Historical Materialism* 10, no. 4 (2002): 51–88.
Bourdieu, Pierre. *Distinction: A Social Critique of the Judgement of Taste*. Translated by Richard Nice. Cambridge: Harvard University Press, 1984.
———. "The Field of Cultural Production, or: The Economic World Reversed." *Poetics* 12 (1983): 311–55.
Bradshaw, William R. *The Goddess of Atvatabar. Being the History of the Discovery of the Interior World and Conquest of Atvatabar*. New York: J. F. Douthitt, 1892.
Brody, Jennifer DeVere. *Impossible Purities: Blackness, Femininity, and Victorian Culture*. Durham, N.C.: Duke University Press, 1998.
Brown, J. MacMillan. *Limanora: The Island of Progress*. Second edition. London: Oxford University Press, 1931.
———. *Riallaro: The Archipelago of Exiles*. Second edition. London: Oxford University Press, 1931.
Bulwer-Lytton, Edward. *The Coming Race*. 1871; reprint edited by David Seed. Middletown, Conn.: Wesleyan University Press, 2007.
Burroughs, Edgar Rice. *A Princess of Mars*. 1912; reprint, New York: Del Rey, 1985.
———. *At the Earth's Core*. 1914; reprinted with an introduction by Gregory Benford. Lincoln: University of Nebraska Press, 2000.
Butler, Octavia. *Lilith's Brood*. New York: Warner, 2000. First published as *The Xenogenesis Trilogy: Dawn*. New York: Warner, 1987; *Adulthood Rites*. New York: Warner, 1988; *Imago*. New York: Warner, 1989.
Butler, Samuel. *Erewhon: or, Over the Range*. 1872; reprint edited by Hans-Peter Breuer and Daniel F. Howard. Newark: University of Delaware Press, 1981.
Campbell, John W. *The Best of John W. Campbell*. Edited by Lester Del Rey. New York: Ballantine, 1976.

Čapek. Karel. *R.U.R.* 1923; reprint translated by Claudia Novack; introduction by Ivan Klíma. New York: Penguin, 2004.
———. *War with the Newts.* 1937; reprint translated by Ewald Osers. North Haven, Conn.: Catbird Press, 1985.
Carnegie, Andrew. "Wealth." In *Darwinism and the American Intellectual: An Anthology,* edited by R. Jackson Wilson, 96–104. Chicago: Dorsey, 1989. First published in *North American Review* 148 (1889): 653–64.
Chesney, George Tomkyns. *The Battle of Dorking: Reminiscences of a Volunteer.* *Blackwood's Edinburgh Magazine,* May 1871; reprinted in *British Future Fiction,* edited by I. F. Clarke, 6:7–40. London: Pickering & Chatto, 2001.
Christensen, Timothy. "The 'Bestial Mark' of Race in *The Island of Dr. Moreau.*" *Criticism* 46 (2004): 575–95.
Clareson, Thomas. "The Emergence of Science Fiction: The Beginnings through 1915." In *Anatomy of Wonder 4: A Critical Guide to Science Fiction,* edited by Neil Barron, 3–61. Providence, N.J.: R. R. Bowker, 1995.
———. "Lost Lands, Lost Races: A Pagan Princess of Their Very Own." In *Many Futures, Many Worlds: Theme and Form in Science Fiction,* edited by Thomas Clareson, 117–39. Kent, Ohio: Kent State University Press, 1977.
———. *Science Fiction in America, 1870s–1930s: An Annotated Bibliography of Primary Sources.* Westport, Conn.: Greenwood, 1984.
———. *Some Kind of Paradise: The Emergence of American Science Fiction.* Westport, Conn.: Greenwood, 1985.
Clarke, I. F., ed. *British Future Fiction.* 8 volumes. London: Pickering & Chatto, 2001.
———. "The Tales of the Last Days, 1805–3794." In *Imagining Apocalypse: Studies in Cultural Crisis,* edited by David Seed, 15–26. New York: St. Martin's Press, 2000.
———. *Voices Prophesying War: Future Wars, 1763–3749.* New York: Oxford University Press, 1992.
Collier, John. *Tom's A-Cold: A Tale.* London: Macmillan, 1933.
Conan Doyle, Arthur. *The Lost World: Being an Account of the Recent Amazing Adventures of Professor George E. Challenger, Lord John Roxton, Professor Summerlee, and Mr. E. D. Malone of the "Daily Gazette".* 1912; reprinted with an introduction by Michael Crichton. New York: Modern Library, 2003.
Conrad, Joseph. *Heart of Darkness and Other Tales.* Edited with an introduction and notes by Cedric Watts. Oxford: Oxford University Press, 2002.
[Constable, Frank Challice]. *The Curse of Intellect.* Edinburgh: Blackwood, 1895.
Csicsery-Ronay, Istvan. "Science Fiction and Empire." *Science Fiction Studies* 30 (2003): 231–45.
Cyrano de Bergerac, Savinien. *Other Worlds: The Comical History of the States and Empires of the Moon and the Sun.* 1656; reprint translated by Geoffrey Strachan. Oxford: Oxford University Press, 1965.
Daly, Nicholas. *Modernism, Romance, and the Fin de Siècle: Popular Fiction and British Culture, 1880–1914.* Cambridge: Cambridge University Press, 1999.
Darwin, Charles. *The Descent of Man, and Selection in Relation to Sex.* 1871; reprinted

with an introduction by John Bonner and Robert M. May. Princeton: Princeton University Press, 1981.

Davis, Lynn Ann. "Photographically Illustrated Books about Hawai'i, 1845–1945." *History of Photography* 25 (2001): 288–305.

Debelius, Margaret. "H. G. Wells and the Riddle of the Sphinx." *Journal of the Eighteen Nineties Society* 26 (1999): 3–11.

Defoe, Daniel. *The Life and Strange Surprizing Adventures of Robinson Crusoe of York, Mariner.* 1719; reprint edited with an introduction by J. Donald Crowley. New York: Oxford University Press, 1972.

Delany, Samuel R. "About 5,750 Words." In *The Jewel-Hinged Jaw: Notes on the Language of Science Fiction*, 21–37. New York: Berkley, 1978.

———. *Silent Interviews: On Language, Race, Sex, Science Fiction, and Some Comics.* Hanover, N.H.: Wesleyan University Press, 1994.

———. *Trouble on Triton: An Ambiguous Heterotopia.* With a new foreword by Kathy Acker. Hanover, N.H.: Wesleyan University Press, 1996.

De Mille, James. *A Strange Manuscript Found in a Copper Cylinder.* New York: Harper, 1888.

DePaolo, Charles. "*The Time Machine* and the Descent of Man." *Foundation* 85 (Summer 2002): 66–79.

Derrida, Jacques. *Writing and Difference.* Translated, with an introduction and additional notes, by Alan Bass. Chicago: University of Chicago Press, 1978.

Dick, Philip K. *Confessions of a Crap Artist.* New York: Entwhistle Books, 1975.

———. *The Man in the High Castle.* New York: Putnam, 1962.

Evans, Arthur B. *Jules Verne Rediscovered: Didacticism and the Scientific Novel.* New York: Greenwood, 1988.

———. "Jules Verne's English Translations." *Science Fiction Studies* 32 (2005): 80–104.

Fabian, Johannes. *Time and the Other: How Anthropology Makes Its Object.* New York: Columbia University Press, 1983.

Fichman, Martin. *Evolutionary Theory and Victorian Culture.* New York: Humanity Books, 2002.

Finney, Jack. *The Invasion of the Body Snatchers.* New York: Dell, 1955.

Fitting, Peter. *Subterranean Worlds: A Critical Anthology.* Middletown, Conn.: Wesleyan University Press, 2004.

Fletcher, Angus. *Allegory: The Theory of a Symbolic Mode.* Ithaca: Cornell University Press, 1964.

Forster, E. M. "The Machine Stops." In *Science Fiction: The Science Fiction Research Anthology*, edited by Patricia S. Warrick, Charles S. Waugh, and Martin Greenberg, 41–63. New York: Harper & Row, 1988. First published in *Oxford and Cambridge Review*, Michaelmas Term, 1909.

Frankenstein. Directed by James Whale. Universal Studios, 1931.

Franklin, H. Bruce, ed. *Future Perfect: American Science Fiction of the Nineteenth Century.* Revised and expanded edition. New Brunswick, N.J.: Rutgers University Press, 1995.

———. *War Stars: The Superweapon and the American Imagination*. New York: Oxford University Press, 1988.
Freedman, Carl. *Critical Theory and Science Fiction*. Middletown, Conn.: Wesleyan University Press, 2000.
———. "Towards a Theory of Paranoia: The Science Fiction of Philip K. Dick." *Science-Fiction Studies* 11 (1984): 15–24.
Freud, Sigmund. "Psycho-Analytic Notes on an Autobiographical Account of a Case of Paranoia (*Dementia Paranoides*)." In *The Standard Edition of the Complete Psychological Works of Sigmund Freud*, 24 volumes, translated from the German under the general editorship of James Strachey, in collaboration with Anna Freud, assisted by Alix Strachey and Alan Tyson, 12:1–82. London: Hogarth Press, 1958.
———. "Totem and Taboo: Some Points of Agreement between the Mental Lives of Savages and Neurotics." In *The Standard Edition of the Complete Psychological Works of Sigmund Freud*, 24 volumes, translated from the German under the general editorship of James Strachey, in collaboration with Anna Freud, assisted by Alix Strachey and Alan Tyson, 13:1–162. London: Hogarth Press, 1955.
Fuchs, Miriam. *The Text Is Myself: Women's Life Writing and Catastrophe*. Madison: University of Wisconsin Press, 2004.
Gernsback, Hugo. "A New Kind of Magazine." *Amazing Stories* 1, No. 1 (April 1926): 3.
Gillmore, Inez Haynes. *Angel Island*. New York: Henry Holt, 1914.
Gilman, Charlotte Perkins. *Herland*. New York: Pantheon, 1979. First published in *The Forerunner*, January–December 1915.
Gomel, Elana. "From Dr. Moreau to Dr. Mengele: The Biological Sublime." *Poetics Today* 21 (2000): 393–421.
Graves, Joseph L., Jr. *The Emperor's New Clothes: Biological Theories of Race at the Millennium*. New Brunswick, N.J.: Rutgers University Press, 2001.
Green, Martin. *Dreams of Adventure, Deeds of Empire*. New York: Basic Books, 1979.
Griffith, George. *The Angel of the Revolution: A Tale of the Coming Terror*. With illustrations by Fred T. Jane. London: Tower Publishing, 1893.
Guillory, John. *Cultural Capital: The Problem of Literary Canon Formation*. Chicago: University of Chicago Press, 1993.
Haggard, H. Rider. *The Annotated She*. 1887; reprinted with an introduction and notes by Norman Etherington. Bloomington: Indiana University Press, 1991.
———. *She, King Solomon's Mines, Allan Quatermain*. 1885–1887; reprint, New York: Dover, 1951.
Hamilton, Edmond. *The Best of Edmond Hamilton*. Edited by Leigh Brackett. New York: Ballantine, 1977.
Harpold, Terry. "Verne's Cartographies." *Science Fiction Studies* 32 (2005): 18–42.
Hawkins, Mike. *Social Darwinism in European and American Thought, 1860–1945: Nature as Model and Nature as Threat*. Cambridge: Cambridge University Press, 1997.
Headrick, Daniel R. *The Tools of Empire: Technology and European Imperialism in the Nineteenth Century*. New York: Oxford University Press, 1981.

Healy, Raymond J., and J. Francis McComas. *Adventures in Time and Space: An Anthology of Science Fiction Stories*. New York: Random House, 1946; reprint, New York: Ballantine, 1975.

Heinlein, Robert A. *The Puppet Masters*. Garden City, N.Y.: Doubleday, 1951.

Hobsbawm, Eric. *The Age of Capital: 1848–1875*. New York: Scribner, 1975; reprint, New York: Vintage, 1996.

———. *The Age of Empire: 1875–1914*. New York: Pantheon, 1987; reprint, New York: Vintage, 1989.

———. *Industry and Empire: The Birth of the Industrial Revolution*. Second edition. New York: Penguin, 1999.

Holberg, Ludwig. *A Journey to the World Underground*. Reprint of *Journey to the World Under-Ground*, by Nicholas Klimius, London: T. Astley, 1742. New York: Garland, 1974.

Homans, Margaret. "Bearing Demons: Frankenstein's Circumvention of the Maternal." In *Bearing the Word: Language and Female Experience in Nineteenth-Century Women's Writing*, 100–19. Chicago: Chicago University Press, 1986.

Horkheimer, Max, and Theodor W. Adorno. *Dialectic of Enlightenment*. Translated by John Cummings. New York: Seabury, 1972.

Hudson, W[illiam] H[enry]. *A Crystal Age*. 1887; reprint, London: Duckworth, 1919.

Huntington, John. *The Logic of Fantasy: H. G. Wells and Science Fiction*. New York: Columbia University Press, 1982.

———. "*The Time Machine* and Wells's Social Trajectory." *Foundation* 65 (Fall 1995): 6–15.

Huxley, Aldous. *Brave New World*. London: Chatto & Windus, 1932.

Huxley, Thomas H. *Evolution and Ethics and Other Essays*. 1896; reprint, New York: AMS, 1970.

Invasion of the Body Snatchers. Directed by Don Siegel. Allied Artists, 1956.

Irving, Washington. "The Men in the Moon." In *Future Perfect: American Science Fiction of the Nineteenth Century*, edited by H. Bruce Franklin, revised and expanded edition, 250–54. New Brunswick, N.J.: Rutgers University Press, 1995. First published in *A History of New York by Diedrich Knickerbocker*. New York, 1809.

James, Edward. "Rewriting the Christian Apocalypse as a Science-Fictional Event." In *Imagining Apocalypse: Studies in Cultural Crisis*, edited by David Seed, 45–61. New York: St. Martin's Press, 2000.

———. "Science Fiction by Gaslight: An Introduction to English-Language Science Fiction in the Nineteenth Century." In *Anticipations: Essays on Early Science Fiction and its Precursors*, edited by David Seed, 26–45. Syracuse, N.Y.: Syracuse University Press, 1995.

Jameson, Fredric. *Archaeologies of the Future: The Desire Called Utopia and Other Science Fictions*. London: Verso, 2005.

———. *The Political Unconscious: Narrative as a Socially Symbolic Act*. Ithaca: Cornell University Press, 1981.

———. "Postmodernism, or The Cultural Logic of Late Capitalism." *New Left Review* 146 (1984): 52–92.

———. "Progress versus Utopia; or, Can We Imagine the Future?" *Science-Fiction Studies* 9 (1982): 147–58.
———. "Reification and Utopia in Mass Culture." *Social Text* 1 (1979): 130–48.
Janvier, Thomas A. *The Aztec Treasure-House: A Romance of Contemporaneous Antiquity.* New York: Harper, 1890.
Jauss, Hans-Robert. *Toward an Aesthetic of Reception.* Translated by Timothy Bahti. Minneapolis: University of Minnesota Press, 1982.
Jefferies, Richard. *After London; or, Wild England.* 1885; reprint, London: Duckworth, 1911.
Jones, Gwyneth. *North Wind.* New York: Tor, 1994.
———. *Phoenix Café.* New York: Tor, 1998.
———. *White Queen.* New York: Tor, 1991.
Kaplan, E. Ann. *Looking for the Other: Feminism, Film, and the Imperial Gaze.* New York: Routledge, 1999.
Katz, Wendy R. *Rider Haggard and the Fiction of Empire : A Critical Study of British Imperial Fiction.* Cambridge: Cambridge University Press, 1987.
Keith, W. J. *Richard Jefferies: A Critical Study.* Toronto: University of Toronto Press, 1965.
Khouri, Nadia. "Lost Worlds and the Revenge of Realism." *Science-Fiction Studies* 10 (1983): 170–90.
Kincaid, Paul. "On the Origins of Genre." *Extrapolation* 44 (2003): 409–19.
King Kong. Directed by Merian C. Cooper and Ernest B. Schoedsack. RKO, 1933.
Kuttner, Henry, and Catherine L. Moore. "Vintage Season." In *The Science Fiction Hall of Fame, Volume Two A,* edited by Ben Bova, 233–74. Garden City, N.Y.: Doubleday, 1973. First published in *Astounding,* September 1946.
Lach-Szyrma, W[ladislaw] S[omerville]. *Aleriel: or, A Voyage to Other Worlds.* London: Wyman & Sons, 1883.
Lang, Andrew. "Realism and Romance." *The Contemporary Review* 52 (1887): 683–93.
Larbalestier, Justine. *The Battle of the Sexes in Science Fiction.* Middletown, Conn.: Wesleyan University Press, 2002.
Lenin, Vladimir Ilyich. *Imperialism: The Highest Stage of Capitalism.* 1916; reprint, New York: International, 1939.
Lévi-Strauss, Claude. *Structural Anthropology.* Translated from the French by Claire Jacobson and Brooke Grundfest Schoepf. Garden City, N.Y.: Anchor Books, 1967.
Liliuokalani. *Hawaii's story by Hawaii's Queen.* Boston: Lee and Shepard, 1898; reprint, Honolulu: Mutual, 1990.
Llewellyn, Alun. *The Strange Invaders.* London: G. Bell and Sons, 1934.
London, Jack. *The Complete Short Stories of Jack London.* Edited by Earle Labor, Robert C. Leitz, III, and I. Milo Shepard. 3 volumes. Stanford: Stanford University Press, 1993.
———. *The Iron Heel.* New York: Macmillan, 1907.
López, Debbie L. "'Invisible Anthropophagi' and Asymmetrical Conclusions in London's Naturalist's Tale: 'The Red One.'" *Excavatio: Nouvelle Revue Emile Zola et le Naturalisme International* 17 (2002): 394–402.

Lukács, Georg. *The Historical Novel*. Translated by Hannah Mitchell and Stanley Mitchell. Boston: Beacon, 1963.

——. *History and Class Consciousness: Studies in Marxist Dialectics*. Translated by Rodney Livingstone. Cambridge: MIT Press, 1971.

MacColl, Hugh. *Mr. Stranger's Sealed Packet*. Second Edition. London: Chatto & Windus, 1889.

MacDonald, Robert H. *The Language of Empire: Myths and Metaphors of Popular Imperialism, 1880–1918*. Manchester: Manchester University Press, 1994.

Macherey, Pierre, and Etienne Balibar. "Literature as an Ideological Form: Some Marxist Propositions." Translated by James Kavanaugh. *Praxis* 5 (1981): 43–58.

The Manchurian Candidate. Directed by John Frankenheimer. M. C. Productions, 1962.

Manning, Laurence. *The Man Who Awoke*. New York: Ballantine, 1975.

Marx, Karl. *Capital: A Critique of Political Economy*. Volume One. 1867; reprint introduced by Ernest Mandel. Translated by Ben Fowkes. New York: Vintage, 1976.

McClintock, Anne. *Imperial Leather: Race, Gender, and Sexuality in the Colonial Contest*. New York: Routledge, 1995.

Merritt, A[braham]. *The Moon Pool*. 1919; reprint edited and with an introduction by Michael Levy. Middletown, Conn.: Wesleyan University Press, 2004.

Miéville, China. "Editorial Introduction." *Historical Materialism* 10, no. 4 (2002): 39–49.

Miller, David. *W. H. Hudson and the Elusive Paradise*. New York: St. Martin's Press, 1990.

Miller, George, and Hugoe Matthews. *Richard Jefferies: A Bibliographical Study*. Aldershot, England: Scolar Press, 1993.

More, Thomas. *Utopia*. 1516; reprint edited by George M. Logan and Robert M. Adams. Cambridge: Cambridge University Press, 2002.

Morgan, Lewis Henry. *Ancient Society*. New York: Henry Holt, 1878; reprint, Tucson: University of Arizona Press, 1985.

Morris, William. *Collected Works*. 24 volumes. London: Longmans Green and Company, 1912.

Mulvey, Laura. "Visual Pleasure and Narrative Cinema." *Screen* 16, no. 3 (Autumn 1975): 6–18.

Orwell, George. *Nineteen Eighty-Four, a Novel*. London: Secker & Warburg, 1949.

Paine, Albert Bigelow. *The Great White Way*. New York: J. F. Taylor, 1901; reprint, New York: Arno, 1975.

Palmer, J. H. *The Invasion of New York; or, How Hawaii Was Annexed*. London and New York: F. Tennyson Neely, 1897.

Parrinder, Patrick. "From Mary Shelley to *The War of the Worlds*: The Thames Valley Catastrophe." In *Anticipations: Essays on Early Science Fiction and its Precursors*, edited by David Seed, 58–74. Syracuse, N.Y.: Syracuse University Press, 1995.

Petersen, Per Serritslev. "Jack London's Medusa of Truth." *Philosophy and Literature* 26 (2002): 43–56.

Philmus, Robert M. *Into the Unknown: The Evolution of Science Fiction from Frances Godwin to H. G. Wells*. Berkeley: University of California Press, 1970.

Poe, Edgar Allan. "The Facts in the Case of M. Valdemar." In *The Science Fiction of Edgar Allan Poe*, collected and edited with an introduction and commentary by Harold Beaver, 194–204. New York: Penguin, 1976. First published in *American Review*, December 1845.

Pratt, Mary Louise. *Imperial Eyes: Travel Writing and Transculturation*. New York: Routledge, 1992.

Reesman, Jeanne Campbell. *Jack London: A Study of the Short Fiction*. New York: Twayne, 1999.

Richards, Thomas. *The Imperial Archive: Knowledge and the Fantasy of Empire*. London: Verso, 1993.

Rickett, J. Compton. *The Quickening of Caliban: A Modern Story of Evolution*. London: Cassell, [1893].

Rieder, John. "Patriarchal Fantasy and the Fecal Child in Mary Shelley's *Frankenstein* and its Adaptations." *Romantic Circles Praxis Series: Frankenstein's Dream*, edited by Jerrold Hogle. February 2003: http://www.rc.umd.edu/praxis/frankenstein/rieder/rieder.html.

———. "Science Fiction, Colonialism, and the Plot of Invasion." *Extrapolation* 46 (2005): 373–94.

Robinson, Kim Stanley. *The Wild Shore*. New York: Berkley, 1984.

Rose, Mark. *Alien Encounters: Anatomy of Science Fiction*. Cambridge, Mass.: Harvard University Press, 1981.

Said, Edward. *Culture and Imperialism*. New York: Knopf, 1993; reprint, New York: Vintage, 1994.

Scott, Walter. *Waverly, or, 'Tis Sixty Years Since*. 3 volumes. Edinburgh: Ballantyne, 1814.

[Seaborn, Adam]. *Symzonia: A Voyage of Discovery*. New York: J. Seymour, 1820; reprinted with an introduction by J. O. Bailey. Gainesville, Fla.: Scholar's Facsimiles & Reprints, 1965.

Seed, David. "Introduction: Aspects of Apocalypse." In *Imagining Apocalypse: Studies in Cultural Crisis*, edited by David Seed, 1–14. New York: St. Martin's Press, 2000.

Serviss, Garrett P. *Edison's Conquest of Mars*. Los Angeles: Carcosa, 1947. First published in *New York Evening Journal*, 12 January–10 February 1898.

Silva, Noenoe K. *Aloha Betrayed : Native Hawaiian Resistance to American Colonialism*. Durham, N.C.: Duke University Press, 2004.

Shanks, Edward. *The People of the Ruins*. London: Collins, 1920.

Shelley, Mary. *Frankenstein, or The Modern Prometheus*. 1831; reprint edited with an introduction and notes by M. K. Joseph. New York: Oxford University Press, 1969; reprint, Oxford World's Classics, 1998.

Shiel, M. P. *The Yellow Danger*. London: Grant Richards, 1898.

Smyth, Edmund J., ed. *Jules Verne: Narratives of Modernity*. Liverpool: Liverpool University Press, 2000.

Sobchak, Vivian. *Screening Space: The American Science Fiction Film*. Second Edition. New York: Ungar, 1987.
Stableford, Brian. *Scientific Romance in Britain, 1890–1950*. New York: St. Martin's, 1985.
Stafford, Robert. "Scientific Exploration and Empire." In *Oxford History of the British Empire*, edited by Andrew Porter, 3:294–319. Oxford: Oxford University Press, 1999.
Stapledon, Olaf. *Last and First Men* and *Star Maker*. 1930, 1937; reprint, New York: Dover, 1968.
———. *Odd John: A Story between Jest and Earnest* and *Sirius: A Fantasy of Love and Discord*. 1935, 1944; reprint, New York: Dover, 1972.
St. Clair, William. "The Impact of *Frankenstein*." In *Mary Shelley in Her Times*, edited by Betty T. Bennett and Stuart Curran, 38–63. Baltimore: Johns Hopkins University Press, 2000.
Stepan, Nancy. *The Idea of Race in Science: Great Britain 1800–1960*. Hamden, Conn.: Archon, 1982.
Stevenson, Robert Louis. *The Strange Case of Dr. Jekyll and Mr. Hyde*. London: Longmans, Green, 1886.
———. *Treasure Island*. London: Cassell & Co., 1883.
Stiebel, Lindy. *Imaging Africa: Landscape in H. Rider Haggard's African Romances*. Westport, Conn.: Greenwood, 2001.
Stocking, George W., Jr. *Victorian Anthropology*. New York: Free Press, 1987.
Street, Brian. *The Savage in Literature: Representations of "Primitive" Society in English Fiction 1858–1920*. London: Routledge & Kegan Paul, 1975.
Suvin, Darko. *Metamorphoses of Science Fiction: On the Poetics and History of a Literary Genre*. New Haven, Conn.: Yale University Press, 1979.
———. *Victorian Science Fiction in the UK: The Discourses of Knowledge and of Power*. Boston: G. K. Hall, 1983.
Swift, Jonathan. *Gulliver's Travels*. 1726; reprint edited with an introduction and notes by Paul Turner. London: Oxford University Press, 1971.
Taylor, Brian. *Richard Jefferies*. Boston: Twayne, 1982.
Unwin, Timothy. *Jules Verne: Journeys in Writing*. Liverpool: Liverpool University Press, 2005.
———. "Jules Verne: Negotiating Change in the Nineteenth Century." *Science Fiction Studies* 32 (2005): 5–17.
Verne, Jules. *Journey to the Center of the Earth*. 1864; reprint translated by Robert Baldick. New York: Penguin, 1965.
———. *The Master of the World*. 1904; reprint translated by I. O. Evans. London: Arco, 1962.
———. *Twenty Thousand Leagues Under the Sea*. 1870; reprint translated by Mendor T. Brunetti. New York: Penguin, 1994.
Wallace, Alfred Russel. *An Anthology of His Shorter Writings*. Edited by Charles H. Smith. Oxford: Oxford University Press, 1991.
Wallerstein, Immanuel. *The Capitalist World-Economy*. Cambridge: Cambridge University Press, 1979.

Warrick, Patricia S., Charles S. Waugh, and Martin Greenberg, eds. *Science Fiction: The Science Fiction Research Anthology*. New York: Harper & Row, 1988.
Weinbaum, Stanley. *The Best of Stanley Weinbaum*. New York: Ballantine, 1974.
Wells, H. G. *Certain Personal Matters*. London: Lawrence & Bullen, 1898.
———. "The Country of the Blind." In *The Country of the Blind and Other Stories*, 536–68. London: Thomas Nelson, n. d. [1911]. First published in *The Strand Magazine*, April 1904.
———. *A Critical Edition of the War of the Worlds*. 1898; reprinted with an introduction and notes by David Y. Hughes and Harry M. Geduld. Bloomington: Indiana University Press, 1993.
———. *The Definitive Time Machine: A Critical Edition of H. G. Wells's Scientific Romance*. 1895; reprinted with an introduction and notes by Harry M. Geduld. Bloomington: Indiana University Press, 1987.
———. *Early Writings in Science and Science Fiction*. Edited by Robert M. Philmus and David Y. Hughes. Berkeley: University of California Press, 1975.
———. *First Men in the Moon*. 1901; reprinted with an introduction by Ursula K. Le Guin. New York: Modern Library, 2003.
———. *The Island of Dr. Moreau: A Critical Text of the 1896 London First Edition, with an Introduction and Appendices*. Edited by Leon Stover. Jefferson, N.C.: McFarland & Co., 1996.
———. *The Island of Dr. Moreau: A Variorum Edition*. 1896; reprint edited by Robert M. Philmus. Athens: University of Georgia Press, 1993.
———. *Mr. Blettsworthy on Rampole Island*. Garden City, N.Y.: Doubleday, Doran & Co., 1928.
———. *Seven Famous Novels*. New York: Knopf, 1934.
———. *The Time Machine: An Invention*. 1895; reprint edited by Nicholas Ruddick. Peterborough, Ont.: Broadview, 2001.
Williams, Raymond. *Marxism and Literature*. New York: Oxford University Press, 1977.
Wodehouse, P. G. *The Swoop!: or, How Clarence Saved England: A Tale of the Great Invasion*. London: Alston Rivers, 1909.
Wood, Ellen. *Empire of Capital*. London: Verso, 2003.
Wright, Sydney Fowler. *Deluge*. 1927; reprint edited and introduced by Brian Stableford. Middletown, Conn.: Wesleyan University Press, 2003.
———. *The World Below*. New York: Longmans, Green and Co., 1930.
Yeats, William Butler. *Poems*. Edited by Richard J. Finneran. Volume 1 of *Collected Works of W. B. Yeats*. New York: Macmillan, 1989.
Zamyatin, Yevgeny. *We*. New York: Dutton, 1924.
Žižek, Slavoj. *The Sublime Object of Ideology*. London: Verso, 1989.

Index

Abbott, Edwin, *Flatland,* 65–66
Adorno, Theodor W., 28
adventure fiction, 4, 35–40, 41, 64, 75, 92.
    See also lost-race fiction; quest romance; romance revival
After London (Jefferies), 81, 124, 126–31, 135, 143, 147
Aleriel (Lach-Szyrma), 65
Allan Quatermain (Haggard), 24, 38–39, 41–42, 45, 55
allegory, 72
Allen, Grant, 127; *The British Barbarians,* 78–79
All-Story, 159n4
Amazing Stories, 17, 61, 65, 113, 119
Ancient Society (Morgan), 5–6, 7
Angel Island (Gillmore), 52
Angel of the Revolution, The (Griffith), 140–41
Animal Farm (Orwell), 107
anthropology, 2, 70–72, 79–80, 98, 103, 134; and anachronism, 5–6, 7–9, 30, 52–53 (see also colonial gaze; science fiction, anachronism in); and race, 98, 100–101
Arabian Nights, The, 70
Argosy, 159n4
Astounding Stories, 16
At the Earth's Core (Burroughs), 43–44, 54, 56
Aubrey, Frank, *The Devil-Tree of El Dorado,* 41–42, 44, 55, 57; *The Queen of Atlantis,* 57
Aztec Treasure House (Janvier), 45, 51, 53, 55

Ballard, J. G., *The Drowned World,* 147
Battle of Dorking, The (Chesney), 124, 125–26, 127, 129, 135, 147

Bellamy, Edward, 39; *Looking Backward,* 29, 77–78, 125
Bennett, Robert Ames, *Thyra,* 42–44, 56
Beresford, John Davys, *The Hampdenshire Wonder,* 78–80
Blake, William, 17
Bleiler, Everett, 27, 34–35, 157n7
Bould, Mark, 62, 96
Bourdieu, Pierre, 17–18, 24–25, 118
Braddon, Mary Elizabeth, 70
Bradshaw, William, *The Goddess of Atvatabar,* 39, 56, 68–69
Brave New World (Huxley), 74, 139–40
British Barbarians, The (Allen), 78–79
Brown, Harold V., 10
Brown, John MacMillan, 98, 124; *Limanora,* 69, 72–74, 112; *Riallaro,* 69, 72
Browning, Robert, "Childe Roland to the Dark Tower Came," 92
Bulwer-Lytton, Edward, *The Coming Race,* 16
Burroughs, Edgar Rice, 15, 41; *At the Earth's Core,* 43–44, 54, 56; *A Princess of Mars,* 43; *Tarzan of the Apes,* 103
Butler, Octavia, *Lilith's Brood,* 163n15
Butler, Samuel, *Erewhon,* 5, 21, 69
"By His Bootstraps" (Heinlein), 160n5

Caleb Williams (Godwin), 19
Campbell, John W., "Forgetfulness," 16; "The Last Evolution," 142, 147; "Who Goes There?" 147–51, 154
Čapek, Karl, *R.U.R.,* 113; *War with the Newts,* 113
Carnegie, Andrew, 116
cartography, 22–23

Chesney, George, *The Battle of Dorking*, 124, 125–26, 127, 129, 135, 147
"Childe Roland to the Dark Tower Came" (Browning), 92
"Circle of Zero, The" (Weinbaum), 160n5
Clareson, Thomas, 27, 29, 157n7
Clarke, I. F., 131
class, domestic versus global, 26–27, 87–89, 140–41; and reading audience, 27–28; in Wells, *The Time Machine*, 85–89
Collier, John, *Tom's A-Cold*, 127, 143
Collins, Wilkie, 70
colonial gaze, 6–10, 30–31, 59–60, 71, 93, 103, 152. *See also* anthropology, and anachronism; science fiction, anachronism in
colonial ideology, 2–3, 20–21, 104–8, 123–24, 126, 129–31, 152–55; ambivalence in, 6, 15, 94–96, 115, 134, 152 (*see also* science fiction, polarization of); and capitalism, 26; and gender, 39–40, 47–50; in lost-race fiction, 40–60. *See also* ideology of progress; Social Darwinism
colonialism: and capitalism, 25–28; defined, 25; and racism, 97–98; and science, 2, 4, 6, 22–23, 26, 52–60, 68, 104; and science fiction disasters, 124; versus imperialism, 25
Comical History of the States and Empires of the Moon and the Sun (Cyrano), 1, 2
"Coming of the Ice, The" (Wertenbaker), 113–14
Coming Race, The (Bulwer-Lytton), 16
Conan Doyle, Arthur, 15; *The Lost World*, 13, 21–22, 43, 50, 58–61
Confessions of a Crap Artist (Dick), 14
"Conquest of Two Worlds, The" (Hamilton), 142–43
Conrad, Joseph, *Heart of Darkness*, 76–78, 87, 89, 92
Constable, Frank Challice, *The Curse of Intellect*, 101, 102–4, 111
"Country of the Blind, The" (Wells), 23–24, 66–68
Crystal Age, A (Hudson), 80–84, 127
Cummings, Ray, "The Giant World," 160n6
Curse of Intellect, The (Constable), 101, 102–4, 111
cyborgs, 19–20, 69, 111–17, 119–22

Cyrano de Bergerac, *Comical History of the States and Empires of the Moon and the Sun*, 1, 2

Darwin, Charles, 13, 22, 56, 69, 86, 109–10; *The Descent of Man*, 103, 110; *The Origin of Species*, 30, 133
Defoe, Daniel, *Robinson Crusoe*, 35–36
Delany, Samuel R., 56, 63
De Mille, James, *A Strange Manuscript Found in a Copper Cylinder*, 5, 37–38, 52, 69–72
Derrida, Jacques, 4, 26
Descent of Man, The (Darwin), 103, 110
Devil-Tree of El Dorado, The (Aubrey), 41–42, 44, 55, 57
Dick, Philip K., 63; *Confessions of a Crap Artist*, 14; *The Man in the High Castle*, 147
Donnelly, Ignatius, 39
Drowned World, The (Ballard), 147
dystopian fiction, 139–40

Edison's Conquest of Mars (Serviss), 136–38
England, George Allan, 17
epistemology, 59–60, 64–68, 89–91, 96. *See also* science fiction, subject of knowledge in; utopia, subject of knowledge in
Erewhon (Butler), 5, 21, 69
ethnography, 7–10, 13, 55–56, 74–75, 127–28, 134
eugenics, 73–74, 98, 107, 112
evolutionary theory, 2; and biogeography, 56; and human origins, 2, 87–88; and ideology of progress, 79–80, 109, 111, 115–16 (*see also* Social Darwinism); and origin of racial difference, 30, 76, 98, 101–2, 110 (*see also* scientific racism); and problem of nature versus culture, 30, 76, 86, 98, 105, 108–9, 134

Fabian, Johannes, 6
"Facts in the Case of M. Valdemar, The" (Poe), 61, 64–65
fantasy, literary genre of, 62
Finney, Jack, *Invasion of the Body Snatchers*, 147

First Men in the Moon (Wells), 74–75
Flagg, Francis, "The Machine Man of Ardathia," 114
Flatland (Abbott), 65–66
"Forgetfulness" (Campbell), 16
Forster, E. M., "The Machine Stops," 139–40
Frankenstein (1931 film version), 118
Frankenstein (Shelley), 19, 99–101, 102–3, 106, 107, 111
Freedman, Carl, 63
Freud, Sigmund, 119; *Totem and Taboo*, 6
future war narratives, 18, 125, 131–32, 140

Galton, Francis, 107
Gartley, Alonzo, 7–10
genocide, 43, 110, 124, 133, 138, 140–43, 146
genre, 15–21, 23–25, 63–64, 68, 71, 127
Gernsback, Hugo, 15–16, 17, 18, 24–25, 57, 61, 136
"Giant World, The" (Cummings), 160n6
Gibson, William, 30
Gillmore, Inez, *Angel Island*, 52
Gilman, Charlotte Perkins, *Herland*, 21, 23–24
Goddess of Atvatabar, The (Bradshaw), 39, 56, 68–69
Godwin, William: *Caleb Williams*, 19; *Political Justice*, 100
Graves, Joseph, 110
Great White Way, The (Paine), 47
Green, Martin, 35–36
Greg, Percy, 39
Griffith, George, *The Angel of the Revolution*, 140–41
Grotius, Hugo, 31
Gulliver's Travels (Swift), 2, 35–36, 78, 106, 108

Haggard, H. Rider, 35, 39, 61, 100, 103, 127; *Allan Quatermain*, 24, 38–39, 41–42, 45, 55; *King Solomon's Mines*, 21–24, 38, 41–42, 44–45, 51, 54–55, 87, 92, 127; *She*, 24, 38, 48–49, 53, 60
Hall, Austin, 17
Hamilton, Edmond: "The Conquest of Two Worlds," 142–43; "The Man Who Evolved," 114–16, 118

Hampdenshire Wonder, The (Beresford), 78–80
Hawthorne, Julian, 39, 127
Hay, William Delisle, *Three Hundred Years Hence*, 141
Heart of Darkness (Conrad), 76–78, 87, 89, 92
Heinlein, Robert A.: "By His Bootstraps," 160n15; *The Puppet Masters*, 147, 154
Herland (Gilman), 21, 23–24
historical novel, 29, 125
History of New York by Diedrich Knickerbocker, A (Irving), 4–5
hoax, 60–61, 64–65
Holberg, Ludwig, *Journey to the World Underground, by Nicholas Klimius*, 36–37
Horkheimer, Max, 28
Hudson, William Henry, *A Crystal Age*, 80–84, 127
"Human Evolution, an Artificial Process" (Wells), 105, 108
Huntington, John, 87, 88
Huxley, Aldous, *Brave New World*, 74, 139–40
Huxley, Thomas H., 85, 87, 109
hybrids, 111–13, 119, 163n15

ideological fantasy, 30–32, 37–38, 106–7
ideology. *See* colonial ideology; ideological fantasy; ideology of progress
ideology of progress, 29–33, 76–77, 79–80, 115–16, 134. *See also* Social Darwinism
imaginary voyage, 1–2, 4, 6, 32, 35–39, 65, 76
imperialism, 26–27, 124–26; and arms race, 28–29, 32–33, 140; and capitalism, 138–39; versus colonialism, 25; and militarism, 41, 131; and nationalism, 129, 136–39
"In the Penal Colony" (Kafka), 107
"Into the Subconscious" (Meyer), 119
invasion, tales of, 33, 124, 126, 144, 147–48, 150–52, 163n15
Invasion of New York, The (Palmer), 138–39
Invasion of the Body Snatchers (Finney), 147
Invasion of the Body Snatchers (1956 film version), 147, 154

Invisible Man, The (Wells), 19
Iron Heel, The (London), 61
Irving, Washington: *A History of New York by Diedrich Knickerbocker*, 4–5; "Rip Van Winkle," 77
Island of Dr. Moreau, The (Wells), 14, 30, 98, 101, 102, 104–10, 111–12, 118, 155

Jameson, Fredric, 29, 118
Janvier, Thomas, *The Aztec Treasure House*, 45, 51, 53, 55
Jefferies, Richard, *After London*, 81, 124, 126–31, 135, 143, 147
Johnson, Leslie J., "Seeker of Tomorrow," 16
Jones, Gwyneth, 163n15
Journey to the Center of the Earth (Verne), 54
Journey to the World Underground, by Nicholas Klimius (Holberg), 36–37

Kafka, Franz, "In the Penal Colony," 107
Keller, David H., "Revolt of the Pedestrians," 163n10
Khouri, Nadia, 50
Kincaid, Paul, 16–17
King Kong, 13, 59
King Solomon's Mines (Haggard), 21–24, 38, 41–42, 44–45, 51, 54–55, 87, 92, 127
Kipling, Rudyard, 39
Kuhn, Thomas, 58
Kuttner, Henry: "Time Locker," 160n5; "Vintage Season," 151–55

Lacan, Jacques, 62
Lach-Szyrma, Wladislaw, *Aleriel*, 65
Lang, Andrew, 103; "Realism and Romance," 38–39
Last and First Men (Stapledon), 90–91, 113–14, 163n12
"Last Evolution, The" (Campbell), 142, 147
Leinster, Murray, "The Runaway Skyscraper," 160n6
Lenin, Vladimir Ilyich, 26, 140
Lévi-Strauss, Claude, 20–21, 40
Lilith's Brood (Butler), 163n15
Limanora (Brown), 69, 72–74, 112
Llewellyn, Alun, *The Strange Invaders*, 143–46

Locke, John, 31, 100–101
London, Jack, 15; *The Iron Heel*, 61; "The Red One," 91–96, 97; "The Unparalleled Invasion," 141
Looking Backward (Bellamy), 29, 77–78, 125
lost-race fiction, 21–25, 27, 31, 34–60; anachronism in, 22–23, 43, 52–53; civil war in, 22, 40–47; closure in, 45, 51–52; ethnography in, 55–57; first contact in, 41–42; maps in, 22–23, 54–55; ordeal of entry in, 22, 51, 65; priests in, 22, 44–46; princesses in 22, 47–50; races and species in, 42–44; repetition in, 22; scientist narrators in, 53–54; specimens in, 56–59; treasure in, 22, 47–51; two strains of, 21–22, 23–25, 41, 45, 52
Lost World, The (Conan Doyle), 13, 21–22, 43, 50, 58–61
Lovecraft, H. P., 45
Lucian, 17, 35
Lukács, George, 29, 116

MacColl, Hugh, *Mr. Stranger's Sealed Packet*, 42–43
MacDonald, Robert H., 41
"Machine Man of Ardathia, The" (Flagg), 114
"Machine Stops, The" (Forster), 139–40
Mackaye, Henry Steele, *Panchronicon*, 160n6
Manchurian Candidate, The, 148
Man in the High Castle, The (Dick), 147
Manning, Laurence, 114–15; "The Man Who Awoke," 163n12
"Man Who Awoke, The" (Manning), 163n12
"Man Who Evolved, The" (Hamilton), 114–16, 118
"Martian Odyssey, A" (Weinbaum), 57–58
marvelous journey. *See* imaginary voyage
Marx, Karl, 48, 116, 139
Master of the World, The (Verne), 32
McClintock, Anne, 39–40, 47
Meek, S. P., "Submicropsopic," 42
Merritt, A., *The Moon Pool*, 49–51, 54
Meyer, Ray Avery, "Into the Subconscious," 119
Milton, John, *Paradise Lost*, 99, 103

Moon Pool, The (Merritt), 49–51, 54
Moore, Catherine L., "Vintage Season," 151–55
"Morals and Civilisation" (Wells), 109
More, Thomas, 31; *Utopia*, 2, 37
Morgan, Lewis Henry, *Ancient Society*, 5–6, 7
Morris, William, 127; *News from Nowhere*, 77–78, 81
Mr. Blettsworthy on Rampole Island (Wells), 13–15, 106
Mr. Stranger's Sealed Packet (MacColl), 42–43
Mulvey, Laura, 7
Murchison, Robert, 22
myth, 20–21, 40; concept of race as, 98–99, 110–12, 117

News from Nowhere (Morris), 77–78, 81
Next War, The (Wallace), 141
1984 (Orwell), 139–40

Odd John (Stapledon), 160n7
Oedipus at Colonus (Sophocles), 71
"Of a Book Unwritten" (Wells), 19, 134
"Origin of Human Races and the Antiquity of Man Deduced from the Theory of 'Natural Selection,' The" (Wallace), 132–33
Origin of Species, The (Darwin), 30, 133
Orwell, George: *Animal Farm*, 107; *1984*, 139–40

Paine, Albert Bigelow, *The Great White Way*, 47
Palmer, J. H., *The Invasion of New York*, 138–39
Panchronicon (Mackaye), 160n6
Paradise Lost (Milton), 99, 103
Paul, Frank R., 10, 119–22
People of the Ruins, The (Shanks), 143
Plato, 39, 90
Poe, Edgar Allan, 17; "The Facts in the Case of M. Valdemar," 61, 64–65
Political Justice (Godwin), 100
postcolonialism, 124, 147–48, 150, 154–55
Pratt, Mary Louise, 9–10, 31
Princess of Mars, A (Burroughs), 43
Puppet Masters, The (Heinlein), 147, 154

Queen of Atlantis, The (Aubrey), 57
quest romance, 35, 38–39, 92, 94, 129–31
Quickening of Caliban, The (Rickett), 101–2, 104

racial warfare, 140–43
racism, 30–31, 41, 80, 94–95, 97–99, 109–12, 117; compared to gender ideology, 99–100; in science fiction, 97–117. *See also* evolutionary theory, and origin of racial difference; scientific racism
realism, 9, 16, 92, 94, 127–28, 146
"Realism and Romance" (Lang), 38–39
"Red One, The" (London), 91–96, 97
"Revolt of the Pedestrians" (Keller), 163n10
Rhodes, Cecil, 26
Riallaro (Brown), 69, 72
Rickett, J. Compton, *The Quickening of Caliban*, 101–2, 104
"Rip Van Winkle" (Irving), 77
Robinson, Kim Stanley, *The Wild Shore*, 147
Robinson Crusoe (Defoe), 35–36
romance. *See* quest romance
romance revival, 19, 34–35, 38–39, 45, 100–101, 103, 127, 131
Ruins of Empire, The (Volney), 100
"Runaway Skyscraper, The" (Leinster), 160n6
Rupert, M. F., "Via the Hewitt Ray," 163n10
R.U.R. (Čapek), 113
Russell, Eric Frank, "Seekers of Tomorrow," 16

Said, Edward, 3, 71
satire, 64–75, 81, 84, 105–6; and colonial travel, 2; in imaginary voyage, 1, 35–38; in lost-race fiction, 21, 23–24, 46–47; trope of reversal in, 4–5, 37, 69, 79; versus science fiction, 68–69, 72–74
science fiction: anachronism in, 10, 32–33, 93, 117; apocalypse in, 123; coherence as formal problem in, 56, 62–64, 84–85, 89–90, 119–22; compared to critical theory, 14; definitions of, 16–17, 157n7, 160n3, 162n6; emergence of, 2–3, 15–16, 34–35, 63–64, 127–28; genealogies of, 17, 24–25, 158n8; generic complexity of, 64–65, 68–75, 92, 95–96; impossibility

science fiction (*continued*)
in, 62; polarization of, 15, 21, 25, 33, 75, 118–22, 131, 136–38; post-apocalyptic scenario in, 126–27, 143; reading audience, 25, 27–28, 119–22; subject of knowledge in, 64–68, 92–96; technological breakthrough in, 32–33; versus satire, 68–69, 72–74
Science Wonder Stories, 119, 142
scientific racism, 30, 70, 101–2, 106–7, 109–10
Scott, Walter, 19; *Waverly*, 99, 125
Seaborn, Adam. See *Symzonia*
"Seeker of Tomorrow" (Johnson and Russell), 16
sensation novel, 70
Serviss, Garrett Putnam, *Edison's Conquest of Mars*, 136–38
Shanks, Edward, *The People of the Ruins*, 143
She (Haggard), 24, 38, 48–49, 53, 60
Shelley, Mary Wollstonecraft, 98; *Frankenstein*, 19, 99–101, 102–3, 106, 107, 111
Shelley, Percy Bysshe, 17
Shiel, M. P., *The Yellow Danger*, 141
Sidney, Sir Philip, 39
Simak, Clifford, "The World of the Red Sun," 114
Sirius (Stapledon), 113
Social Darwinism, 2, 13, 30, 73–74, 85, 93–94, 109, 112, 116, 132–35, 136, 146
Sophocles, *Oedipus at Colonus*, 71
space opera, 147
Spencer, Herbert, 13, 85
Stapledon, Olaf, 98; *Last and First Men*, 90–91, 113–14, 163n12; *Odd John*, 160n7; *Sirius*, 113
Star Trek, 147
Star Wars, 35, 147
Stevenson, Robert Louis, 21, 39, 127; *The Strange Case of Dr. Jekyll and Mr. Hyde*, 107, 111; *Treasure Island*, 23
Strange Case of Dr. Jekyll and Mr. Hyde, The (Stevenson), 107, 111
Strange Invaders, The (Llewellyn), 143–46
Strange Manuscript Found in a Copper Cylinder, A (De Mille), 5, 37–38, 52, 69–72
"Submicropsopic" (Meek), 42
Suvin, Darko, 17, 24–25, 27, 52, 62, 88, 157n7

Swift, Jonathan, 39; *Gulliver's Travels*, 2, 35–36, 78, 106, 108
Swoop!, The (Wodehouse), 162n3
Symzonia, 36–37, 50, 159n3

Tanner, Charles R., "Tumithak of the Corridors," 89–90
Tarzan of the Apes (Burroughs), 103
Three Hundred Years Hence (Hay), 141
Thyra (Bennett), 42–44, 56
"Time Locker" (Kuttner), 160n5
Time Machine, The (Wells), 14, 19, 27, 61, 77, 80–81, 84–89, 98, 107, 109, 111–12, 132, 140
time travel, 6, 76–89, 113–16
Tom's A-Cold (Collier), 127, 143
Totem and Taboo (Freud), 6
tourism, 9, 151–55
travel writing, 6, 55–56, 64
Treasure Island (Stevenson), 23
"Tumithak of the Corridors" (Tanner), 89–90
Twenty Thousand Leagues Under the Sea (Verne), 16, 32, 61

"Unparalleled Invasion, The" (London), 141
utopia, 70–72; and colonial travel, 2; in lost-race fiction, 21, 36–37, 46–47, 50; purgation in, 73, 124; subject of knowledge in, 65, 73, 77–78; in time-travel stories, 29, 77–78, 81, 84
Utopia (More), 2, 37

Verne, Jules, 6, 15, 17, 54; *Journey to the Center of the Earth*, 54; *The Master of the World*, 32; *Twenty Thousand Leagues Under the Sea*, 16, 32, 61; *voyages extraordinaires*, 34
"Via the Hewitt Ray" (Rupert), 163n10
"Vintage Season" (Kuttner and Moore), 151–55
Volney, Constantin-François, *The Ruins of Empire*, 100

Wallace, Alfred Russel, 56, 109; "The Origin of Human Races and the Antiquity of Man Deduced from the Theory of 'Natural Selection,'" 132–33
Wallace, King, *The Next War*, 141

War of the Worlds, The (Wells), 5–7, 10, 18, 19, 43, 98, 105, 111–12, 113, 124, 129, 131–35, 136, 144–49, 155
War with the Newts (Čapek), 113
Waverly (Scott), 99, 125
We (Zamyatin), 74, 139–40
Weinbaum, Stanley: "The Circle of Zero," 160n5; "A Martian Odyssey," 57–58
Weird Tales, 159n4
Wells, H. G., 2, 6, 15, 17, 143; "The Country of the Blind," 23–24, 66–68; *First Men in the Moon*, 74–75; "Human Evolution, an Artificial Process," 105, 108; *The Invisible Man*, 19; *The Island of Dr. Moreau*, 14, 30, 98, 101, 102, 104–10, 111–12, 118, 155; "Morals and Civilisation," 109; *Mr. Blettsworthy on Rampole Island*, 13–15, 106; "Of a Book Unwritten," 19, 134; *The Time Machine*, 14, 19, 27, 61, 77, 80–81, 84–89, 98, 107, 109, 111–12, 132, 140; *The War of the Worlds*, 5–7, 10, 18, 19, 43, 98, 105, 111–12, 113, 124, 129, 131–35, 136, 144–49, 155; *When the Sleeper Awakes*, 77
Wertenbaker, G. Peyton, 17; "The Coming of the Ice," 113–14
When the Sleeper Awakes (Wells), 77
"Who Goes There?" (Campbell), 147–51, 154
Wild Shore, The (Robinson), 147
Wittgenstein, Ludwig, 16
Wodehouse, P. G., *The Swoop!*, 162n3
Wonder Stories, 114, 142
"World of the Red Sun, The" (Simak), 114
Wright, Sydney Fowler, 63

Yeats, William Butler, 146
Yellow Danger, The (Shiel), 141
Yellow Peril, 141

Zamyatin, Yevgeny, *We*, 74, 139–40
Žižek, Slavoj, 30, 37, 107

About the Author

John Rieder is a professor of English at the University of Hawai'i at Mānoa and the author of *Wordsworth's Counterrevolutionary Turn: Community, Virtue, and Vision in the 1790s*.